DESERT(ED)

IAN O'HARA

Printed in the United States of America

First Printing, 2018

ISBN: 978-0-692-09887-5

Ingram Spark Publishing

www.IngramSpark.com

Mom and Dad, I love you.
Friends, I thank you.
Special thanks to Robert Storms for answering all of my questions, and Andrew Cohn for letting me run with his idea. I hope you all enjoy the journey.

"An artist needn't fear the censor."

-Andrew Ryan / *Bioshock*

BOOK

I

ONE

NAMIBIA, AFRICA: GARDEN OF EDEN MILITARY OUTPOST YEAR 2157 JUST ON THE OUTSKIRTS

"Hurry! Faster! It's gaining speed!"

Caleb Hendrickson ran as fast as he could. The cracked desert earth beneath his feet groaned and gnarled as he could hear the terrible rumbling around him. Hell had come once again for him and his team. A bulk build of a man—mid-fifties, gray, and all-around smart ass and qualified leader—he was used to this kind of weather. "God's Wrath." That's what they'd called it. Man must have done something fierce years ago to piss off the Almighty. Today wasn't going to be any different. Wrath had homed in on his team and was full of hunger. The roaring of the desert storm picked up faster and was louder as the team continued to run, sand blowing each and every way, getting ever so closer and engulfing them.

"Just another day on the job, huh, sir?" shouted his first lieutenant Rebecca Masters—a young girl in her early thirties, spunky and a leader through and through. But she'd never tell Caleb that. He was far too proud and more of a father figure to her than anyone else on the team. She removed her sand-infested mining hat and dumped it out. She gave her bushy brown hair a few quick shakes and put her helmet back on.

Caleb looked at her. "You really think that's going to help? What did I always tell you? Buckets off when we reach base!"

He pointed to a blurred image in the distance. He could barely see through his goggles and could barely be heard through his oxygen mask that was protecting his breathing. It was a precaution. Nothing like trying to breathe with just a scarf and having sand crawl up your nose or into your mouth. You're liable to inhale too much trying to breathe and end up choking to death.

He rotated his wrist palm up and squinted down through his sand-covered goggles. He ever so carefully kneaded the tattered cloth on his wrist. The color of his skin was a sun-bleached white. There was a light scar that could be seen going directly down the middle of his forearm, about two inches in diameter. He pressed it with his thumb, and the scar made a whir-like sound as the skin protruded from the rest of his arm. It made a small rectangular shape and split itself into opposite ends. There were no visible wires or other really enhanced cybernetics to speak of. All that could be seen was bare, bloody tendon. And a percentage: 65%.

"Good," he whispered to himself. He pressed the skin just below the incision, and the two rectangular halves came together and settled back to their original position, his flesh becoming whole once more. He wrapped his cloth tighter around his wrist this time, making sure not to get any sand trapped.

"Problem, boss?" called out private first class Jerome Tucker. Tucker was a string bean of a kid in his mid-twenties. He had only been with the squad for a few months, but Caleb looked after him as he did Rebecca. Jerome was the type of guy to tell the stupidest jokes, but they made Caleb either laugh or shake his head in bewilderment.

"Nah," said Caleb. "Nothing to worry about. C'mon, Wrath's not letting up anytime soon!" He motioned for Tucker and Rebecca to get a move on. The storm was all around them now. They could barely keep a foothold and had to hold on to each other for support. Golden, jagged specs hit them all over their entire bodies. It was as if thousands upon thousands of tiny needles was stabbing them multiple times.

The sun was starting to set, but the team couldn't tell for spit. They were engulfed in Wrath. Doing their best, they slowly made their way to Eden. Rebecca tripped, and Jerome was right there to catch her. He put out his hand, feverishly searching for Caleb's pack. A few moments went by, and Caleb's hand grabbed his wrist and pulled them along. Jerome secretly called Caleb the "Wise Ox," behind his back. Jerome assumed that he probably knew, but Caleb wasn't into nicknames. It wasn't his style. He just wanted to be called Caleb. Plain and simple.

The trio finally made their way to Eden. It wasn't a regular type of outpost with grand walls or guards on watch. It was a giant cavern. The storm burst its fury toward the three companions. There was just one tiny problem: there was a giant scarred blast door blocking their entrance. The three companions made their way to the door, Wrath gaining speed, ready for an ultimate assault against them. Jerome quickly ran to the other end of the blast door, Rebecca took the middle, and Caleb stayed where he was on the far-right side. They looked at each other and nodded. There were three slots with jagged inserts. The team reached into the neckline of their shirts and grabbed their individual keys that hung there around their neck, nestled under their clothing. They inserted the keys into the slots and turned them to the right simultaneously.

There was a groaning sound as they removed their individual keys. A small square flip pad now replaced each of the keyholes. The team opened the pads and looked at each other again. They uncovered their thumbs and pressed down on the pads' readers. The pads glowed a faint blue and made a faint robotic jarring sound. The three removed their thumbs from the pads, and the scanner made a positive chirp. The three devices retracted into their respective slots and became keyholes once more.

The blast door could be heard whirring, various gears grinding as it struggled to open. At twenty-four meters, it was a *slow* process, but the team loved hearing that sound. It was safe, and it was home. The doors slid open wider and abruptly stopped. Dust flew down from the top of the cavern's entrance as one by one the team quickly entered. When Jerome arrived inside, Caleb flipped a box port, entered a numeric sequence, and shut the doors. The sand and wind roared toward them as the blast doors shut, slightly muting the eternal roar of Wrath. What was once a loud roar of sand and wind was now only a deep hum. The trio was surrounded by darkness now. They were thankful for that.

"Lights," Caleb said. *Christ, that was close.*

Slowly, various rows of lights could be seen illuminating the cavern itself. Crevices and different stalagmites and stalactites were appearing one by one. The sound of running water could be heard in the distance. If one wanted to, they could just walk down a few yards and swim to an underwater cove. The group did this almost religiously whenever they came back from the outside. It was peaceful. And relaxing.

They went their separate ways, and undressed out of their sand-drenched clothes. It was annoying at times. But damn it, it was a bittersweet reward from digging their way down to the bottom of a gigantic hole looking for things to eat.

Rebecca reached her room, which was just a makeshift corridor of stalagmites uprooting from the ground. A tight squeeze to be sure.

She took off her cap first, shaking out the excess sand and dirt. Her frizzy brunette hair was knotted and a gigantic mess. *What I wouldn't give for a comb.* She removed her tattered outer layer of clothing next. This was the hard part. It was so hot outside that their clothing stuck to their bodies like a second skin. And hers was no different. It was like taking off a Band-Aid on a patch of hair-covered skin. Very painful, and *very slow.* She looked down at herself. Her chest was marked up something fierce. Her abdomen was bruised to hell.

Nothing like being pelted by different sized grains of sand making you look like a freaking pincushion test subject. The markings would go away eventually. But it was annoying to see herself battered from the elements. *Fuck. You'd think you would be used to it by now. Nope.*

She took off her final wears below her waist and checked herself out some more. Nothing but old scars and bruises, with the same pincushion effect as was on her torso and chest. Her skin felt like it was on fire. *Maybe if I close my eyes, I'll be in a soft bed with a decent meal in my stomach. Yeah right. If wishes were horses . . .*

She went to rub her tired eyes and felt plastic and more dust and sand.

"Shit." She forgot to take off her goggles. *Of course you did, idiot.*

Closing her eyes, she carefully pulled off her goggles, feeling the sand and dirt crack and fall gingerly on her eyelids. With her hands now free, she wiped her eyes and brushed away the rest of the dirt and dust from her naked body. She suddenly remembered she was naked. A cool breeze washed over her, and she started to shiver from the shock of the cool sensation. Enough of checking herself out. Time to eat and relax. She threw her clothes into a crumpled pile on the ground a few feet across from where she was standing. A moment passed by and she looked herself over one last time. "Fuck."

TWO

Jerome needed a break. And a drink. Unfortunately, he could only afford one, and he didn't have to guess. He walked to his hollowed-out space and took off his outerwear. Like Rebecca, he had a tough time getting comfortable. He had gotten used to the hot, dry heat, but it was still a pain in the ass afterward.

His dark skin blistered like no tomorrow. The "uniform" was supposed to keep them cool to a certain number of degrees outside. It didn't. When it's 124 degrees outside, there's only so much the material it was made with could withstand. *Something called polymer threading.* Yeah, that was the name. It was a strange substance from a time long ago. Caleb knew what it was. "Wise Ox strikes again," he said.

He took off his outerwear and craned his neck. His body was blistered and sore. He tried to make do with his hair, but it was to no avail. *Try to look decent for once. Can't even do that.*

Jerome stretched his legs and arms. The cracking of various joints soothed his nerves. It meant that he was alive. And that he had to do it all over again tomorrow. But for now, he was at peace and ready to relax.

He threw his clothes onto the ground and walked out of his enclosed space (which was almost the same size as Rebecca's, save for a few varying crevices here and there).

Jerome walked naked down to the cove at the end of the long, looming cave. It was a long hallway of sorts, but seeing the blue watery glow was very satisfying. It was where the three would go after they had endured a full day of the outside. Rebecca was already relaxing, her head up and her eyes closed. Her fingers flicked the water, playing with it gingerly. Jerome entered opposite of her.

"He's late again," she exclaimed as she lifted her head to look at her friend.

"You know how he is, always puttering around, never enjoying the simple things in life," said Jerome, who was settling into the cool, shallow waters.

"Yeah, he seriously needs to put a stop to it," Rebecca said.

Jerome splashed some water and looked around. "I wonder what he does?"

Caleb was rummaging through old scraps of ancient machinery. It was tossed aside from years of unkempt wear and rust. He tossed a pair of empty 10-gauge shotgun shells off to the side. *What's a 10 gauge? Must have been used for something . . .*

Weaponized machinery had long been turned into a giant rust pile. Humanity had died off years ago; by what, Caleb and the others didn't know. Why were they the only ones here, in this new Eden? Caleb couldn't coin an answer immediately. He decided to store it in the back of his mind for now. He looked toward the direction of where the pool was and decided not to join the others. Not right away. There was something else he wanted to do.

He looked around some more and went to his secluded crevice. It was not much bigger than Rebecca's. But it could fit his bulk frame. The crevice was the only one opposite of the other two.

He picked himself up from his muttering, sat his old bones down in a weather-beaten chair, and slowly rocked back and forth. It reminded him of a distant memory that was on the tip of his brain, but he couldn't quite place it. It was as if he was supposed to remember something important and he was running through a maze of doors trying to find the answer.

He finally gave up and leaned back, closing his eyes. The chair, it was the best thing he could hope for. Sure, the pool was relaxing, but nothing beat just sitting down in some sort of cushioned comfort.

He was too tired to take off his outerwear, though he did take off his sanded goggles and cap and oxygen mask. "Just resting his eyes," as he would say time and again to Rebecca and Jerome. *Good kids*, he thought to himself. He reminded himself that he'd wake up in a few minutes to join the others in the pool just over the ridge.

Caleb began to dream. The dreams came to him not in motion, but a flashing of images. He dreamed of what the world was before. Though he had no clue.

He was a boy again. Running through vast oceans of green. The images around him weren't clear. It was a moving painting. He kept running though, bursting his hands through each wall of green. Caleb looked around. His head turned to the left and then to the right, confused. Everything was green. Soon it began to change color.

The ocean that was green was now turning into a sick black. It scared him. Adult Caleb breathed heavily. Young Caleb curled and screamed as the darkness began to envelop his body. He tried to run, but his feet were stuck in the black. It rose up his body, higher and higher. Eventually, he was enveloped in this darkness. He opened his mouth to scream, but all that came out was a muted sound.

Caleb reached out with his blackened hands and desperately tried to tear the blackened mass of his face, but it was to no avail. He screamed again, shaking and convulsing.

"Caleb!" a distant voice said. "Wake up! Wake up, man!"

The voice was familiar. It was Jerome.

Caleb woke up with a shock and grabbed Jerome by the throat, squeezing it tightly and choking him.

"Caleb, no!" shouted Rebecca. She tried prying Caleb's arm away. Caleb was too strong and screamed.

Rebecca smacked Caleb across the face. Multiple times. That didn't work. Caleb was still in hallucination from the nightmare. She made a fist and punched her friend in the face. Caleb's lips bled, and he finally calmed down and released Jerome from his death-like grip. He looked around feverishly. Jerome collapsed on the ground, gasping for sweet air, rubbing his throat. Rebecca rubbed her hand that she punched Caleb with and stretched it out.

"Dammit, Caleb," she said.

Jerome coughed and wheezed. "Why's it always gotta be the black guy?" He got up, still catching his breath. "W-what the hell?"

Caleb looked at his two friends. It all came back to him where he was. He wasn't covered in darkness. Tears welled up in his eyes as he realized what had transpired. There was a sting. He felt his bleeding lips with his hand. They were pulsating from the pain.

"I'm sorry. I'm so sorry . . ." he trailed off.

Jerome nodded in compliance. "What happened?"

"Bad dream," Caleb said. He looked at Rebecca. "You throw a hell of a punch."

"Sorry," she said. "I didn't really have any other choice. You were screaming and we ran over."

There was a slight pause.

"What . . . was it about?" Do you remember?" asked Jerome.

Caleb tried to remember. Flashes of the nightmare entered his conscious. He shook his head. "No. No, I don't."

Rebecca leaned in gently and put her hand on his cheek. "You know we're here for you, right?"

Caleb nodded. “Yeah, I do.” He got up and nearly lost his balance. Rebecca and Jerome rushed to help him, but he waved them off. “It’s okay. I’m alright. Just a bit tired . . . and feeling like shit with all this crap on me.”

“Get out of those clothes, man. Take a swim,” said Jerome.

The pool sounded refreshing. Rebecca smiled as they headed back to the cove.

“I’ll see you guys in a bit. Promise,” he said as he began to take off his outer gear.

“You better!” replied Rebecca.

Caleb turned around and removed articles of clothing. His body ached and his hands shook. He calmed his nerves by breathing slowly. *Just a dream.* That’s all it was. Just a nightmare. He was now naked. Various types of scars entombed his body. He’d had a rough life, but that was in the past. It was time to look toward the future. And speaking of future, he was still hungry,and needed to find something more to eat. Not without the others though. It wasn’t fair that he eat and they didn’t. They go together. That was the rule.

He put a shaking hand on his growling stomach. *Food will have to wait.* He double-checked his belongings and headed to where his friends resided.

The three sat in the clear water and just took it in. Nothing could be sweeter. It was an especially hard day. They hadn’t caught much food—yes, vultures and field mice here and there, but no fruits or vegetables to really speak of. There were roots and small amounts of grass that had sprung up from the cracked desert ground, but nothing to conquer their pallet.

Caleb raised his head and looked up at the dancing reflection of the water against the cavern’s walls. The water brushed against his body as he sunk deeper into the pool.

“So, who wants to go first in washing their clothes?” asked Jerome.

"You can go first," exclaimed Rebecca. "You take the longest, anyhow. I want to relax some more." She sank deeper into the pool, lightly kicking her legs under water.

Jerome looked at Caleb. "Is that okay, boss man?"

Caleb nodded a yes in reply. He too didn't want to go anywhere. "Use the rope," he said.

"But of course," said Jerome. "Safety first, right?"

"Mhmm. And don't go down too fast! I'm tired of you breaking your equipment!"

"But that's the fun part! And I call total bullshit of being accused of always breaking my stuff!"

"You broke it last week," proclaimed Rebecca. "And the week before that."

"I was testing out its maximum potential! How was I supposed to know it would break!?"

"Because it has a warning sticker on it, numb-nuts! You go down too fast and the locking mechanism gets jammed!" Caleb yelled. He didn't enjoy raising his voice at Jerome. But sometimes the string bean would go too far and really piss him off. "You're damn lucky that we were able to repair it and get you back up here in the process!"

Jerome held up his hands. "Okay, okay. I won't exceed the maximum force while going down."

". . . Good," said Caleb. "Go. Wash your clothes. Send a wave if you need anything."

Jerome stood up and walked out of the pool. It was cold. He was shivering a bit, but he briskly walked to his crevice and retrieved his belongings. He double-checked to make sure he had everything. Especially his ropes. Just a few weeks ago, he had found an old backpack on one of their excursions for supplies. It was the greatest link to the past they had.

Jerome walked briskly past the pool. He was cold. But the fast-paced walking helped. It kept his blood going. Even though he was a string bean of a person, he was still muscularly toned. It had taken a couple of weeks to get used to being naked almost 24/7 around the other two. His mind, as well as theirs, had to get used to the realization this was the world they inhabited now.

The cavern did not narrow; it only widened into a steep cliff that went far down. There was barely any reflection to speak of. But one could hear the faint whisper of a waterfall in the distance.

Jerome set his clothes down and took the rope out. He entwined it and gave it some slack. It wasn't coarse or rough. It was smooth, almost like silk. He took the end of it and pressed a silver button. The end morphed into a three-clawed metallic prong. With a steady hand and a good eye, he measured the angle of where he wanted the claw to hit. Within a split second, the prong shot out and clamped securely into the ground.

The prongs dug themselves deeper into the ground, making a mechanical hum and then a beep signaling that the claw itself was embedded into the ground securely.

Jerome took out his harness and secured it around himself tightly. He placed the directional clamp onto the rope and hooked himself up. There was a chirp, and the rope lit up with many LED lights faintly illuminating his position. He threw the elongated rope down. It faded into the darkness of the cavern below. He took a slight breath, turned his back, and jumped from the ground into the abyss.

THREE

EDEN OUTPOST: THREE YEARS AGO

"Shit! Shit! Shit! Open the door! Please for the love of God, open the fucking door!"

A young man pounded on the blast door with each fist as hard as he could. He was on an excavating mission for food when he had heard a roar. It was Wrath, and it was hungry. Jerome quickly looked back. He could hear Wrath roar with hunger. It was getting closer.

"C'mon! Hurry!" he screamed.

He pounded on the door again, nearly breaking his hand in the process. He cried out in pain and looked at it. He was still able to move his wrist and fingers—albeit slowly.

His ear twitched. Sweat tinged his earlobe, but he could hear it very clearly. He breathed heavily and looked back, eyes widened in horror. Wrath was nearly at the doorstep. *Shit. Shit!*

There was a loud whir of machine and groaning. The blast door finally opened. A hand reached out and grabbed him by the back of the collar and violently pulled him inside. The young man fell to the ground, exasperated.

He looked on as the storm was nearing its destination. Closing his eyes, he was ready to be engulfed. That was his fear. Not being able to breathe. The door slowly closed as the storm rushed to take Jerome out. There was a loud boom as the door closed followed by a giant thud. Wrath didn't get its intended target and slammed against the blast door in all its rage.

"You alright, son?" asked a gravelly voiced Caleb.

Jerome blinked once, then twice. He outstretched his arm, and Caleb helped him up.

"Yeah, yes, sir. Thank you!"

"Yeah, don't sweat it," said Caleb. "What in God's name were you doing out there? You could have gotten yourself killed."

He got to his legs, still shaking. He looked around and noticed that he was in a giant cavern.

"What, what is this place?" he stammered.

"First, answer my questions," demanded Cal. "What were you doing out there, kid?"

The man tried to think. His brain and body itself were drained by fear and extreme heat. He couldn't think straight. Images flashed through his mind. His sister dead on the desert ground. Another image. His parents lifeless and dismembered bodies crumpled against the side of their home. Another image. Hiding underground with his sister, covering both their mouths. Trying not to make a sound, their eyes widened in utter horror. The past nine days were a complete blur.

"Son . . . ?" Caleb said calmly.

Jerome's mind snapped back into the right head space. He saw Caleb more clearly, and Rebecca, who had been resting, walked toward the two men.

"Everything alright?" she asked.

Caleb looked at the stranger cautiously. "I don't know yet . . ."

The young man blinked again and looked at Caleb and Rebecca and said, "I-I'm sorry, I'm okay. Yes, we're okay. The name's Jerome. Jerome Tucker."

EDEN OUTPOST: PRESENT DAY

The Abyss—the nickname was well suited for it. By no means was this a small extension of the cavern itself. This was a gigantic room. Like a cathedral with a vaulted ceiling.

It was almost pitch black, but thankfully Jerome's rope illuminated some of the area around him, like a firefly at night. He slowly descended into the darkness, and his eyes gradually adjusted to the lack of light. In the distance a faint sound of running water could be heard. He looked around; all he could see was the faint crevasse of the hollowed earth around him.

Jerome wished he could lower himself down faster. This was taking too long. It felt like an eternity, but he didn't want to piss Caleb off any more than usual. There was only so much the old man could take from him. Jerome was a smart ass most of the time, but he had it where it counted. Trust and good faith in people—the only two people he knew, and they counted on him.

He looked around and exhaled. He was bored. This was going to be a long trek down. He looked out into the distance and listened. He hadn't heard anything the past three years since he was with the unit. *Must be my mind playing tricks on me. Get your head out of your ass, man.*

Caleb had spoken once of winged creatures that could sleep upside down. *What were they called? Wait . . . bats.*

Bats. But they had long been extinct, since 2042. Not one member knew what the cause was. Caleb had told stories of these creatures—how they were the size of an average human; how they could fly, hiss, and use their clawed wings to attach to their prey and pierce the neck of their victims with their razor-like fangs and suck all the blood out, killing you in a matter of mere moments. It was indeed a terrifying thought. *Not going to happen to me. Not me.*

He gulped at just the thought. He closed his eyes and shook his head of the bad visions. Jerome looked down and could faintly see the ground below him. *Thank the maker!*

A squawk from his radio receiver made him jump. He rolled his eyes and reached into his backpack and grabbed the transceiver. He flipped a switch, and a static voice came on.

"Hey, you okay?"

It was Rebecca.

"Yeah, almost down to ground level," he said in reply, again looking down at the rocky ground down below.

"Good. Just checking to make sure you're alive and all. Caleb was starting to get worried."

"No I wasn't, String Bean."

"Yes you were. You're the one who told me to contact him to make sure he was still alive."

Jerome chuckled. "I'll be fine, guys. I won't take long, promise."

"Roger, Jerome," replied Rebecca.

There was a light click of the receiver turning off. Jerome clicked it off and put it back in his bag. His feet touched the ground. It wasn't sharp or rocky, but flat and rough. The souls of his feet were tough and used to the ground. Calluses had formed long ago from always being barefoot. He liked this state of being the most. Clothes, to him, seemed so primitive and unnatural. There was a sense of belonging when his feet touched the hard earth. *This is home.* He looked around for a moment and made sure that the rope was still secure. It was. He looked in his bag and found a small crank-controlled light. It was ancient. Someone had kept it in working order. Jerome had found it on one of the team's excursions in the desert. He had Caleb take a look at it, and as a team they decided to keep it for going into the Abyss and dark places that were hard to see. The machine wasn't like anything he'd seen before.

A different time period, that's for sure. It worked, and that's what was important. He cranked it a few times, and a flicker of light erupted illuminating his surroundings. It wasn't like the rope.

This was a duller, more faded light. Not what he was used to. He cracked his neck and started out toward the sound of the waterfall in the distance.

He held the light aloft and let it guide his path. It wasn't a far walk, thankfully. Just a lot of careful footing. While the path where the rope hung was flat, the walkway to the waterfall had little rocks that could cut one's feet if stepped on wrong. He set his bag down and opened it up. With his dusty, dirt-filled clothes there were beat-up shoes. The size on the tongue was faded, but they fit his feet (even though they were a size too big). He put them on, laced them up, and began walking toward a darkened opening. His mind raced back to what Caleb had talked about. The bats. He hated that word. *Bat!* Jerome looked up and imagined thousands upon thousands of bats sleeping on the ceiling, waiting for him, ready to strike without warning. He shuddered and started to move at a more quickened pace. *Stop thinking about those things! They're gone. End of story.*

Quicker down the path he went as small pockets of water splashed beneath his boots as he trekked onward toward a darkly lit passage. He walked inside, cranking the light source again. The sound of water was deafening now. It was still amazing to him. When everything outside was agony at times, he could come here and have some sort of peace of mind. He bent down and put his hands in the water; feeling the cool sensation on his skin revitalized him. His rough, beaten hands were tired and needed relief. He probably would never tell the others how he felt about the water, but it was some sort of godsend to him, wherever they were. He pooled some water, took a sip, and began to wash his dirty clothes.

FOUR

"Harder! Come on! Fuck me harder!" screamed Rebecca as her body thrust back and forth in ecstasy. She moaned and closed her eyes tight as she was being penetrated over and over again. The one doing the penetrating was a slack-jawed mooch by the name of Kyle. He was ordinary looking, but he had beautiful green eyes. It drove her wild. And she was horny. So horny she wanted to consummate with the first man she saw. And that lucky bastard was Kyle Redding. Not the brightest crayon in the box, but he'd do. They'd met at a local dive one night. Kyle sitting at the bar, entrenched in his beer and looking at the clock wondering whether he should go home to that bitch of a wife of his. *A few more sips . . .*

The bar door opened and in walked Rebecca Masters, a hot dish that was ready for action. They'd hit it off really well. What seemed like a victory for Kyle, was agony for Rebecca. They talked and talked until the night started to wind down. It was 1:00 a.m. A few drinks led to kissing, and kissing led to Rebecca suggesting that they go back to her place.

"I'm goin'! I'm goin'!" he declared as he thrusted harder into her. He grabbed onto her ass and squeezed. Hard. Rebecca let out a yelp of excitement and started slamming her rear into him, trying to make the motions faster and the sex hotter.

"Come on! Do it! Fucking do it! Yeah! Yeah! Yeah!" she yelled at the top of her lungs as her breasts shook from the pleasure of having someone attending to her needs. "Keep going! Keep going! Don't stop!"

She looked back at him, wanting to see the expression on his face. She wanted him to know that he was fucking the most beautiful woman alive. He had an expression alright. His eyes were a hollow, puss-filled mass, his lips dry and teeth full of decay. Rebecca's expression was not that of horror, but confusion.

"Kyle? Baby? Why'd you stop? Seriously? You're stopping? It was just getting heavy . . . what the hell?" she asked.

Kyle sat motionless. His hips kept thrusting, but he started to turn into grains of sand, and piece by piece he drifted away.

Rebecca quickly opened her eyes. Still lying in the pool, she blinked a few times to get her focus back, and looked around. She was alone. *A dream.* It was nothing but a dream. *What the fu—? Who the heck is Kyle?*

She suddenly felt a strong sensation in her nether region. It was overpowering, satisfying, and it also angered her. She put her hand on her forehead and gritted her teeth questioning what she had just dreamed. Rebecca honestly didn't know. She just knew she hadn't had any good sex in a long time. There was Jerome, but her feelings toward him were platonic. *Still . . .*

No, she thought. *It'd be too weird.*

She shook her head and wiped her lips with the back of her hand. Gingerly she stood up and walked back toward the entrance to grab her clothes. She looked over to see Jerome sleeping, curled in his makeshift bed. His clothes were drying by the blast door. Rebecca then checked on Caleb. He too was fast asleep. And snoring. Rebecca moved past him with great ease, not to disturb him.

"You okay?" Caleb whispered.

"Yeah," she said. "How long was I out?"

Caleb squinted one eye open and said, "About two hours, give or take. You closed your eyes and were out like a light. Figured you didn't want to be bothered by me or String Bean."

Rebecca smiled. "Thanks. I'm going to go wash my clothes. Did you do yours?"

Caleb shook his head, "Not yet. You go ahead. I can wash mine tomorrow. Got a big day and . . . all." Caleb yawned and quickly fell back asleep.

Rebecca walked softly over to the old man and gingerly touched his hair. A sweet man, a nice man. It was a wonder they'd made it this far in life. She turned around, put her boots on and descended to the lower depths of the cavern. She wondered what Caleb meant by it being a big day tomorrow.

FIVE

The sun slowly rose. Beams of its rays warmed the cool landscape. Caleb awoke first. He yawned and stretched his arms in the air. *Nothing like a good night's sleep on a hard surface. What I wouldn't give for a bed. And a good hard drink.* The old man slowly got up and looked at the others. Still asleep. He took a look around him and found his sandy clothes. *Screw it.* He could wear them again. They weren't *that* dirty. Just sand filled. A few sweat stains here and there but nothing that horrible.

Bathroom. That's what he needed most. An alarm went off in his bladder, loud and clear. He went to the keypad and typed in a few codes, and the blast door opened. The sound woke Rebecca and Jerome.

"Rise and shine, boys and girls! Got a big day today!" he ordered as he walked outside the blast door. Rebecca and Jerome went back to sleep.

Caleb walked down the side of the cavern; the sun caressed his naked skin. He put the side of his hand to his forehead and looked upward. It was another bright day. He did this almost every morning. It was his way of wishing good fortune to the day. He put his hand down and proceeded around the cavern's exterior rocky walls.

The outside was like a rock fortress. He put his hand out and felt the surface. It was sharp and jagged, but it was home. He didn't remember what had happened before; he just knew that Eden was his home.

He walked around a corner and looked out at the horizon. It was just endless desert. There were white bones sticking out of the ground in the distance at different points. They were sea creatures varying in size, but he couldn't tell any of the different species.

There was an ocean, but it was almost dried up. It was as if the sun had scorched the earth and taken out a piece of it. Caleb could see a faint tint of dark color in the far distance, but the journey itself would be too far for them. They would need a month's worth of supplies in order to even attempt it. He held onto himself and went to the bathroom. A breeze emanated from the east, and it made him smile. The tide was coming in. Caleb finished up and walked back to the entrance of the cavern. Rebecca and Jerome were still sleeping. He just looked at them and shook his head. *Amateurs. Every time . . .*

"Hey!" he yelled. "Wake the hell up!"

The two finally woke up, squinting at Caleb. "We're up, Cal . . . We're up," said Rebecca, stretching.

"Amateurs. Can't even get up early. C'mon, we've got a lot of packing," he said.

"For what, boss?" asked Jerome, standing up and stretching.

"Food! We're out of it. Hurry up."

Rebecca and Jerome looked at each other for a moment and quickly got their clothes on. They checked their supplies and gathered as much water as they could carry in their bags. *So, this is what he meant*, Rebecca thought to herself. *Could have told me last night.* She grumbled under her breath as she loaded her heavy pack onto her back. Jerome quickly got his supplies together and put his pack on his back. It was heavy. Heaviest he'd ever had it. This was going to be a long journey. Food was scarce. He guessed it was time to find a new food source. Caleb had told him that food used to grow on these things called trees. Succulent things called apples, and oranges, and something called a pineapple.

Jerome wondered what the hell happened to the world that was before. Many theories entered his mind, but they were just that. Theories. He put his oxygen mask in his bag and checked the percentage of the current tank in his arm. It was at 100%. He put extra oxygen packs into his bag and headed outside with Caleb and Rebecca. Caleb opened his flip switch on the blast door and input a code, and it roared as it closed. They waited until it was fully shut, and headed out toward the warming horizon.

"Where to?" asked Jerome.

"There," said Caleb, pointing to the east. "Figure we hike that way and see what we come up with."

"Sounds like a plan," said Rebecca.

The three companions set out to the east. They'd traveled that way before, but today was going to be the farthest they'd ever traveled. They balanced their packs on their shoulders and backs and headed outward. The desert was heating up. Their skin was beginning to burn. At least Wrath hadn't caught up to them. Yet. The horizon became a blurred visage around them. Rebecca looked back at the fading image of Eden and continued to march forward.

The air was a sticky sensation that was felt all around their bodies. The companions still kept a steady pace. It was early morning, but they knew in a few hours it was going to get hot. If it weren't for the uniforms they were wearing, they would die of exhaustion. Their clothes kept them relatively cool. They heard the faint sound of crows and vultures in the distance and tried to pinpoint which direction it was coming from. They determined it was northeast and headed that way. Food was food. And they were hoping they would find tons of it.

Caleb and the others started a slow, steady sprint, paused, and looked around. The sound was closer, but they couldn't see anything. No crows. No vultures. They slowed their breathing and focused their hearing to where the sounds were coming from. They looked in all directions. Nothing.

"Where're you hearing it most?" Caleb asked the others.

They turned their ears to the loudest point of origin of the sound. There was nothing. Then, a squawk.

"Over there!" said Jerome, running toward it as the others followed his lead.

They covered their eyes with their hands to get a better view in the distance and looked up to the sky. Two to three Vultures were circling in the sky. The team looked down to see what had died on the cracked earth. There was no sign of a carcass.

"Do you want to do the honors, boss man?" asked Jerome.

"Don't I always?" replied Caleb, who took off his bag and set it down. "Remember the plan. Come and get me when I have them both or at least one."

"Yes, sir!" said Rebecca.

Caleb slowly walked toward the circling kettle. He stopped, looked back at his friends, and lined up his body almost perfectly underneath the birds. He lay down and closed his eyes, pretending to be dead. He put his arm out and rested his head on it. He concentrated his hearing to the circling swarm in the sky, waiting for the moment they were going to dive down and try to feast on his flesh. *Like that's going to happen . . .*

Caleb felt a breeze come across his body. He opened one eye to peek at the two birds to make sure they were still circling and interested in him. They were. The two birds dive-bombed down and landed next to him. He lay motionless but could clearly see they were very large. Their wingspan was at least five to six feet wide. They were disgusting beasts to him, but at least they were edible. The two carrion eaters circled Caleb and squawked at each other, probably communicating whether or not to eat this large meal before them. Caleb slowly opened his eyes to a blurred visage of the two vultures arguing among themselves. They were in the perfect spot. Like a flash, Caleb grabbed both of them by their necks and squeezed tight. They screamed and squawked, trying to break free, pecking and biting his hands and trying their best to claw his arms with their sharp talons, wings flapping wildly.

"Now!" he screamed to his friends. They ran toward him as he struggled to keep the birds in both hands. His muscles flexed as he tried to keep his tight grip on their necks. There was a break in the chaos, and with his right hand, he broke one of the necks, dropping the bird to the ground. With his other hand, he squeezed harder and took his now free right hand and with both broke the remaining vulture's neck, letting it fall to the ground. He looked at his cut-up arms and hands. They were bleeding and severely scratched. It didn't matter to him. He had gotten his team food.

"Dear gods, they're huge!" said Jerome.

"Probably the biggest we've ever had," replied Rebecca. "Are you alright?"

"I'll live," Caleb replied. He picked up the two vultures by both necks and held them up. "Not bad. Looks like a good week's worth of meat."

Jerome handed him a slender rope and watched as Caleb strung both birds together. It was an art how he did it. He always made these fancy loops and knots that baffled Jerome. It was because he wanted to make sure they were secure. One day he would ask Caleb to teach him.

Rebecca took a large sack out of her bag and held it open for Caleb. He put the two large birds in, and they closed it, setting it on the ground. Caleb knelt down and pressed his thumb against the surface of the bag. A pad materialized, and he pushed a button labeled Freeze. The inside of the bag became ice cold. An interior freezer. It could keep the meat preserved for at least two whole days.

"I can carry it, boss," said Jerome. "They aren't that heavy."

"Thanks."

Jerome put the frozen sack in his bag, barely being able to close it. It was a tight fit, but it worked. He hoisted his now heavier bag to his shoulders, and they looked around.

"Where to next?" asked Rebecca, looking at the desert-filled horizon. She wanted to get back to Eden, but they needed food. Restocking was a pain in the ass. Why did they have to be born into a world that was on the brink of extinction? It didn't make sense. Sometimes at night she would wish that the world would just explode and destroy everything and everyone. This was no way to live. But at other times, she would hope that maybe, just maybe trees would grow again, that everything would turn green and good again. Those were stories though. Just stories. How could anything good come out of this damning place?

"How about over there?" pointed Jerome, to a large blurred land mass in the distance to their right. It was a far walk, but he was sure they could make it.

Who knows? It could be fruitful for their stomachs and whetting appetites. Caleb looked in the direction where Jerome was pointing. He thought about the walk a few moments and did the math in his head.

"Think we can make it?" asked Rebecca.

"Yeah . . . yeah, I think we can. We'll have to ration our food supply of course, but I think we can make the long haul."

The company marched onward to their new destination. It was getting hotter. They conserved as much water as they could but spent more of it sweating from the intensifying heat. Rebecca took out a headband and wiped her brow and her neck. She tied it around her after she was finished. Jerome perspired the most. He should have been used to this the most, but on this day, it was agony. Caleb just grunted in frustration and carried onward. The vulture's claws had dug deep, and his arms were throbbing. *Probably got some goddamned bird disease now. Just what I needed.* He took his canteen and took a sip of water. It was still cool. The canteen was insulated to keep liquids cool. He didn't really care. As long as he had something to drink, he was content. Except when it wasn't so damned hot.

There were no edible plants to speak of. It was just a barren field of desert and wind. The air was dry, but it was the best they could do. They continued on, looking toward the horizon to where the black mass stood that Jerome had pointed out.

Jerome started to wonder if it was worth it or if he had sent them out to their demise. Caleb didn't venture outside of the outpost too often, for fear of heat stroke and getting lost.

He usually was able to find supplies close to Eden, but this time —this time it was not so easy. Humanity was dwindling to the point of a pin.

Caleb knew there were other humans around, but no one had shown up except Rebecca and Jerome. He couldn't remember how Rebecca came into being on his doorstep. It was just him all those years ago, in the dark. Caleb wiped that memory from his thoughts. He was responsible for them and didn't want to be the cause of their deaths by drifting off into his head.

Time went on, and the sun was slowly setting in the west. Rebecca looked at the fiery star and quickly squinted, covering her head with her hand. She quickly looked back and continued on with the others. They said nothing. There was nothing to speak of, just getting to the dark mass that was on the horizon. They could see it more clearly. But it was still a sea of heat from the sun reflecting off of the ground.

Another drink. And then another. Jerome set his things down and took his breathing mask out. Caleb and Rebecca followed suit. It was getting hard to breathe, let alone being able to walk. They were exhausted and felt they were no closer to their destination.

"Let's rest here for the night," instructed Caleb, who was taking out his belongings from his bag. "No sense in going any farther, not until tomorrow."

Fortunately, he had prepared for this. He took out a folded tent he had found a few years ago and got it standing upright. It could fit a max of five people, so they would have plenty of room. The three made their way inside and said nothing. Rebecca tried to look upward at the darkening sky, but couldn't. Her eyes closed, and she drifted off to sleep. Caleb and Jerome quickly followed suit. It was nice to finally rest.

The ground shook. The three quickly awoke and ran outside. The sun's morning light blinded them. They quickly gathered their belongings and packed everything. The desert shook some more and then suddenly stopped.

"Everyone alright?" asked Rebecca.

"Yeah, just . . . what *was* that?" asked Jerome, looking around wildly.

"Earth-shake," replied Caleb. "Hasn't been one of those in a long time." He folded the tent and picked up his belongings. "Everyone have everything?"

"Yeah," replied Jerome.

"Do we still head toward that direction?" asked Rebecca, adjusting her backpack. The ground shook again, this time less violently.

"We move forward!" said Caleb. "We've come too far to turn back. I'm not going to let something like an earth-shake be the end of us."

They gathered the rest of their things and continued their way onward toward the dark point of the horizon. Hours passed; it was late afternoon when they came upon a large object before them. It was a gigantic hole that went down as far as the eyes could see. Around it lay strands of green vines that encircled the entire edge, crawling downward into the depths. The team stared in amazement. This was clearly nothing like they had ever seen before.

"So, what should we do?" asked Jerome.

"I'm not sure. This wasn't the earth-shake," said Caleb. "This has been here for a long time."

Rebecca took a step forward and looked down. "Wouldn't happen to know how long, would you?"

"If I did, I would tell you," exclaimed Caleb, joining her looking down. He kicked some loose rocks downward. Moments passed. There was no sound or echo in return. "Hmph. We'll eat first and decide what to do about this."

Four hours passed. They de-feathered the vulture carcasses, chopped the necks, cooked, and ate them. Even though they were big in size, yet still scrawny. When they were finished, they surveyed the massive hole.

"Do you think we can maybe climb down on those vines?" asked Rebecca.

"I wouldn't risk it," replied Caleb. "They could come loose and you could fall. Think harder."

"I suppose I can't talk you out of not going," said Jerome, looking at Rebecca.

"C'mon, Jerome. It'll be fun!"

"Oh yeah. Loads of fun!" he said.

"Well," said Caleb, "let's get moving."

They unpacked their gear and took out their illuminating ropes. Each member put in a numerical sequence on their lowering equipment and angled their clawed ropes to the ground. The prongs dug themselves into the hard sun-scorched earth and clamped down hard. They put another set of codes into their equipment. Caleb, Rebecca, and Jerome each looked at one another as they secured their harnesses. They were going to enter the unknown.

SIX

Darkness. A feebleness-inducing state that was ever so calming, and yet, it felt like home. This was Fred. And Fred—well, Fred was dead. At least the part of him that was human, anyway. You see, Fred Comstock—or Freddy, as he was known to his peers—had taken a turn for the absolute worst. He didn't remember what happened to him, but knew he had to wake up and somehow get out of the current predicament he was in. Freddy was impaled on a sharply pointed stalagmite erupting from the bottom of the ground. He opened his eyes—cracked and full of dried puss—and widened them, stretching his sockets as best he could. He was hoping to see something, but it was just a black swirl; like being wrapped in a felt blanket.

But then he heard it. It was something familiar . . . something that he couldn't quite put his finger on. A sound that was extremely faint, but there was something else. Something he could *smell.* That was another perk. His sense of smell was in overdrive. If he could just reach it, he'd be more than satisfied.

Like a toy that hasn't been on for a long time, he opened his rotted jaw. His teeth were black; his mouth oozed a thick, dark slime. Bits of dust and pebble escaped from his mouth, and his tongue stretched out for the first time in what seemed like forever, his vocal chords slowly humming to life as he tried to speak, but could only utter a soft moan.

Fred lifted up his head and looked around, trying to get a sense of his surroundings. That was the horrible part about being in a state of suspended animation, becoming aware again was both terrifying and surreal.

With all of his might he tried to get up, but could barely move. He was weak. He moaned, this time in frustration. His guts were hanging there, splayed out like loose curtains as he tried to push himself up from the impalement. He raised his arms and tried to pull himself up, but gave up. Fred closed his eyes. Darkness was consuming him once again. *No.* He thought. *Feed. Feed.*

But Fred could hear it again. The noise was louder; the smell was wafting over his senses. He couldn't take it anymore. The need was too great. He let out a long moan, trying to scream, but couldn't find the right connections. So, he just lay there, waiting for his meal to come to him. That was the best plan he could come up with. The sound was coming closer; he knew that for sure. It was only a matter of time. He had a newfound hunger, and it was on its way. Fred would be feasting soon.

Down and down they descended into the unknown. The company had never been this far out. The fact that they were was nothing short of a miracle. Their illuminated ropes slowly swayed as they gave pause and made sure they were still tethered to the surface. The jagged wall formations around them were slowly getting darker and began to mesh together. It was beginning to look the same. The three tugged on their ropes again, again making sure they were taught. They were. That's one of the things that Rebecca and Jerome found gratifying about Caleb: the man knew the placement of things. That's for damn sure.

The team descended some more as their rope sensors kicked in and somewhat illuminated their surroundings. They were now in complete darkness, save for their ropes.

Gotta love the simple things, Rebecca thought to herself as she looked upward and saw that the opening was now the size of a quarter. *So far away . . .*

Rebecca continued down and looked at her friends. Both Caleb and Jerome were next to her, concentrating on their descent. She smiled. It was nice to have friends that cared for her as much as she did for them. The feeling made things at least bearable in this new world.

"You still with us?" asked Jerome.

"Yeah, just thinking how much longer it's going to be when we hit bottom . . . if we ever do," she said, once again looking up at the opening. A feeling of dread washed over her, as if she wasn't going to see the surface ever again. She quickly shook her head clear of it. *Get ahold of yourself, damn it. For fuck's sake!*

Caleb chimed in, "We're probably almost down to ground level. Just a few more minutes."

"Oh yeah?" asked Jerome. "How can you be sure?"

Caleb pulled out a contraption from his jacket pocket and examined it. "Because of this. Says we're about forty fathoms down and . . . only twenty more to go." He put the machine back in his pocket and looked at his friends. "That's if I'm reading the damned thing right."

Jerome rolled his eyes, "So, it's a guess, then?"

"Pretty much, son," replied Caleb.

Should have known . . . Crap, thought Jerome, *always something with us, isn't there?* He looked down and had to take a double take. He squinted and leaned in as the party continued to go downward.

"Hey, hey, guys! I think I see the bottom!" he said as he pointed.

They both looked where he pointed, and squinted. It was ground alright, smooth and it looked faintly copper in tone, though that was because of the illumination of the ropes themselves. They all smiled, and Rebecca and Jerome hurriedly made their way to the ground.

"Damn it! Wait!" ordered Caleb as he began to chase after his companions.

"Hurry up, old man!" exclaimed Rebecca, who was looking up at Caleb closing in on them. Jerome laughed and pressed the button that made his descent faster.

"Jerome, remember what—" said Caleb before he was interrupted by Jerome.

"Yeah, yeah, I got it, C!"

Jerome landed feet first, followed quickly by Rebecca.

"Beat ya," he said. "You get to wash my clothes for a week, pretty lady."

Rebecca punched him in the arm. "Bullshit. We never made a bet." She unhooked herself, as did Jerome.

Caleb landed with brute force. He unhooked himself and yanked his two friends by their jacket collars. "What. Did. I. Tell. You?" he said very slowly, looking at them sternly.

"Oh, come on, sir, we were just having some fun. We landed, didn't we? Safe as spit," said Rebecca, stretching her legs and her body.

"Yeah . . . right," grumbled Caleb, who looked around their surroundings. Since the sun was still out, they could see very faint objects in the distance. *Probably more rock.* Caleb pressed his feet firmly on the ground to make sure his team was on a sturdy surface. He stepped back once, twice, and on the third time, felt nothing but air.

"Damn it!" he said, and grabbed hold of Rebecca and Jerome, both caught off guard and immediately pulled him back. He quickly opened another pouch in his vest and pulled out a flare. With a quick motion, he broke off the ignition end, and the object erupted in flames of bright teal. He pointed it down to the surface where they were standing. The other two followed the flare. It was a surface, but in actuality, it was a very wide ledge.

"Holy shit," said Rebecca and Jerome at the same time as they stared down. There was more rock and jutting wall below, and something else. It was metal. A metal beam. The three had puzzled looks on their faces. What was a beam doing this far down?

"Oh-kay . . ." said Jerome, trying to make sense of what it was doing here.

Rebecca and Jerome took out their flares and lit them up. They raised them over their heads, as did Caleb. What they saw left them speechless. In the vast distance there stood looming structures, that were seen more clearly. It was a city.

"Ah, shit," exclaimed Caleb.

SEVEN

"And you didn't know this was down here, because—?" asked Jerome, still in awe of the visage before him. *An underground city*, he thought. It had, of course, long since been abandoned and almost fully destroyed. Few remnants remained though: partially tall skyscrapers, various freeways and sidewalks. There was even a postal mailbox, which surprisingly didn't look damaged, as far as they could tell. As for the rest of the decayed Atlantis, there was destruction on almost all sides from what they could see with their flares.

"Oh yeah, like I knew about this. I'm in as much shock as you are, Boy Scout."

"Well, this is different," said Rebecca, who was still holding her flare steadfast.

The companions looked around, trying to find a way down. Although there was the metal beam that could be seen jutting outward toward them, they still couldn't make the leap. Skulls would be cracked, stomachs impaled. No, they had to find a different way down. Caleb looked at the two. He already knew what they were thinking.

"Let's get the ropes and head down. Flares out," he said. "Careful, and if anything goes wrong on our way down, we evac back up. Understood?"

The two understood, crystal clear. They all turned and pressed a button on the back of their harnesses that recalled the ropes. There was a slight whir as the ropes returned to their respective origins. A few moments later, there was a faint click of the ropes locking themselves back in place.

Jerome hoisted the supply case on his back to get a better sense of balance.

They looked at the metallic structure they had seen from the ledge. Up close it was a rusted dust-filled pile of scrap, a silent homage to a distant past.

The harnesses whirred as they slowly made their way downward. The beam continued to rise above them slowly as they descended. Bolts and rivets were missing, and it looked like it would topple over any second.

Caleb and the others squinted in the distance, trying to see more of the city's vast landscape. It was futile. Not only was the beam blocking most of their view, but it was also almost pitch black as they made their way down to the bottom.

Thank the gods we're almost at the bottom, thought Rebecca. She was anxious to start exploring as soon as she touched the ground. She looked up to see the opening. It was now a dot with faint light coming through it. She looked downward and shivered. It was cold here. Not freezing, but she wasn't used to this condition. The others felt it too, though they didn't show it. *Men. Never showing their emotions.*

"Hey, you okay?" asked Jerome, sporting an expression of concern.

"Yeah, just a bit cold is all. Not used to being away from the heat."

"You're telling me. I'm kind of missing it. But look on the bright side," he said, "no Wrath and no sand getting in your hair."

Rebecca smiled. He was right, after all. No Wrath and no damn sand and no pock marks on her body. "Very true."

“Eyes open, people,” interjected Caleb. “We’re almost at bottom.”

Jerome and Rebecca nodded and refocused their attention to the task at hand. Their feet touched down, and they unhooked themselves from their ropes. They dropped the flares to the ground and took out their lanterns. They cranked the handles, and light illuminated the surrounding area. The metal beam was still lying next to them, but now they had a better view of the city.

Each looked toward the looming structures and still could not believe what they were seeing. An ancient city, made of concrete, wood, and brick. There were tattered windows and cracked roads, like that of veins on a human’s body. As the company moved forward, they could also see objects in the windows. They were hanging, ever so silent.

Bodies, thought Jerome. *There must be thousands.* Jerome looked to his left and then to his right as they made their way into what was to be considered the entrance. Besides the bodies, there was also something else. Silence. Not even a breeze. The only sounds that the team could hear was each other’s breathing. That frightened them more than the bodies hanging about like rag dolls.

“Keep moving . . . ,” said Caleb, who was on pins and needles.

Rebecca looked at Caleb and did as she was instructed. Something suddenly slithered up her nose. It wasn’t physical; it was a smell. It stung her nose upon entry, and she covered her mouth. The others did the same. It was the smell of rotted death.

“Goddamn that wreaks!” she exclaimed as she could feel her eyes tearing up from the putrid smell. It was like someone had just dumped thousands upon thousands of pounds of crap and puke and let it sit out in the sun for a few days. It was revolting. “Don’t suppose you have any plugs, boss?”

“Nope . . . Just—try and breath through your mouth,” he said.

“Easier said than done, Cal. Like Becky said, this shit wreaks! What’s with all the bodies anyway? What the hell happened here?”

Caleb paused and tried desperately to come up with an answer. "Jerome, I'm with you on this one. I have no fucking clue. Best we just keep our guard up and take it slow."

"Yeah . . . sure," said Jerome. He never liked darkened places. It reminded him of how he and his sister had to live after their parents died. Garden of Eden took some getting used to. Yes, there were lights, but it was only light for a short time. He never got used to the dark. *Bad things happen in the dark, and I don't like this.* He shouldered the large thermo-pack some more and followed his friends.

Light! Light guiding the way to salvation! Feed! Feed! Closer . . . Closer, yes! Sound . . . coming closer! Whispers in the darkness, remember . . . try to remember. No. Move. Must . . . move. Can't speak. Can't move. Pain. So much pain. Food. Hunger. Feast. Flesh. Blood of my blood. Flesh of . . . flesh. Yes! Must have flesh. Closer . . . Closer the sound . . . no! Soundssss. They come closserrr. Feed. Feeeeed. Almost time. Almosssst tiiime. Tiiiime. Wherre amm I? So . . . hungryy. Soo . . . hunggrrrryyyyy. Feeed. Almosst tiime. Time . . . Feeed . . .

Fred flared his rotted nostrils and widened his eyes. He was still impaled on the damn stalagmite. But he had to wait. Just a bit longer. His food would come. It had been so long since he ate *anything*. He didn't have the strength. Yet. But soon, his agonizing wait would pay off. The sounds could be heard closer now. He couldn't understand what the sounds were saying though. He just saw darkness. But there was a slight hint of red now. Like walking down a tunnel, he saw red. That must have been what the light was! The red light of salvation illuminating in his mind.

He tried to remember how to laugh. But all that was coming out was dust and a black ooze. So, he just stared up into the vast black and ever so slowly he tried with all his might to smile. It hurt, but he knew that it felt *good.* A deep wheezing breath was inhaled and immediately exhaled, followed by a hacking of phlegm and acidic puke. He didn't care. He was going to have his meal, and he'd be goddamned if *anyone* or *anything* was going to get in his way.

Fred closed his eyes and started to dream about his feast. His mouth transformed into a widened grin and he continued to wait.

Yess . . . Food. Sweeeeet fooooooooood.

EIGHT

They were getting close now. He could taste it. The sweet nectar of the gods. Fresh meat. Fred opened his eyes and looked around. He could hear them. His food was close. Ever so close. *Voooiiicesssss . . . so verry louuud . . .*

The trio made their way deeper into the catacombs of the city's structure. They all started cranking their lanterns again. The darkness was all around them. Caleb looked around, squinted, and paused mid-step. Something was off. He couldn't put his finger on it. But there was just *something . . .*

"Stay here," he ordered as he slowly took a step forward. He wished he had more to say, but the hair on his arms was standing straight up. *I don't like this.*

"Boss? What is it?" asked Jerome, looking onward. Silence. Complete and utter silence around them. He looked at Caleb and then to Rebecca. He could see that her breathing had increased, her pupils were dilated. Jerome put his hand on her shoulder. She stood, still hyperventilating, but managed to calm down and looked at her friend.

"Hey, you okay?" he asked.

"Yeah . . . yeah, I'm fine. Just nerves is all," she replied, holding his hand in reassurance.

Jerome nodded. "Okay . . . good to hear."

Caleb motioned for them to move forward as he squinted his eyes again, looking forward.

"Everything cool?" asked Rebecca.

"Yeah . . . ," he replied. "Just didn't feel right is all. You two okay?"

"Yeah, of course!" Jerome said nervously as he let his eyes look upward at the fading giant building in front of them.

"C'mon," said Caleb.

The three companions made their way toward the front entrance of the city. They stopped and, together, took to the shattered and broken streets of a once thralling city. Around them were flashes of cracked and broken sidewalks, what looked to be a bridge of some sort in the distance, and bruised buildings that were just about to give way and collapse around them. They had to step carefully, for they could only see so far around them.

They walked forward, looking at the ancient structures that surrounded them. Caleb had heard stories about what they used to be. *Shopping malls, fountains, fr . . . freeways.* All gone. They were now derelict and slowly crumbling, only being held together by their beams and giant steel rebar shooting out from each end.

The team kept moving forward, listening for any sounds in the muddled darkness. They were beginning to feel claustrophobic—like they were going to be swallowed whole.

"Not even a chirp," whispered Jerome to Rebecca as he tightened his grip on the cooler. "Feels like we're going deaf or something . . ."

She put her hand on his arm and gave it a gentle squeeze. "Yeah, but don't worry; I've got your back."

Jerome nodded in compliance. *And don't forget I've got yours, girl.* He looked at Caleb, who continued being steadfast and alert. Jerome realized he should probably do the same. They were in unknown territory, after all. He realized he was already missing the surface. As of now, there was no turning back. Curiosity had gotten the best of them, with their new surroundings and all.

Caleb held up a fist to alert the others. They froze in their steps. And listened intently. Around them was crumbling cement and various cracked fixtures. Caleb looked down at the semi-illuminated sidewalk. It was blistered and cracked in every which way. The light in his lantern suddenly went out.

"Stupid piece of shit," he said to himself, cranking the handle again. "Remind me to fix these."

"Yeah. Sure." Rebecca answered as she sped up to Caleb's location. Jerome followed suit. She felt safer being next to him, as did Jerome. They were a unit, after all. They should continue as one.

The city seemed to rise upward into infinity into the darkness. The trio couldn't tell for sure how far the buildings extended, but they knew the once beautiful structures must have been a pinnacle of perfection.

Jerome quickly looked back behind him. They were deeper now. To him, it was as if the city had enclosed around them and had locked its doors. While that wasn't true, it sure did feel that way. He refocused ahead of him. *That is some crazy bullshit. Yep.*

"Freeze," instructed Caleb.

Jerome and Rebecca followed the command, tensely looking around.

"What is it, Pops?" Jerome asked.

Caleb turned around and faced him. "What did you just call me?"

"Pops . . . what? Not appropriate?" Jerome asked.

Caleb squinted his eyes, an expression of confusion across his face. "No!" He pointed a finger. "And I'm not that old!"

"Okay, okay," replied Jerome. "Sorry."

They made their way slowly deeper into the vast cityscape. Caleb lifted his lantern and squinted into the distance. There was an unusual object he could see. It was faint. He got the other two's attention, putting his hand back, signaling to slow down. They noticed what Cal was staring at.

"What is that?" asked Rebecca, trying to get a clearer view.

They moved closer to the object and lifted their lanterns higher to cover more ground in front of them.

Rebecca sniffed, and suddenly her nose began to sting. The same reaction happened to Caleb and Jerome. They placed their hands over their nostrils. The *smell.* The damned smell. It was foul—like a mixture of gas and shit. With the emphasis on *shit*. Permeating around the area was a rotting aroma. The three wanted to puke.

"Blech! What the hell!" Jerome asked fervently.

"My thoughts exactly!" said Cal, who was trying desperately to breathe through his mouth. The smell still crept in and left an awful bitterness that his taste buds could feel, and it tinged his senses. He ordered them to keep moving forward. The shape was becoming much clearer now that they had stepped further inward. He suddenly stopped in his tracks.

"Ah, shit," he blurted out.

They all saw it. "It" was a body.

NINE

The sound! The smell! Yes! Yess! Feed! Food is here! Must be patient . . . must time right! So hungry . . . Feed! Warm, hot flesh! Feed! Feed!

"You've gotta be kidding," said Rebecca, trying hard not to puke. *The smell! That's where it's coming from. Fuck!*

They all stared at it, mesmerized. The corpse was impaled on a stalagmite that protruded from the ground. The thing's guts were a blood-soaked mess that was hanging all about. Caleb moved the lantern closer to get a better look. He examined it more without daring to touch it.

"Must have been here for years," he said as he nervously paraded the lantern around it.

"Yeah? Like how many?" asked Jerome, cautiously moving closer to Caleb.

"Hard to say . . . but at best guess, ten, maybe fifteen years at least," he said. "Becky, come here."

She stayed put. There was no way she was getting closer to that thing. The smell seemed to get stronger and even more foul. "No, I'm going to stay here, thanks."

Caleb looked at its face. The skin, or what once was the skin, looked like runny oatmeal and was dried in random spots. There was something else—in the eyes, which were closed. He leaned his lantern in closer. There was movement underneath the eyelids. It was like tiny swirls and dots were dancing underneath.

"What the—" he whispered.

"FRED!" exclaimed Jerome, pointing at the tattered name tag on the shirt. "This guy's name was Fred."

"*Was* being the operative word," chimed Rebecca, who was still standing a few feet away.

Now! Feed now! Noww! Feeeeeed!

Without warning, Fred opened his eyes.

"Holy fuck!" screamed Caleb, immediately darting backward. Jerome's eyes widened, and he fell backward.

Fred opened his mouth and let out a harrowing moan, as black ooze dripped from his encrusted dried-blood lips.

"What the actual FUCK!" screamed Jerome, scrambling to his feet and hurrying to Rebecca's side, staring in horror at what had just taken place. *This isn't real! This isn't real! This isn't real!*

The eyes! Caleb thought. Fred had eyes, but they were engulfed with dozens upon dozens of maggots, wriggling about, trying to break free.

Fred reached out, desperately trying to clasp the fresh meal that was now before him.

Different! Different! Get free! Try something different! Flessh! Feed! Feed!

He moaned again, and with what strength he had, exerted himself forward toward his meal. Caleb and the others stepped back, still not sure what to think. Maggots began falling out of Fred's eye sockets, which were blacker than the night sky. Black ooze poured from his mouth once more, splattering the ground making a thop sound.

With both arms outstretched, he extended himself more, and at long last his torso (what was left of it) finally began to give way and pull apart. Dead skin and sinew was tearing itself. What was left of blood was pouring out as the dried intestinal tract swayed to and fro. It was eventually cut on the jagged rock of the stalagmite.

Caleb and the others could see acidic liquid and other juices pour from the openings.

Fred moaned and continued his approach toward his three meals. His torso gave way and he fell to the ground with a hard thud. A moment passed, and the amputated body started to animate again.

The three friends were still drop-jawed and in disbelief at what they were witnessing.

Fred's innards poured out over the ground as he began to crawl faster toward them.

Caleb could see Fred's legs still in motion. Then he realized that Fred's torso was still connected by a thin sliver of spinal tissue that hadn't been severed.

Fred's eye sockets contained fewer maggots, but the visage was still grotesque. His nose oozed black gunk as he opened his mouth again and let out another gasping moan.

Caleb couldn't take it anymore. Something exploded inside of him. It wasn't anger. It was utter fear, and he was scared, not only for himself, but also for his friends. His hand balled into a fist, and he leaped at Fred on all cylinders. Caleb raised his arm and began punching Fred in the sides of his skull. The skull. To his surprise, it wasn't the hard-cranial protector anymore. It was like punching a rotten piece of grapefruit. His fist smashed the skull again. And again. The head finally imploded, Caleb's fist and part of his forearm going in deeper. He could feel the brain matter, the oozing slime wrapped around his hand. Slowly he retracted it, exposing the bits of brain matter and frayed nerve endings and fragments of blood.

The odor stabbed at his nostrils. Caleb gagged and threw up haphazardly into Fred's mutilated rotted skull. He wiped his mouth and stood up, backing away. Rebecca and Jerome gave him looks of worry.

"You okay?" she asked, putting her hand on his shoulder.

"Fine," he said, looking down at Fred's now officially dead corpse. "Let's just get the hell out of here."

Rebecca and Caleb turned around and began to walk.

Jerome stood still and kept looking at Fred. "Shit, you don't have to tell us twice."

The walk back to their ropes seemed long and arduous. Each of them kept looking over their shoulders, as if to make sure they weren't being followed. So far, they weren't.

What the fuck was that thing? "Let's double-time it, people!" ordered Caleb.

They jogged past the buildings, looking straight ahead, lanterns dangling from their belt loops. They were almost to the entrance, and the team saw a faint glow in the distance.

The ropes! Thank the gods! Jerome jogged faster toward them.

Faster they ran; it was a sight of sweet and glorious freedom. They had reached the metal beam and immediately latched themselves onto it. Caleb glanced at Rebecca, her face radiating a soft glow from her lantern.

"I-I'm sorry. I—" he stammered.

"Let's just get the hell out of here," she interrupted.

Up and up they climbed, the cool touch of metal felt like the best thing since running water. Moments later, they had reached the top of the cliff face. With all of their might they pushed themselves upward and immediately grabbed their lighted ropes.

Together they ascended to the surface. The opening at the top was slowly getting larger in size.

Rebecca smiled as they were getting ever so close. *Yes! Just a bit more!* She started going at a faster pace, leaving her friends below her.

BOOM!

An explosion.

BOOM!

Another explosion. And then another!

Objects shot out from the jagged wall in front of them. Jerome felt it first. Then Rebecca, and finally Caleb.

"Holy shit!" screamed Jerome. *Hands!*

Decayed forearms and tendril fingers grasping desperately for their warm flesh.

Get off! Get off! Rebecca thought, fighting the onslaught that was trying to get every bit of her they could. She was mortified; her eyes widened as another decayed arm burst through the rocky wall and attached itself to her face. She couldn't breathe. She felt the slimy crab-like fingers dig into her cheeks and could smell the rotted meat engulf her senses. Her eyes rolled into the back of her head, and she passed out.

Caleb punched and kicked every degrading hand he could. It was an uncontrollable feeling. The feeling of survival. With his right foot, he kicked a protruding arm that was clawing at his pant leg. He looked around and could see Jerome punching and kicking the hands that were trying to cling to his boots. Caleb then looked up and saw that Rebecca wasn't moving.

"Becky!" he shouted.

Jerome looked up in her direction. "Rebecca!" he shouted, kicking off another onslaught of hands, which were grasping at his feet and chest.

"We'll get her! We have to push our way through!" yelled Caleb as more and more hands and arms burst through the rock. "C'mon!"

The two raced to Rebecca's aid; she was still passed out. Caleb took the hand that was clasped onto her face and broke it off. Literally. There was a muffled scream that could be heard coming from within the rock face. Blood oozed from the dismembered stump as the hand fell to the ground below.

Caleb gently smacked Becky to rouse her. Jerome was keeping the other outstretched arms at bay as best he could. Rebecca moaned softly.

"Hey, c'mon. C'mon . . . ," he said softly.

She finally awoke with a fright. She inhaled and exhaled furiously and leaned over and puked, immediately remembering the toxic, nauseating smell. There were cuts to her face, light gashes from where the fingers had been.

"C'mon. Up and at 'em. Let's go," he said to her. "It's okay. Hey, hey we're here. Go, we'll cover your back."

Rebecca looked at Cal and nodded, wiping her lips, embarrassed. She flipped a few switches and continued her fast ascent upward, Caleb and Jerome following behind. *Finally.*

BOOM!

Four outstretched arms erupted from the wall and quickly latched onto her, strangling her body as she was caught off guard. She writhed in pain, trying desperately to break free.

BOOM!

More explosions could be heard as hands and arms burst through, grabbing onto both Cal and Jerome, who feverishly kicked their attackers every which way they could.

Rebecca screamed as she felt her skin being pulled and tugged on. She grabbed a slime-riddled hand and pulled it off her waist. In doing so, she unhooked herself from her rope. She began to free fall.

TEN

I'm flying. Is this what freedom feels like? Being able to go anywhere, or do anything? Wait. No, not flying. I'm falling. Fast. My body hurts. Blood. So much blood. All around me. Caleb. Jerome. Screaming . . . can't make it out. What? I can't—I don't—understand what you're saying! Fall? Grab? Grab onto what? Hundreds. Hundreds of them. Hands. All decaying . . . smell. The awful smell. Jerome? Where are you? Caleb? Oh God! I'm falling! Back to reality! Now! No, this can't be real! I was flying . . . no. Wait . . . not yet. Not now. I . . . wasn't . . . flying. Falling. That's right. I'm falling. Get it together, girl! Get your brain straight! Shit! Nearly to the ground. Fuck! Fuck! Food! No! Have to re-position myself. On my backside. Quick, you dumbass! Have to roll onto my stomach. Have to grab onto something . . . anything. A hand! I need a hand! Jerome and Caleb, they're too far away. Damn it! What the hell! Wait! There! A hand! Gotta try and brake my fall with it. Try to survive. Angle it just right . . .

"Holy shit!" Rebecca said as a decayed hand burst through the rock side. She grabbed ahold of it and held on with all of her strength. The arm continued to emerge, and locked up at the shoulder as the weight of Rebecca acted as a counterweight.

She looked up and saw her friends fending off the massive hordes in front of them. "Guys, I'm okay! I'm—"

Suddenly she realized she saw herself hovering in the air, holding on for dear life to the dead bastard in the rocky wall. The arm was rotted meat and tendon. She started slipping and grabbed onto its forearm, and the thing was giving way. A head could be seen now. It was like Fred. Dead and puking what was now a mixture of black ooze and dirt. The stuff fell on her brow and smelled awful. Its eyes were blackened holes with white, milky pupils. No colored iris, just death and full of an undisputed look of hunger.

The thing pulled further down, her body weighing more than the sickly thinned bastard. Something had to be done, and fast.

No! I won't die! Not like this!

She climbed up its body, gritting her teeth. She was now face-to-face with the disgusting bastard. She howled at it, her fierce eyes piercing straight into its dead ones. With all of her strength, she then lifted her legs and wrapped them around the thing's waist. She flipped herself over and was straddling its shoulders. It started moving downward more. It realized what was happening and was flailing its arms, trying to grab onto its foe. Rebecca, however, had other plans. She grabbed both of its arms and used them as a rein. Rebecca leaned in and whispered, "Time for a ride, asshole."

The bastard lifted its head snapping its decayed maw at her viciously, trying to get its teeth into her tasty soft flesh. She let go of one "rein" and made a fist and started beating the thing in the skull, bashing it to a bloody messy pulp. She lifted her hand and saw a gathering of blood and brain. She flicked her hand and wiped it on the thing's back. Then she leaned forward more and let gravity take control. Looking up at her friends, who were finally making their way down to her level, Becky let out a glorious howl and flashed a sick smile of triumph. The other two heard it as they saw the two bodies go down the jagged rock.

"Cripes!" yelled Caleb, wide-eyed.

"Is she serious?" asked Jerome. "She's serious." He took a rotten arm that had burst out at him and broke it off.

"Wooo! I'll see you boys down there!" Becky yelled.

She rode the body at an almost ninety-degree angle. She was scared, thrilled, and praying to whoever was listening that she wouldn't die. Dust flew up into her face as well as bits of rock.

The bastard's skin fell off of its face, pieces flapping about, puss and what looked like blood flying around in the air. *At least the smell's gone down.*

It felt like an eternity going downhill. But she finally reached the bottom. They flew-tossed into the air and crash landed at the bottom. Thankfully the bastard did indeed break her fall. She hit her head hard and blacked out. *Fuck.*

It felt like hours had passed. She would hear faint voices in the distance. She couldn't make out where they were coming from, but she knew they sounded familiar. Darkness now surrounded her. It was pitch black, and all she could feel was a presence over her. It wasn't fearful. It was . . . friendly. *Wake up, damn it!*

She dreamed. Rotten teeth and spider-like fingers were clawing and gnashing at her legs. She was pinned on the ground, rotted hands uprooting from the floor, pinning her body down, scratching and tearing at her sweet, warm skin. Her eyes opened wide and she screamed.

"Hey, B! It's okay! It's okay! It's us!" a reassuring voice said. It was Jerome, both hands on her shoulders, widened eyes looking at her.

She breathed heavily and looked around. There was an orange glow around her. Caleb was holding his lantern over her.

"You alright?" he asked, surveying the wall above them.

"Ye-yeah. Just took a hard tumble is all," she said, looking at the dead body a few yards from her. It wasn't moving. She let out a sigh of relief. Jerome outstretched his hand, and she took it, smiling. They turned their attention to the towering wall. They could see the bastards clawing their way out, their bodies emerging from their dirt-filled wombs.

The three saw the things falling. One by one they were hitting the upper cliff headfirst, aided by broken necks. Some, though, were "lucky" enough to land on their shoulder or backside. Those that did immediately continued to crawl toward their adversaries.

"Time to go," said Caleb, who made an about-face and headed toward the crumbling city, the others following his lead. It was official. Their way of escape was now forfeit.

ELEVEN

They could hear the sounds fade into the distance as they made their way deeper into the ancient city. At first it was as if the bastards were closing in on them. Closer and closer they seemed to come. Jerome looked behind him. There was nothing. Just darkness combined with the orange glows of their wind-up lanterns. He squinted and felt droplets of water blur his vision. It was sweat. He quickly wiped his eyes and brow and looked at his hands. There was a mixture of sweat and rocky ash on his palms, with the added sting of the claw marks and the slight throbbing of his joints. His muscles were sore, but he was more concerned about his friend. *Balls of steel that girl. Crazy woman, she is.*

Caleb had the same reaction. Stingy, salty sweat. They were down below, but not close enough to the Earth's core. They continued on, each of them wondering the same thing. How were they going to get the hell out of this mess?

Hours passed. Slowly the trio walked, cautiously back into the crumbling city streets. They had rationed off more of the carcass. Jerome's bag felt lighter. He was missing the weight of it for some reason. It felt off and weird. He, like the others, trekked on, trying to see if there was a different path they could take back up to the surface.

So far, it wasn't looking like it. He noticed Becky looking up toward the blackened emptiness.

"What?" he asked her.

"Sun's gone. Stars are out now," she said while taking a drink from her canteen. "It's strange . . . we've only been down here a while, but I'm already starting to miss them."

Jerome put his hand on her shoulder. "Come on, let's find a way out of here."

She smiled, and the two caught up with Caleb, who was a few steps ahead of them.

Caleb. The man was intelligent and had a stone-cold demeanor about him. But his heart was in the right place. Always was. He never really talked about what his life was like before. Both Rebecca and Jerome wondered if he had seen the tall buildings that would go on forever and almost touch the clouds. He never said. He was the silent type and only spoke when needed to be heard. He liked it best that way. It was *familiar.*

He took out his canteen from his pouch and gulped down some water. He put the cap back on and shook it. *Almost gone.* It was time to find a water source. Or else they'd be royally screwed. He stopped in his tracks. "Okay, mount up."

Jerome and Rebecca stopped and looked at their friend.

"How are you two on water?" he asked them.

"Halfway," replied Rebecca.

"Got about a quarter or so left, boss," Jerome answered.

"Okay . . . I'm almost gone as well. We're going to need to find a source as soon as possible," he said, looking down the central path of the crumbling landscape. "We'll head down that way. Maybe we'll find a spring or, hell, something useful. Any questions?"

No one asked.

"Here's hoping we don't run into any more of those things," he said.

His two friends nodded in agreement. If they found a giant horde of them down there, they were dead. There was no denying they were all scared. But it was better to move ahead. At least they stood some sort of fighting chance and could maybe find some sort of weapon to fight off those things, if any should come in their path.

Silence. No wind or rustling of anything. They had walked on, passing Fred, who was very much dead. Becky and Jerome glanced at his remains. The eye sockets were just now two blacked abysses. *Maggots must have gotten their fill and moved on*, thought Rebecca, who, like Jerome, quickened her pace.

Caleb lifted his lantern and sniffed the air. Nothing. He surveyed the area and led the team to a crossroad. They each took a spot and with lanterns in hand, looked for clues, anything they could find. *A way out, water, hell, one of those magic carpets would be fantastic!* He went to the left and lifting the lantern, tried to get a better look in front of him. It was a crumbling building. Only it looked like it was of special importance. There was a large marquee with bold lettering scrolled across. It spelled out a strange title, but it was incomplete. It was burned at the edges, so it was missing the final word.

REVENGE OF THE JE–

He lowered his lantern and saw there were steps leading to wooden doors, but they were blocked by giant cement slabs. Caleb could see that he could still possibly fit through. It was going to be a tight fit for his frame. He turned toward the others, who were across the way, looking around at the various buildings and shops.

Rebecca focused her attention on a shop called Gelsons. Jerome was studying the ground. There were large objects with writing that was either faded or burned off.

"I'll be back in a bit!" Caleb called out to his friends.

They looked at him.

"We'll come with you!" said Becky.

"You continue looking for a water source. I'm just going to check something out. I'll call you on comm if anything goes wrong."

"Okay . . . be safe," said Rebecca.

Jerome looked at her. "Is he for real? We should be going with him!"

"He's gonna do what he wants. There's no arguing with him. We've got comm if anything goes wrong," she said.

Jerome shook his head, finally surrendering the argument.

Caleb made his way over the giant slabs to the door. It was ajar a bit, but he was able to squeeze through. Lantern in hand, he looked around. He noticed a large cylindrical beam in front of him. He climbed over it and realized he had entered an open area. He slowly made his way to the center and saw that there were two stories to the building. Beside him was a shattered glass barrier, and a counter was directly across from him. It was full of dust and broken pieces of ceiling and strange food strewn about on the cracked tile floor and on the counter itself. *Food. Nothing that I've seen before. Only talked about . . .*

The food was popcorn. It was also covered in a thick coat of dust, and spiders had made it their home, as he could see thick webs hover over it. There was also an oily stench that could be traced to the machine behind the counter where more popcorn was sitting. *Yeah, not appetizing at all.*

He wandered around the corner of the counter and saw the rotting bodies. His own body tensed up in anticipation that the meat bags would rise up and attempt to snatch him. He inched closer. He lifted his lantern and squinted at them. They were sprawled out on the floor, but there was something peculiar. The pair he was staring at was holding hands, cuddled next to each other. Caleb felt a great emotion of sadness wash over him. There were a number of questions he had. What were they doing just before they died? Who were they? And most importantly, how did all of this happen?

These questions would have to wait. He had to continue his search for water and hopefully a way out.

He turned around and headed to what was a *T* section of the building. There were rooms on both ends, with fallen debris and bodies lying in the hallway. They didn't move. He turned to the left and was in front of two doors. The handles were dust ridden. He carefully placed his hands on them and opened the door. It was pitch black, save for the illumination of his lantern's light around him. But he could see the severely damaged walls. Carpet and wallpaper were cracked and ashen. Slowly he made his way up a dust-filled ramp and could see a giant torn screen with hundreds of torn seats with debris fallen on them. His lantern began to flicker and went out. He cranked the handle, and the light came back to life. *Nothing . . . shit.*

CRASH!

Caleb put his attention to the back of the theater. He wasn't alone . . .

"What do you think of this?" asked Jerome, studying a burnt sign that was lying on the dirt-filled ground next to his feet. "Don't know what it means. You?"

Rebecca stopped looking at the different stores and looked at what Jerome was seeing. She too couldn't tell what the sign meant.

"Howdy Doody. What the hell is a Howdy Doody?" she asked.

He shook his head in confusion. "Got me, girl."

He was now on the balls of his feet, squatting down. He saw something underneath the giant sign. "Hey, can you . . ."

"Yeah, sure," she said.

Together they lifted the sign up as high as they could and moved it over a few inches. Underneath the sign they saw it. A doll. It wasn't Howdy Doody. It was a child's doll. And it was being held by the hand of a little girl, who was decapitated. Both of them heaved and nearly threw up. It wasn't just the smell; it was the very thought of someone's child. The body was clothed in a torn ashen dress. The body was a pale gray color, that was somehow still preserved in the cold darkness. The age of the girl could only have been about five or six years old.

That part hurt Rebecca the most. Someone so young could have their life snuffed out in a matter of moments. Jerome tried to look for the girl's head, but couldn't find it. He lowered his lantern so Rebecca would have more light to view the body.

"What should we do with her?" he asked.

"What can we do?" she replied, looking at him, a tear falling down her cheek.

"The only thing that would be right would be to bury her. As deep as possible. Would only seem fitting, right?" he asked.

"Yeah," she said. "Yeah, it would."

Piece by piece, they moved various bits of wreckage and objects and placed the girl's body into the ground, covering it with the dirt and what they thought were fitting mementos and tokens of respect. Jerome was saddened by the fact that they didn't have a complete body.

"In my culture, we believe the spirit wanders the earth if the body is not complete. It is not hell, but simply a waiting period until they can ascend to the heavens."

"What happens if the body will never be complete?" Rebecca asked.

"Then the spirit will walk the earth until the end of time. Always searching."

"That's pretty fucked up," she replied.

"I know . . . that is why I am saying a prayer for her spirit to find peace."

Rebecca couldn't escape the feeling of utter loss and loneliness that had washed over her. How long had this girl been down here? She shook her head and put the last of the items on the girl. They stepped back.

"Would you like to say anything?" Jerome asked.

She wanted to, but she couldn't find the words. What can one say about someone that they never met or even knew existed? She swallowed a deep pit in her throat and shook her head. "No."

Jerome nodded. They focused their attention to the theater.

"Cal went in there, huh?" he said, a worrisome expression on his face.

"Yeah. And I don't like it," said Rebecca.

Just as soon as she had finished her sentence a soft moan erupted. Her eyes widened as did Jerome's. *Not now. Goddamn it, not now! Fucking hell!* She turned to see where the sound originated. Jerome quickly turned around, and his ears perked, focusing intently. *Another* moan. It was closer. Much closer.

Another one. It was louder this time. The two quickly turned around and saw them. They were a few yards away, darkened by the night, their bodies barely illuminated by their lanterns. But they came closer, *faster.* The gaping maws and soulless eyes were there. Hungry, and desperate for a meal. The Bastards; puss filled, blackened eyes, and slack-jawed mouths. The smell was getting worse. It was like a sick beacon warning Rebecca and Jerome. The Bastards weren't just a few. They were *many.* Some drudged on foot, while others were crawling over every inch of trash to get just a taste of the two meat sacks.

Hand in hand, they both decided to head into the theater. The Bastards were getting closer: the smell wreaking havoc on their nostrils. A few yards closer, the moans more sorrowful and much more hungry and "alive."

Better to die together than to die alone, I guess, Rebecca thought to herself as she led Jerome toward the steps of the dilapidated construct. Together they leaped over the fallen structures blocking their path. Jerome quickly jammed his fingers against the door frame and began to pull. There was no budging. The damn thing was stuck.

Feed! Feed! Flesh! Flesssh! More! Must have moore!

The Bastards were now closing in. Quickly they moved and homed straight in on Rebecca and Jerome. They were now inches away from devouring them.

"C'mon! Pull!" she shouted; the veins on her biceps and forearms beginning to pulsate as her fingers also clamped down as hard as they could on the door frame, helping Jerome.

"Almost got it, girl! Almost! Just a little more!" said Jerome.

Slowly the door moved along with the large cement slab that was blocking the entrance. They could now feel it—the hot breath of the Bastards literally on their doorstep, decayed arms outstretched, the stench of shit and puke wafting over their senses.

"Becky, go! *Now!*" Jerome ordered.

She didn't even hesitate, and squeezed her body into the door frame. She turned around and held out her hand as Jerome squeezed himself in. She pulled on his arm as hard as she could.

He pushed his way through the small sliver of an entrance just as the Bastards' scaly thin fingers were about to grab him and rip his flesh limb from limb. He fell on top of her, who in turn fell on top of the large slab that lay a few inches behind her.

Jerome quickly got off of her and turned around, his mouth gaped open. The two could see the slimy, blood-soaked hands viciously trying to claw their way inside. They tripped over the slab outside, their gray-boned tendrils that were their fingers clawing their way up the wooden frame, thinking of how to open the door.

Both Rebecca and Jerome rushed to the door and quickly slammed it shut, in the process slicing a few Bastard fingers off. They could hear a moan coming from what had happened. Apparently, they still felt pain, that much was certain.

"Quick!" whispered Jerome. "Get that slab and bring it here!" he said, pointing to a piece of slab on the ground a few yards from their position. Rebecca took her lantern and placed it next to the slab they were lying on moments ago. She raced over and lifted the medium-sized slab of concrete and handed it to Jerome, who placed it near the entrance of the door.

"That's not going to hold!" she said.

"I know. Just a placeholder is all! Help me with the giant one! We gotta push! With all our strength!" he said, exhausted, as bangs could be heard from the outside. The door vibrated with each powerful bang.

He hurried behind the larger slab, and Rebecca followed.

"Now . . . PUSH!" he ordered.

With all of their combined strength, they slowly pushed the giant slab toward the door.

A few moments later, the giant cement slab was leaned against the door frame, with the smaller piece on top, for good measure. The banging continued outside. For now, at least, Jerome and Rebecca knew the Bastards weren't getting inside. And they also realized they were trapped inside.

MINUTES EARLIER

CRASH!

Caleb looked up, squinting in the black, his lantern overhead as he heard the sound of glass shatter and break. He also heard a wet thump. A shadowy figure fell . . . and seconds later rose up.

"Crap . . ." he whispered under his breath.

The Bastard, from what Caleb could tell, had on a strange attire. Very regal looking and prestigious. He deduced that the thing used to work here. It opened its mouth, and Caleb could see its orange-silhouetted lips puke its black ooze as it started shuffling faster, moaning, its arms stretched out, making its way around the tattered chairs. It suddenly tripped trying to go downstairs. It slid down the steps and tried to balance itself on one step, then lost its balance again, falling down one more time.

Caleb walked up the steps and looked at the decayed figure, sprawled on its back, trying to figure out how to get upright again. He put the lantern over the thing's face. Its cheeks were sunken in, eyes were the usual blackened holes, it's mouth full of grotesque-looking bugs and other dead insects. It saw Caleb's boot and looked up at him.

Food . . . Food!

It reached up, trying to somehow grab Caleb's boot. It wasn't successful. Caleb's rage increased inside of him. With one hand he grabbed the thing's right arm and slammed it down on the ground, with his right foot stomping on its wrist, holding it there. He continued and grabbed ahold of the left arm and did the same procedure, only with his left foot. The damned thing writhed and, like a scared animal, began to chomp violently at its aggressor. It spit up bugs and ooze, trying to get a piece of Caleb. It bent its fingers trying to claw at Caleb's boots. Anything that would let it get the soft, meaty flesh. Caleb stared down at it.

"Uh-uh," he said.

The thing chomped at him even more ferociously. Caleb could see the anger in its darkened eyes.

"One of your things is easy. But a handful of you fuckers . . . holy shit."

Caleb bent down at the waist and stared intently at the thing silently.

The Bastard finally got it through its feeble mind that it wasn't going anywhere. It widened its eyes and looked at Caleb. Moments passed as they both stared at each other. They seemed to be studying each other, trying to find each other's weaknesses. Finally, the thing gave a mewing scream of rage and hate. Caleb had had enough. With one fist he bashed the thing's melon from end to end. The head exploded from the inside, and brain and guts covered Caleb's hand, while bits of tender skull and other parts of brain adorned the carpet. He could see the thing's hands twitch, nerve endings slowly dying. Caleb wiped his hand on the wall next to him. *Disgusting. Nasty as hell.*

He looked back up at the projection room. *Nothing coming from there. Good.* He turned around and saw the large screen torn and lights broken. All was quiet. He saw two doors that had Exit signs posted on the top. Unfortunately, they both were blocked off by fallen debris of wood and cement. He took his lantern and attached it to his vest. He heard faint sounds coming from the outside. *Rebecca. Jerome.*

He took one last look around the room. *No water here.*

Caleb walked out of the theater's room. It was still dark inside the hallway. He made his way back to the wooden doors and noticed that the large cement slab was against the door frame. He could hear the moans of the Bastards outside. There was no way he could move it, not by himself, and why would he want to? He had to find the others. Becky and Jerome were in here somewhere. He took out his comm and spoke into it.

"Becky . . . Jerome . . . ," he said softly.

There was no answer. Just static. "Shit."

He looked around and made his way back inside the theater's open space. *Time to get moving.*

TWELVE

MOMENTS AGO

"That should hold them!" Jerome said as he helped Becky up off the floor. She had collapsed from all the exhaustion of pushing the giant slab against the door.

BANG!

BANG!

The Bastards were using what strength they had and bashing their heads against the entrance. From the sounds of it, more had arrived. Both Becky and Jerome were hearing louder voices of moans, as more had arrived at the door.

The two decided to race to the first room they could find and hole up there.

"We've gotta find Cal," said Rebecca. "He's here somewhere. Hey, try your comm."

"Okay," Jerome answered, taking his comm from his vest pouch. He pushed the button to communicate. "Cal? Cal, it's Jerome! Over!" Nothing but squawks and static. He looked around, holding the device up toward the ceiling to try to maybe get some sort of signal. It was hopeless. He was still just receiving bursts of static in return.

"Damn it," Rebecca said.

They looked around and saw two doors behind a large archway that was rusted and dust filled. They both looked at each other and ran to them. Caleb had to be inside. Rebecca was sure of it. They went around the archway and opened the doors. They were in a similar room, but it was much smaller. They knew that. This room barely had any damage on the inside. There were a few broken pillars and dust-laden seats, but one could almost call it mint. Almost.

The two raised their lanterns, the bulbs began to flicker, and they tried to get a better sense of awareness around themselves. In the faint, dark distance, they could see bodies slumped over. Joints were twisted and broken, heads and various limbs were missing. The air was fermented in their nostrils. Death was all around them. It stung, and they covered their mouths.

"Breathe through your mouth. Less impact of the stink," said Jerome. "Can't believe this happened . . . however it happened."

Heads were backward on the bodies. Flies accumulated for what seemed like years, laying their eggs on the corpses' eyes and other parts of their bodies.

Jerome and Rebecca looked toward the front of the room and saw a stage.

The stage was intact for the most part. There were fallen beams and lights, but there was a large hollow space that could be seen jutting out from the bottom portion of where the steps were supposed to be. The wood that made it up was rotten and crumbling away. *That hollow*, thought Rebecca, slowly starting to walk toward it. Jerome grabbed her shoulder and it caused her to stop in her steps.

"What—?" she asked.

She soon realized why she was stopped. The entrance to the hollowed-out crevice was large enough, sure, but what took her off guard was that there were sea shells and other sea-like fossils adorning the jagged walls and entrance. It was strange. Had they actually reached sea level?

We reached sea level? Must have if there's sea life. But why is only this area affected? Doesn't make any sense.

"We reached ocean depth?" she asked. "How the hell is that possible? We didn't go that far down, did we?"

"I honestly don't know, girl. You got me. I'm stumped," said Jerome. In his head he was still trying to find how the hell this was possible.

They crept closer, looking behind them to see if anyone or anything had followed them inside. So far, nothing did.

The entrance was a collage of jagged sandstone and wooden planks jutting out to the sides and toward them. It was very odd looking indeed.

"Shouldn't we wait for Cal?" asked Rebecca. She was curious about what was inside but wanted desperately to reunite with her CO and friend.

"What if he went this way? He could be inside wandering around or gods forbid, injured," said Jerome. There was a moment of silence when an idea formed in his head. "Okay, how about this: I'll go in, you stay here. If I find anything, I'll come get you."

"No! You're not going in by yourself! We go together. If it's too much we'll head back out this way," she said. "Deal?"

Jerome didn't like it. But with Rebecca, there was no arguing with her. He rolled his eyes begrudgingly. "Alright, fine! But I'm holding your hand."

"Such a gentleman."

Lanterns in hand, Jerome took her hand and clasped it. This was the first time they had any physical contact with each other. Slowly they made their way to the entrance. Immediately they could smell the sea. It was refreshing and a relief. They looked at each other and stepped forward into the new world.

THE PRESENT

The earth shook. Caleb looked around for a safe place to stay in hopes of not getting crushed by falling debris. In the dimmed dark, he saw across from him an indented space. There were machines that had long been silent, screens that now lay dormant and covered in what was a thick coat of dust and cobwebs. *Fuck it. I'll take my chances.*

He ran and hid in the corner, covering his head. The earth-shake lasted for what seemed like a long time. Down here, it felt like an atomic bomb was going off next door. But he knew it wasn't the case. He just hoped that wherever Becky and Jerome were, they were safe. *Not the best way to search for supplies!*

They huddled next to each other. Their lanterns flickered and turned off. They could feel the earth-shake. Only, in there it was more powerful. In the tunnel, the damned thing echoed loudly, like some sort of pulse sonar banging against the walls themselves. It was a thunderous barrage of shaking over and over again. They closed their eyes.

Later the shaking subsided. The two opened their eyes and looked at each other, and then their surroundings. Nothing had collapsed around them, and the tunnel was still intact. It was at that moment they both turned and headed back to the doors, to regroup with Caleb and find a way out. To hell with supplies. For now, at least.

They jogged out of the seashell-laden entrance and rushed to the double doors. They tried to push them open, but they didn't budge. Both of them looked into little windows. Both of them cranked their lanterns, and the lights flickered back on. They held the lanterns up to the windows and tried to make out what was wrong. There were no Bastards. Panic set in. They pushed the doors again, and they wouldn't budge. *They automatically lock when they close? What the heck kind of shit is that!* They tried to push the doors open again. Nothing. Not a damned budge. Jerome looked around and saw the problem. He pointed to it, and Rebecca looked. The earth-shake had caused cement slabs and metal beams to come crashing down in front of the door, each one either landing on top of one another or next to each other. They weren't getting out that way. Frustrated, Jerome slammed his fist against the door.

"Fuck," he said, turning around and making his way toward the sea life enriched opening. Rebecca followed. "Well, only one way to go now."

"What if Caleb comes? He could probably move those—"

"No, they're too heavy, even if C is built like a brick house," Jerome cut in. He was right. Even though Caleb was strong, he would have trouble moving the slabs of concrete, plaster, and wooden support beams.

"Fuck," Rebecca said.

The two continued toward the new entrance and paused. They looked back one last time, hoping against hope that the doors would explode inward and they would be able to escape the room. It was a pipe dream. Jerome faced forward and touched the sand-rock surface and stepped forward. Rebecca frowned, and with lantern in hand, she stepped forward, following Jerome.

His lantern went out. Flickering like a heartbeat and then dead.

"Shit," Caleb whispered as he smacked the damn thing once, then twice. In this new kind of hell, he hated cranking the handle. The noise wasn't the problem. It was what it might awaken. The thing cranked as the light flickered back to life. What sucked was that he couldn't crank it slowly; it had to be fast in order to build momentum and get the flame lit. *You'd think someone would invent something quieter.*

He got back to his feet and looked around, his senses slowly becoming more alert. He focused his thoughts on his hearing. In the dimly-lit corner, his eyes were beginning to adjust, and that meant they could play tricks on him. He was beginning to think the shadows were moving. He could trust his ears though. Right? *Yeah, right.*

He turned his head and looked down the hallway. It seemed to go on forever in the dark. He heard crackles of plaster falling around him and faint noises in the distance. Slowly he crept to his right, backtracking to the entrance. But there was a problem. One giant problem. He could only go seven to eight steps. His path was blocked. It wasn't just a section, no. He squinted his eyes and leaned in closer, using the lantern as best he could.

"Goddamn it!" he said under his breath.

Caleb could see the damage much clearer now. The entire corridor and hallway to the front entrance had collapsed on itself! A tapestry of support beams, plastered walls, and wooden supports could be seen. *Fuck! Fucking fuck fuck fuck!*

His ears perked up and twitched. He heard it. The hunger. The feeding. The Bastards had found a way in. And they had their sights set on Caleb.

THIRTEEN

The sea-infested corridor was narrow and long. Further down the rabbit hole they went, not knowing where they'd end up. Rebecca was hoping the other side or, hell, back to the surface. She knew that was a long shot. Jerome's curiosity was getting the best of him. He kept inspecting almost every bit of detail there was on the rocky surfaces around him. He noticed that Rebecca wasn't in the same mindset as he was. She gave him "the look." He knew it all too well.

"Sorry," he whispered, catching up to her. "It's just, I never got to see any of these kinds of things where I grew up. It's fascinating to me."

She smiled. "It's okay. It is fascinating, you're right. I've just been focused on getting the hell out of here, and regrouping with Cal."

Jerome gave her a look of understanding. "He is like a father to you."

Rebecca smiled. He was like a father to her. Brash, stern, but loving.

"Yeah, he is . . . ," she said, trailing off. A memory had come flooding back. It was the first time she met Cal, with his worn-out face, but eyes full of compassion and also heartache. The memory was just a flash. Nothing more. She heard Jerome's voice echo in her head.

"How did you two meet?" he asked.

She tried to remember, but for the life of her, couldn't.

"I don't remember," she answered. "I was very young, but there he was. I remember being picked up in his arms, his grizzled sun-soaked face, and his eyes. Those beautiful, caring eyes. They looked at me, and I remember myself not being scared anymore. I was safe, because he was there. But . . . there was something else I could tell, in those eyes of his . . ."

Jerome listened intently, looking at her. "What?"

"He was sad. Broken and tired. But the man pushed on, took me in, and now here we are," she said.

The tunnel began to curve to the left, the smell of the sea embracing their senses.

A tear fell down her cheek, and she quickly wiped it away. Jerome put a hand on her arm, gently squeezing it.

"We'll find him. We will."

She smiled and kissed him on the cheek. "I know."

Jerome smiled, and they continued walking. The tunnel began to downgrade, and they slowly made their way to a small opening. Both could fit, but they would have to crawl. They cranked their lanterns again and crawled through. The air was now deprived of moisture and filled with a heat that couldn't be explained. It was like they were wrapped in a warm blanket. The ground, while still firm, was now softer than before. This was different. Rebecca suddenly had the idea to take off her boots. Jerome did the same. The ground was soft, and they looked down. The ground was *sand.* They both knew the feeling was the best feeling either of them had ever experienced, and they needed a much-deserved break. The sand felt cool and refreshing against their toes, especially on the soles of their feet. They walked around for a while, when Jerome felt something hard and dull scrape across his heel.

"Ow! What the—?" he said.

He looked down, focusing the light of the lantern on the object that had struck his heel. The dark sand began to slowly sink around them. As it sank, their lanterns and eyes saw what Jerome had scraped his foot against. It was a finger. More precisely a bone, with cartilage still attached. The sand began to lower faster, and it was revealed after a few moments that the two were standing in a room full of bodies. The expressions on each of the faces was surprise and terror. The one that Jerome had encountered was reaching up toward him. The black sand had finally emptied enough to reveal a hardened surface.

Some of the corpses were preserved, while others, unfortunately, were in a horrid state of decay with looks of asphyxiation. Some had their hands wrapped around their own throats. On the more preserved ones, there were slash marks that were visible on the throat itself. There were also long, deep gashes on the abdomens of the others. It was disgusting.

Who could have done this? Rebecca thought, looking around the room in utter disbelief. These weren't the Bastards. These were innocent people. Victims. She couldn't take any more. She nudged Jerome and signaled that she wanted to leave. They couldn't do anything to help anyway. It was best if they just left them where they lay. *Whoever did this is long gone, and they're lucky. Hope they're burning in a special place in hell.* The two quickly grabbed their shoes and laced them up.

Shouldering the lightened bag, Jerome and Becky made their way through the grave, making sure not to step on any of the bodies. Their lanterns flickered as they passed. There was no way out to their left or right. They could only head straight forward. The ceiling looked as if it was going to collapse.

Jerome raised his lantern higher. Something had caught his eye. He immediately stopped in his tracks. He grabbed Rebecca by the arm and made her stop. He pointed to the ceiling. She slowly looked up and gasped. *Spiders.*

They both stood still, terrified.

The ceiling and parts of the walls moved like a collage in motion. Both Becky and Jerome quickly made a mad dash for the exit. But as they ran, they saw that it began dripping with hundreds of the damned things. They turned around and tried going the other direction. That too was blocked off.

"Argh! This is bullshit!" Rebecca yelled as she looked every which way for a viable exit. The swarm slowly closed in, gathering momentum, wanting to cover the two whole and slowly devour them.

"Well, at least we'll die together . . ." Jerome said.

"Goddamn it!" shouted Caleb.

It wasn't the instant barrage of them. It was a slow trickle. He heard it from the outside—the distant moans of hunger. But then it came out of nowhere.

BANG!

It sounded again.

BANG!

The sound made him jump out of his skin. He was trying to pinpoint where it was coming from. Caleb closed his eyes and concentrated. He let his hearing take over and closed off his other senses. The darkness seemed to wash itself around him as he tried to narrow down his search. *Where is it . . . where are you . . .*

The large wooden entrance. The Bastards were bashing their own heads against the door itself.

BANG!
BANG!
BANG!

The sounds were becoming even more ferocious and sporadic. Caleb was safe for the time being. He turned off his lantern and crouched down. *Nowhere to go right now.* He was tired, but knew he had to stay awake. He thought about Rebecca and Jerome, praying to anyone that would listen, hoping they were safe.

BANG!
BANG!

The damned noise intensified. He heard it now. A sound he was dreading and had hoped in the back of his mind it wouldn't come to pass. It was the sound of splintering wood.

"Goddamn it!" he shouted again, getting himself ready for whatever horrors came through the doors.

And come they did. The Bastards had broken through. Caleb hunkered down more as to try to not be seen, lest heard. Squinting through the black, he tried to adjust his eyes the best he could; he even attempted counting how many were bursting through the frame. He could hear them trip and fall over the barricade, but seconds later, they got up and continued their search for food.

Minutes passed. To Caleb, it felt like years. Just how many of these things were there? He was protected so far by the metallic beams and mountains of ceiling that blocked his path, but for how long? He couldn't stay there in that spot forever. They would eventually find him.

More started trickling through the doorway. He could hear them, same as before, tripping and getting back up.

Dumbasses.

He finally made a decision, and slowly he took a flare from his vest. He took the tip and bit it off, the end exploding in a waterfall of red flame. *Shit shit shit shit!*

They turned their attention to the noise and the faint red glow in the distance. The Bastards knew where their meal was hiding.

Feed! There! There! Fresshh! Flesssh! Feed!

Caleb had only one choice: He was going to have to somehow lure the Bastards away from where he was. The fact that they were able to break through a large wooden door meant that these were strong. And resilient as fuck. The Bastards moaned louder and shuffled faster to where he was hiding. He had one chance. If this didn't work, he knew he was royally screwed. He tossed it as far as he could through the widest opening he could find in the wreckage. It landed near the popcorn stand. They didn't go for it.

Shit! Damn it!

They stretched out their arms, and Caleb could see their white, soulless pupils. Hunger was in their mouths as they moaned vehemently. *I'm dead. I'm so dead.* He closed his eyes and gritted his teeth, waiting for them to break the barrier and lunge at him. He would try to fight off as many as he could, but he knew he was going to die. There was no way around it.

But something happened. The Bastards heard a new sound, as did Caleb. It wasn't the flare. It was coming from the popcorn machine behind the counter. He could smell it as well. *Gas.* The Bastards turned and motioned for the flare and the counter, focusing their attention on the bright flame. And then, moments later, a flash of bright white light. A ringing in his ears and hitting his head on the ground. Hard. It all went dark.

SOMETIME IN THE PAST- NEW EDEN BASE

"Will it always be like this?" asked the boy, standing on the cliff face looking toward the golden-colored hue of the horizon. The sun was setting, and he could see the last bits of day fade into obscurity as dusk started to transform into night. He felt a familiar hand upon his shoulder. It was from a middle-aged man, full of life, and a hard-ass.

"Like what?" asked the old man.

"I mean, like this," the boy answered, pointing to the earth in front of them.

"Oh, you mean dry. You mean dead," said the man, taking a flask out from his pouch and taking a giant swig. He handed it to the boy, who took a sip. "Nah, it won't always be like this. You know why, Cal?"

Caleb shook his head, not understanding, handing the flask back to the man.

"It's because it's going to get much worse. Ya see, this is paradise. But what's coming, ya see, what's coming is hell. A truly agonizing time. For you—" he took a sip, the liquor dribbling down his chin—"and for me too."

The man saw a lizard on the cracked ground. With one giant boot he stomped on it, killing it, but not before letting it squirm, trying its damnedest to get free.

"Heh . . . even for him. We're all fucked. So, you better bite the pillow hard, boy. Life is coming in fast, and as far as we know, it is going in dry! Not even some goddamned spit is going to make it feel tolerable. You understand?"

Cal looked down at the lizard and then put his hand around the old man's, holding it. "I think so, sir."

The old man nodded. "Good. Now . . . WAKE THE FUCK UP!"

PRESENT DAY

Caleb awoke with a start. As far as he could tell, he was still alive and still whole. He blinked furiously, getting his bearings. *What the hell?* Being careful, remembering about the Bastards, he slowly and quietly re-positioned himself, trying to see where they were. Flames danced in the distance as minor explosions popped up here and there. His hands began to shake. He searched for his lantern. It was only a few yards away from his feet.

"C'mon, work. Work!" he whispered, cranking the handle. A few seconds and the light slowly flickered to life. "Thank you, thank you, thank you."

Slowly he got to his feet, lifted the lantern, and checked to see if there were any more of the monsters. They were there, but in pieces. He could see that some more were entering the front doorway still and climbing over the destruction of where the explosion had happened. *Fuck.* He looked around and squinted to his left. He saw what looked like two metal doors and headed toward them.

FOURTEEN

I don't remember the taste of bread. I'm forgetting what water used to feel like going down my parched throat. I don't recall ever knowing what blades of grass looked like, or for that matter felt like.

A warm spring day, a cool summer's eve. Different types of clothing. A dress or a skirt to make myself feel more attractive. To get the boys to notice me. I know nothing of these things. They're all so alien in my mind. Distant concepts from a time that is now long gone. A past that once looked promising, from what I was told when I was a child.

Now that past—this future—is a tattered and torn reminder of how far we've come. I don't hate my life. This is what I was given. I just wish I could have experienced the feeling of nature when it was calm and gentle.

He told me about things that had long been forgotten. Places I only imagined in my dreams. Strange creatures that seemed like something out of legend, but only he knew of their existence!

He was like a man from another time, and I followed him wherever he went. It was like learning the secrets of the universe, passed down to him, who, in turn, passed them down to me. I miss him immensely.

I remember your face. Your warmth and compassion. But most of all, I will always remember how you loved me, though I was not yours by blood.

You, with those big caring eyes of yours. That heart full of love. You, who took me in when I had no one else.

I will never know what had come before, but I do know this:

I love you.

All my love,
Your daughter-

Rebecca

"Oh, you've gotta be kidding me!" shouted Jerome as the swarm of spiders approached furiously. Both exits were still blocked off, the blackened onslaught sliding down from every way.

Both friends held each other close as they silently accepted their fates. *This is not how I wanted to go!* Jerome thought.

Seconds later he looked over his shoulder. The exit—across from them. A sliver of hope. An opening. Just a small hairline of an opening, but that was all he needed.

"Becky, look!" he whispered.

Becky opened her eyes and looked.

"Go! Go now!" he said to her.

As fast as they could, they ran. Hearts were racing, hope was brimming. *Only one shot!* They reached the exit and immediately could feel the heat of thousands of spiders descending upon them. It made the hair on the backs of their necks stand up. The damned things were *close.* Right on top of them. It was a feeling of scratchy disgust. They hated it. They could now feel the prickling sharp legs attach themselves on their necks and heads. The two crawled faster and hurled themselves through the tiny opening.

They quickly stood up and brushed each other off, making sure they got every single one of the little things and that there were no stragglers. Holding his lantern aloft, Jerome pointed. "Look."

Rebecca saw it. They were regrouping. *Fast.* "Shit! Shit! Shit! What do we do now?"

Jerome looked around. On the walls there could be seen a slick, syrup-like substance. He had an idea. Reaching into his vest, he took out an extra flare. *Please let this work. Please, please . . .*

He ignited it and took quick aim. He threw it against the syrupy substance that was coating the cave's wall. The arachnids followed the blinding light like moths to a flame. And what a flame it was.

"Okay, time to go!" he said, taking Rebecca's hand and leading the way.

The flame caught and plumed toward the disgusting mass, setting them ablaze. Tiny screeches were heard as they burned and exploded from the mixture of heat and gas. Jerome and Rebecca ran as fast as they could, Jerome still carrying the cooler on his shoulders. He decided to dump it. The thing was more of a problem now than before. The situation warranted it, he thought.

Rebecca saw what he did. "You sure that's a good idea? We kinda need that to live!"

"No! Keep moving!" he called out.

Rebecca rolled her eyes and moved at a faster pace. Then they heard it . . . a low hum at first, and then an explosion of rock, dust, and other debris. The other debris, of course, being the thousands of carcasses that came flying through the tunnel at them. The two companions dropped to the ground and covered one another, closing their eyes. Minutes passed. The dust slowly settled. Both of them heaved inward and coughed uncontrollably. They took their lanterns and tried to find their way out of the corridor.

With their hands, they slowly felt their way through the jagged rock wall. Rock chips were falling from the ceiling as they moved forward, staggering every step of the way. They had come to an opening. A narrow bridge, easy to move across but did not leave that much room.

"Well, shit," Jerome said, cautiously looking down, holding his lantern over the blackened abyss. "What now? Should we try and cross? It's a long drop."

Rebecca looked down. It was a long drop. Her eyes widened as she began to get scared and her vertigo kicked in. She immediately sat down. Jerome knelt beside her.

"That's too high. Way too high!" she said, staring at the ground, trying to get her nerves under control.

Jerome looked at her and smiled softly. "Hey, it's okay. We don't have to cross. We'll find another way."

She smiled. It was great to know she had such confidence in her friend. They had been through a lot together, after all. This being the worst of it all. She was scared. They both were. But she knew they had to push forward, no matter how scared she was. She brushed his cheek and kissed his lips. It was gentle and sweet. She saw that he was blushing and giggled as they both laughed. *Huh. Not bad. Not bad at all.*

She laid her head on his chest and closed her eyes and fell into a light sleep.

Jerome brushed her hair softly and held her in his arms as they both rested.

"Ow! Son of a—! Goddamn it!" shouted Caleb over and over again. That was the third time he had tripped over his feet in the darkness. He was flat on his stomach and rolled over onto his back. He was tired and pissed off. He breathed in deeply and exhaled, coughing from the dust.

AN HOUR EARLIER

He crawled. He crawled his way past the hallway of corpses strewn over the ground. Some were complete, as in they had all their limbs and other appendages. Some weren't so lucky, however.

Cement beams had fallen on top of the poor souls, crushing their bodies and turning them into spaghetti sauce. The lumpy kind. Their blood and organs, what was left of them, had long dried out and stained the dust-ridden carpet.

He heard them. The moans. The abhorred gasps. They were outside. *More of them.*

He aimed his body for the EXIT door and pushed it open. It budged, but was blockaded from the other side. He held his lantern to the door and studied it. There were burn marks where the locking mechanism was. Not only was it barricaded outside, but someone had made damn sure nothing got inside. Or out.

Could Becky or Jerome have done this? Maybe there are others that have been surviving . . . dunno how though.

Caleb shook his head and headed back down the short walkway of the hall. He looked to his right. There was an open space he could crawl through. It was just wide enough for him to fit through. *Another tight squeeze. Something really doesn't want me to have an easy go at life! Fuck. Although . . . those two could have gone this way.*

Attaching his lantern to his vest, he took one last look around to make sure he hadn't missed anything. He knelt down and slowly crawled through the opening.

The inside was mapped with sand rock. It was a jagged mess, with dead crustaceans attached to it, and some more littered on the ground next to him. He decided that it was best to crawl on his stomach. There was no way he was going to go through on his haunches. He detached the lantern and jimmy-rigged it to fit his shoulder. It was an awkward feeling, but at least he could see his surroundings. The next thing he noticed was the smell. It was the sea. *We're that far down? Nah, can't be. Hell, what am I thinking? I've got things chasing my ass and wanting to eat me alive! And you're worried about reading sea depth.*

"Damn it."

The tunnel was narrow, but he was able to crawl. He was tired of small spaces. He enjoyed being out in the wide open. It was safer that way.

Continuing to crawl, he realized the terrain of the ground had changed. It was no longer the sand-rock he had spent the last few hours exploring. The first thing that tipped him off was the aroma in the air. It was a burning smell, like an explosive had gone off a few meters away from him. The next clue was the ground itself. He had to do a double take. With his hands, he brushed the ashen ground. His brain tried to answer the question of why there was a change in texture. Caleb rolled his eyes. *Screw this. Need to keep moving. Stop overthinking stupid shit.* He started to pick up the pace.

Around him, the narrow space had widened. He was able to stand on his haunches, and bracing his arms against the walls, he slowly made his way forward. Ahead he saw the tunnel widen more and he was able to stand; while not fully erect, it was sufficient for him to hunch over a little. He was doing his best to keep his balance. He needed to take a break from being on his stomach. It was tiring, and he needed to stretch his legs somehow. He stepped again and lost his balance.

"Crap," he said as he fell.

He couldn't see there was a large drop. He tried to fall back, but unfortunately, gravity had other plans.

"Shit! Fuck! Damn it! Ow!" he yelled as he tumbled down.

This wasn't a straight drop, but it was a heavy decline. Caleb managed to curl into a ball, trying to land on either side or shoulders, covering his head with his hands. The added pain of the lantern punching his chest didn't help. He had to try to save it somehow or get rid of it as a last-ditch attempt. *Screw it.*

In one quick motion he unhooked it. He had a thought. At the last moment he decided to keep it and cradle it in his arms. He had flares, but those would run out a lot sooner than the lantern.

He continued to roll downhill and finally reached the bottom, sliding through puddles of water.

"Fuck," he said, finally coming to a stop. He landed on his back, his eyes closed. He was thankful he had stopped, but he could feel the pain throbbing all over his body.

He lay there still, giving himself a moment to catch his breath, looking up into the darkness. With his right hand he took his lantern, which wasn't broken, and cranked the handle. The flame flickered but didn't ignite. He cranked the handle again. Nothing.

"C'mon, you stupid piece of shit! Work!" he scolded, smacking the holding case with his hand. The ignition sparked for a moment, but did not ignite. In desperation, he cranked the handle again. Faster. *Maybe it just needs to be revved.*

It was no use. He opened the container and looked inside. He let his eyes adjust to the dimmed surroundings and examined the cartridge inside. The damn things were oil based, unfortunately. He turned it around in his hands and saw the problem. There was a crack, and he could see oil seeping out.

"Shit," he cursed at himself as the oil leaked onto his hands.

PRESENT

Rebecca woke from her nap in Jerome's arms, smiling and stretching. *So, this is what happiness feels like.* She looked at him. He was still sleeping.

"You snore," he said. "It's cute."

She gave him a playful shove and let her head rest back on his chest. They were both still fully clothed. She felt the safest in her gear, but now, she felt even safer in her friend's arms. *Protected.* She leaned over and kissed his lips.

"You're an ass," she said softly.

He laughed and put his hands around her lower backside. "Why didn't we do this before?"

"Dunno. But I like it."

"Yeah," he said. "Same here." Reaching over, he grabbed his lantern and cranked it. The light exploded inside, and the soft glow caressed their faces. "That's much better," he said, looking at her.

FIFTEEN

Caleb looked up. He could see a faint orange glow in the distance. Or so he thought. He looked around and made sure nothing was coming his way. All he could see was watery puddles, and different-sized mounds of mud were around him. It was odd, though, that he was seeing an orange glow. He needed help.

"H-hello?" he called out.

Both Rebecca and Jerome shot straight up. They took their lanterns and peered over the edge. They both lowered their lanterns, trying to get a better view. *No way . . . no freaking way.*

"*Cal?*" she echoed through the darkness.

"Yeah! Becky! It's me! Is Jerome—" he started to say.

"Pops! Yeah, I'm here!" Jerome interrupted, hearing his friend's voice.

"I'm going to let that slide! So good to hear you two!" he said, then looked down at his broken lantern. "Hey! My lantern's busted, doesn't light anymore."

Rebecca and Jerome looked at each other.

"How the hell did he survive!" whispered Jerome.

She shook her head and refocused on Cal. "It's okay! I'll toss you mine!"

"No!" interjected Caleb. "I'll climb up to you!"

Rebecca and Jerome smiled. They were finally going to be reunited with their friend.

"Can you see anything that you can grab ahold of? We can't see jack squat from where we are!" said Jerome.

"Hold on! Lemme find something."

Caleb peered deeply and squinted into the darkness. *There's got to be a cliff face or something I can get ahold of.*

Walking, he headed toward the sounds of his friends' voices.

Rebecca and Jerome kept holding their lanterns over the edge, trying their best to give their friend as much light as possible. There wasn't much. They both tried to figure out where Cal was coming from. It wasn't where they were kneeling down. They slowly walked across the bridge, still holding their lanterns over the edge. Cal could see this and tried his best to follow the dim glow.

The two reached into their vests, and each took out a flare and ignited them. They dropped them into the murky ground below. Caleb saw the flares and carefully double-timed to the burning lights. He saw there was a cliff edge. He picked up a flare and gritted it in his mouth, his teeth biting down on the stick. Raising his arm, he grabbed his first rock mound and began to make his way upward.

Rebecca smiled as she could see the faint red glow move. She grabbed ahold of Jerome and gave him a kiss on the cheek, and a giant hug, which almost toppled him over.

"Okay, hun! Okay!" he said, smiling and laughing with excitement.

Caleb slowly made his way toward his friends. The rock face was a crumbling mess, but he was able to find his footing and secure spots for his hands and feet. He paused and looked up. Flashes of hands bursting through the rock entered his mind. *C'mon. Get it together, asshole! They're waiting! Double-time it!*

"Cal!" yelled Rebecca. "You're almost there!"

He continued climbing, excited to see his friends. That gave him hope, and it gave him purpose. Meaning.

His foot was planted in a groove, and it slipped out. He was hanging just by his hands.

"Shit!" he muffled, holding his flare in his mouth. He quickly put his foot back into the groove and regained his balance.

Placing his hands on another rock edge, he hoisted himself up, moving faster in speed. He didn't want to be down in the dark anymore. It was time to head to the light. And that light was his friends.

He grunted and was almost to where Rebecca and Jerome were looking downward.

"You look like shit!" said Jerome.

Caleb grunted again and made his way closer to the top. He turned his head and spat out the flare. "Go fuck yourself."

Jerome laughed, as did Rebecca. Jerome outstretched his hand; Caleb was now only a few feet from them on the rock face. *One more to go.*

He placed his right hand on a rock face and looked directly up and saw that his path was blocked by a smooth rock surface. Nothing to grip onto. He did see the hand reached out, and leaped into the air and caught it. Jerome pulled him up, Rebecca also helping.

Caleb pushed himself up and rolled onto his back, breathing heavily, sweating, and laughing. He was alive. Rebecca and Jerome wrapped their arms around him and carefully helped him to his feet.

He smiled. Seeing his friends was the best thing that had happened. Reunited, they decided to sit down, lanterns lit around them, and told each other stories of what had transpired the past few hours. All of them were amazed and shocked at what each of them had learned. In reality, they were just happy to be together again. A family.

Jerome slept soundly. Caleb stirred and woke up. He stood and stretched his tired and sore limbs. Reaching carefully for Becky's lantern, he went to the side where he climbed up and began to relieve himself.

"Everything okay?" asked Rebecca, who was a few feet from him as he finished up.

"Awkward question to be askin' while I'm taking a piss, darlin.'"

She rolled her eyes. "I wasn't talking about *that*. I meant how are you doing?"

He put away his junk and made himself proper. "Fine, I guess. Just glad to be back."

She looked down to the ground smiling. "Cal—I, I didn't know if you were going to come back."

He turned around. "I didn't think I would either. But here I am."

She smiled and looked at him. He was right. Here they were. Together and breathing. She walked to him and hugged him. He put his arms around her. The smell of him was relaxing and safe. She squeezed his back tighter. He chuckled and caressed her hair, kissing the top of her head. A tear streamed down her cheek. She wiped it away quickly. Caleb looked at her and smiled tenderly. "Hey, enough of that. C'mon."

"Sorry," she whispered.

"Don't be."

"You're the best thing that's happened to me, you know that?"

"Nah. I'm just a mean old man," he said.

She laughed and swatted his vest. The two headed back to where Jerome was lying down. It was time to head out.

Rebecca noticed that Caleb wasn't with her. She turned around. He was gone.

SIXTEEN

"CAL!" Rebecca screamed. She had seen what happened. *They* had gotten him. The Bastards had gotten ahold of Caleb.

Jerome woke hastily from his sleep and frantically looked around. He squinted, and his eyes widened. He saw Rebecca race toward a defenseless Caleb. Getting to his feet, he stumbled to help his friends.

I can't breathe. Everything's gone dark, and I'm being pulled in every direction possible. Shit! What's happening? Slimy, shit-ridden fingers vibrating over my face, grabbing any part of my body they can, trying to tear me limb from limb. The sounds I hear with those blasted hands smelling over me. Their nails dig deep into my skin, clawing away at my flesh.

I can see again, but just barely.

I'm seeing Becky, screaming something. Eyes wide. What? What is she saying? Can't hear. Jerome. He's running. Can't catch up to me. Everything is slowing down. I'm being dragged down below. Back down to that goddamned pit. Awe, shit. Gotta focus. Gotta regain control somehow.

"Get the hell off me, you assholes!"

All he could see was hands. Nothing but hands grabbing at his scalp and trying to peel his skin off. He could feel his lips stretch as their rotten fingers went inside his mouth, cutting the inside.

Fuck this!

Caleb widened his jaw and chomped down, taking off some of the decayed appendages, immediately spitting them out. Blood and black ooze penetrated his taste buds, as well as the rotten smell of dead flesh. His eyes rolled up into the back of his head. *Well, that was a mistake.*

His body hit the floor with a thud. The Bastards were closing in to dine on their meal. Caleb realized what had just happened. The Bastards were hidden in the jagged rock face he had scaled.

"We've gotta go after him! He needs us!" cried Becky, heading to the cliff, about to leap and make her way down. The Bastards seemed busy with Caleb, but a few stragglers were eyeing them.

She felt Jerome's hand grab her wrist, tugging her away. "You will die! You can't take them on by yourself! We can't. There's too many of them!"

Tears washed over her cheeks hearing these words. In her heart, she knew he was right. She balled her hands into fists and began hitting him on his chest. He grasped her and held on tightly as she sobbed in his arms while he kissed her forehead and closed his eyes, hearing the screams and moans of Caleb and the Bastards.

Caleb writhed on the ground as they continued to claw at him. He managed to kick a few off and bash their skulls in, but it seemed like it was never-ending. Then he felt it. Underneath him. The ground began to move. The mounds of dirt shifted, and seemingly all at once, Bastards appeared, clawing out of their quickly made graves to get a piece of Cal. He knew he wasn't going to win.

Suddenly a Bastard extended its jaw and chomped down on Caleb's thigh. He screamed in agony and could see his tissue and muscle exposed as it was being torn apart. Blood exploded as more Bastards surrounded him. In a last-ditch attempt, he pushed the one that had taken a bite out of him. He was able to knock it to the ground next to him.

Fear-stricken, he quickly crawled his way back to the tunnel where he emerged. Hordes of Bastards were shuffling toward him.

He had made it to the entrance when he felt arms explode behind him and wrap themselves around his waist and chest, squeezing tightly.

In the distance, he grabbed a quick glance of Rebecca and Jerome. "Run! Go now!" he shouted. He took a deep breath and smiled. "Live."

He closed his eyes and dreamed of Becky and Jerome.

"DAAAAAD!" Rebecca screamed. She heard the moans and squelching sounds. Caleb was gone.

Jerome led her away to the other entrance ahead, as more of them started to converge on their location. She quickly glanced back. *Maybe—maybe he got out.* She didn't see any sign of her friend. She only saw those white, soulless eyes and shuffling bodies heading in their direction. Some were scaling the walls.

They had to hurry. Rebecca followed Jerome begrudgingly.

Lifting his lantern, he made his way further into the new cavern. He couldn't believe what he had just witnessed. The man that had taken him in was dead. He heard the moans getting louder and then a rumble in the far distance. He wanted to go back and see what it was, but knew it was a fool's errand. He grunted under his breath, frustrated to no living end he couldn't help Cal. *That's not your priority now. Gotta keep moving, right? Get Becky and yourself out to safety. Somehow. That's what he wants. For us to live.*

Rebecca was still in shell shock. It happened all in slow motion. One minute talking to her friend, the next he was gone for good. *All those years . . . . . . gone. Why? Why did this happen? Should have been faster. Should have been there sooner!*

She suddenly remembered something. A memory she had buried, but that had resurfaced.

SIXTEEN YEARS AGO

She ran as fast as she could, smiling. Being happy, Rebecca fell on the hard, dry ground, scraping her knee. It stung. She sat upright and saw blood seeping out. With both hands, she rubbed the wound and placed pressure on it. It didn't help. The scrape stung even worse now.

She heard the crackling of footsteps as tears burst down her cheeks. A large barrier of a man stood in front of her and knelt down.

"What happened, sweet pea?" he asked.

"Cal!" she cried as she was picked up in his huge arms. It was the safest when she was close to him. She felt protected, like he was her angel.

"Oh, that's nothing but a scratch, sweetie. Want me to kiss it to make it feel better?" he asked, smiling.

She nodded, looking down at her injury.

Caleb lifted her leg and kissed her knee. It did feel better, and it had made her feel better.

Rebecca wrapped her tiny arms around Caleb's broad neck and kissed his cheek, burying her head in his chest. She looked up and saw him smile.

PRESENT DAY

"Rebecca . . . Becky," said Jerome, looking at her concerned. She snapped back to reality. Her eyes flashed as she looked to him. "You alright?"

"Y-yeah," she stammered. "Just remembering something."

He looked at her and sighed. "C'mon, we've gotta go." Nodding in compliance and placing her lantern on her vest, she grabbed his hand, and they made their way deeper into the unknown void.

SEVENTEEN

The other end of the entrance wasn't much different from the previous one, as they soon noticed. Both of them turned around. There were moans in the faint distance. They weren't getting closer, but it was still no worse for comfort. The two continued onward in silence, carefully making their way through the rock-covered corridor. Rebecca whispered a prayer that they wouldn't end up back at the entrance. That was the last thing they needed: to make one giant U-turn and get stuck, or worse . . . eaten by other things.

Jerome let go of her hand and grabbed the side of the wall. The corridor had a steep slope. He descended cautiously, Rebecca following his lead. It was bad enough they were tired, but it would have been a lot worse with broken bones, and luckily, neither of them had *that* problem.

They gradually made their way down to a leveled area. A few moments had gone by when Rebecca opened up and said, "Thank you."

"We're not out of this yet," said Jerome. "Tell me that when we're back on the surface and in Eden."

She smiled. The surface. It may have been desolated and barren, but it was her home.

The two companions stopped and looked around their new surroundings. No sign of spiders. That was a good sign. Other things though . . . those were major question marks in her mind, that didn't need to be answered. She didn't want answered. *With everything that's happened so far, I wouldn't be surprised.*

The interior was adorned with more sea life. The two held their lanterns up high overhead and searched for an exit. Below where they stood, there were dubious amounts of puddles containing seawater massaging their boots. It was refreshing, as their feet ached from the walking and running.

The shallow waves crashed against the rocky surface and subsided.

"Wonder where it goes . . ." Jerome said.

"Let's not do that again, please."

He smiled. "Deal." He took one more look. There was an exit. Although it wasn't in front of them or on either side. It was above. "Um . . . hey." He pointed up.

Rebecca followed his finger and smiled. The hole wasn't very high up. The pair could, however, fit through.

"Shall we?" he asked her, clasping his hands together, palms up, and kneeling down, ready to give her a boost up. "Ladies first."

"Such a gentleman!" she said playfully as she planted her left foot on his hands while at the same time attaching her lantern to her vest. Her hands grasped his shoulders for balance.

She removed them as she began to rise up and extend her arms, hands breaching through the opening, and push herself to the other side. Jerome waited a few moments, lifting his lantern upward, and saw her two arms shoot down, motioning him to latch on.

"You sure?" he asked.

"Yeah! Hurry up!" she responded.

Connecting his lantern to his vest, he jumped up and grabbed onto her forearms and with all of her strength, pulled him through. When he was a quarter of the way through, he grabbed hold of the opening and hoisted himself the rest of the way through. He was thankful that they were both relatively the same weight and almost the same height.

They detached their lanterns and surveyed the new area. It wasn't the surface, but they were out of the tunnels. They were back in the abandoned city, miles from where they first entered. Jerome lifted his lantern for a wider view. A large green sign lay at their feet.

NEW MOMBASA – 23 KMS

In the darkened distance, they saw a concrete road. It was fractured and split into pieces, but it could still be traveled upon. Faint markings could also be seen, various numbers and separated lines that designated the middle. Mounted on both sides of the highway were long poles, and attached to them were covers. Some were shattered, others cracked. In a rare occurrence, however, some were in perfect condition.

On the surface of the highway stood automotive machines and other signs of a past that had disappeared. There was something else. Silence. No moans coming from any direction. She punched him in the arm. Hard.

"What was that for?" he asked, slightly rubbing his shoulder.

"Just making sure. Come on."

With both feet, they stepped onto the crumbling ruins of the old road. It was their only clear path. By "clear," it was, in fact, that they only had enough room to maneuver between the desolate vehicles still on the road—which were either still upright, or turned over.

Rebecca peered into one with its driver's-side door broken off. Inside there were the skeletal remains of a person. In the back there could be seen two bodies smaller in stature. Their mouths were open and no skin was visible. She took another look at the driver again. The head tilted to its side and made her jump. *That's the last thing I need!*

The damn thing wasn't alive, but just seeing it lie there didn't ward off her questions that were forming in her head. There were many, but one that stood out the worst was what had happened. Perhaps she, along with Jerome, would never find out. But she secretly hoped they would. She shook her head and headed toward Jerome, who was looking inside the abandoned vehicles as well.

"Find anything?" he asked.

"Nothing. Just remains. You?" she asked, looking back at the vehicle.

"Same," he answered. He reached into his pocket and pulled out a metal contraption. It was cylindrical and was separated by hoops. "I did find this. Dunno what it's used for though."

She raised her lantern to get a better look and raised an eyebrow in confusion.

"Didn't think so," he said, tossing it to the side. It bounced its way over a broken edge and fell to the bottom, crashing to the ground.

They continued on their journey through the crowded twists and turns of the road. Their lanterns went out a few times, leaving them in the black, but they would flicker on soon enough. One would start to question how much gas was in a lantern. The two soon found out, as Rebecca's lantern stopped igniting. She opened the bottom and removed the gas canister and weighed it in her hand, Jerome giving as much light as possible.

Empty. Shit. Just what she needed. Jerome searched for a spare in his vest and handed it to her.

"Last one. Make it count," he said.

She took it and popped it into place, making sure everything was connected.

“Will do.”

She gave the handle a few cranks, and her lantern ignited. She turned around and two glowing white eyes were staring directly at her in the far-off distance. “Ah, shit.”

EIGHTEEN

"Jerome!" she whispered. "Jerome, are you—?"

"Yeah. I see it, girl. I see it."

She steadily lowered her lantern. The two pupils glistened in the darkness. From what she could tell, it didn't move like a Bastard. Whatever it was tilted its head, curiously staring at them.

Jerome squinted trying to see what it was, but the damn thing was too deep in the shadows. *Great. First those things chasing us, then spiders. And now this son of a bitch!* He slowly picked up his lantern and lowered the flame. Maybe he could make out what it was. He focused his eyes to pick up any shadow or shape or facial feature. It was no use; it was too far away.

Rebecca tried as well, but she got the same result. The thing skulked from left to right, staring at them. They could see that it was tilting its head from side to side, trying to figure out what they were, and what should be done. It made no sound, but the two could see the white-eyed shadowy mass grow larger in form, and it seemed to sniff the air. The sniff wasn't boisterous. It was silent.

She and Jerome glanced at each other and back at the shadow. When they looked back at it, they noticed it had moved closer to their location. Their two bodies tensed and stood still. The shadow moved again, but it had moved out of view. They wondered where it had gone off to. Lanterns in hand, they carefully walked to the broken edge of the highway and looked over it to see if the figure was at the bottom somehow. It wasn't. The pair turned around and began to head back up the highway, when they heard a noise. It was whining from behind them.

"Really?" she whispered, taking Jerome's arm as they about-faced.

It was the shadow. The eyes were still glowing white as it stood on the edge looking at them. Slowly, very cautiously, it made its way toward them. Rebecca instinctively jumped, raising her lantern with her hand shaking. Jerome remained steadfast, gently putting his down. The shadow began to take form, and they could finally see what it was.

"Mrow."

"Seriously?" Jerome asked. "A *cat*? That's what we've been so afraid of?"

"I thought these went extinct about ten years ago . . ." Rebecca replied, bending down to coerce the animal near her so she could pick it up. "It's okay, honey. We won't hurt you. Shh. Shh."

The cat looked at them and trotted toward them, purring and nuzzling their legs and hands. It was a tabby. Big hazel eyes, fur that was striped like a tiger, and black spots that were birthmarks on the inside of the mouth, along with long whiskers. Its ears were pointed and huge.

"I guess it's going with us," Jerome said.

"Mrow!" it responded, purring loudly.

A noise was suddenly heard in the distance, coming from the east. The cat turned its head in the direction of the sound, its eyes scanning the dimmed dark as it growled and hissed. It sensed something was off. And that something was getting closer.

Rebecca held the cat close to her chest, its paws resting on her forearm. It was time for them to make it to a safer location.

"We'll find a better spot and we'll get you something to eat, okay?" Rebecca suggested to the friendly feline. It "smiled." "You look famished, little one."

"Mrow . . ." it responded.

"Oh, he definitely likes you," said Jerome.

"He?"

"Yep. He," Jerome said, pointing to the cat's underside.

Rebecca looked. "Oh yeah. Definitely a 'he.'"

The new companions three made their way further along the highway. It was a long and tedious task, unfortunately, but it was the only direction they could go. From time to time, they would look off to the sides, just to try to see if there was any sort of habitable buildings they could possibly use for shelter. There were only crumbling ancient landmarks that didn't have any more identities. Nothing livable.

Rebecca's stomach grumbled as did Jerome's. The cat looked at both of them, tilting his head in curiosity.

"We're hungry, little guy. You must be too," she said. "How did you survive through all of this? Huh?"

"Mrow."

"I see," she said, kissing his head. She looked at Jerome. "Hey, we should name him."

"What did you have in mind?" he asked, pausing in his steps, petting the feline's forehead.

Rebecca looked at him and thought. "Hm . . . what about Spanky?"

The cat gave her a look of disapproval.

"Okay, okay. How about . . . Finn?"

"Mrow!"

"I guess he likes it," Jerome said.

Finn purred and nuzzled both of his new adoptive parents.

"Okay, Finn it is then!" she said.

The three continued to make their way past more and more rows of junkyard vehicles. Finn leaped out of Rebecca's arms and searched for something to eat. He climbed through a shattered windshield, his little butt in the air as he steadily and carefully arched his back downward so as to not get cut by the sharp glass. He put his paws on the dust-filled dashboard and curiously looked at the deceased driver and passenger. He decided to make his way between them and gracefully jumped onto the armrest. There weren't any signs of life in the back seat either. Just mounds of dust, torn leather, and dozens of spiderwebs, among other nasty and oozy things.

Finn made his way to the floor and searched around. He could sense it. It was close. *Food.* With one outstretched arm, he pawed at the object that was under the passenger's seat. Slowly he maneuvered it closer to him and began to play with the plastic-wrapped container.

Rebecca smiled and slowly opened the rear door. There was Finn, on his backside with the object between his paws and feet, nibbling the edges.

"Crackers," she said.

Finn froze, looked at her, and continued playing with the plastic-covered food.

She reached down and slowly grabbed the dried-up food from her new companion. Finn had other plans though as he continued to hold onto the item as she lifted it. He jumped onto her shoulder and meowed. She patted the cat's head, him purring. "I have to see if they're still good, silly!"

Taking hold of the edges with her fingers, she tore open the bag and sniffed the inside. *Doesn't smell bad.*

She lifted her lantern to further examine the contents and found that there was no mold or any other state of contamination. No insects or spiders. *One last test.*

Taking a cracker and breaking it in half, she bit down. It was salty and dry, but it was still edible. Jerome came over, and she handed the other half to him. He raised his eyebrow and said, "You do realize these have been down here for god knows how long, right?"

"Yeah, that crossed my mind," she said.

Jerome inserted it into his mouth and bit down.

Rebecca took another cracker from the plastic bag and broke it into three pieces. She held a piece in front of her after she had eaten hers and handed the other to Jerome. Finn sniffed it and began licking the salt contents of the bread-laden food.

"Finn, eat it. Go on," said Jerome as Rebecca was putting the food close to his mouth. The cat continued to lick the remaining salt and didn't eat.

"Guess he's not hungry."

"Or he's not into this type of food," Rebecca said.

"We'll find you something, okay, little guy?" Jerome said, rubbing Finn's back, making his way to the top of his head. The cat's purrs didn't make things easier, but they were relaxing to Jerome. In all of the darkness, something as small as Finn could bring them so much joy.

Finn crawled down into one of Rebecca's open pouches and settled himself inside. He yawned and closed his eyes, drifting off to sleep.

Two hours had passed. Rebecca and Jerome climbed their way through the cracked and shattered concrete of the highway. They were almost to the New Mombasa turn off. Now the question had become, do they continue straight or venture off the path? There was another question. Do they take a giant gamble and split up in hopes of finding some sort of food or, hell, even a way out?

No. Rebecca thought. *Like hell we're splitting up. Are you really that stupid? C'mon, girl, get your head back on right. Gotta keep moving together. Not separate.* She looked in an overturned vehicle and put her lantern closer to one of the windshields. She found two corpses. One had its head in the other's lap—facedown. Rebecca didn't know what it meant. Her eyes wandered to the rear and checked the back seat. Dust and cobwebs adorned the now torn cushions. Her lantern shone on the holes, and she noticed that the bugs and other unnatural insects scattered anywhere they could to escape the lantern's flame. She pulled herself back and looked down at Finn.

"Nothing in there for us," she said.

"Mrow," the cat echoed as he looked up at her, his paw placed on her chest.

Jerome could be seen leaning inside a locked door, the window shattered. He was throwing out various items. Some were children's toys, and clothes, and plasticware. *Nothing to eat!* He heard Rebecca walk up behind him. "Couldn't find anything. Not a damn thing, Becky."

"Yeah, same here. Just remains and lots of death. It's like the universe has it out for us."

"You're right on that one," he said, looking at the vehicles. "We searched every one so far, right?"

"Yeah. All we found so far was the crackers, and that's it food-wise. Any luck with water?"

"No, luckily it's not unbearably hot, or else we'd be fucked."

"Well, we'll keep looking. There's gotta be a source somewhere," she said, looking at him and Finn.

Finn began to purr, his ears suddenly perked up, and his eyes darted to the right. His nose inhaled the air, and he began to get excited. Placing his paws outside of the vest, he squirmed out of his home and leaped to the ground. Tail wagging, he stuck out his tongue and licked his snout. He trotted in the direction his senses were telling him to go.

Jerome looked at him curiously, as did Rebecca.

"Find something, boy?" he asked, kneeling next to the feline.

"Mrow . . ."

Finn slowly crept passed the derelict vehicles and paused at the edge. He extended his neck and peered down, his irises homing in on the smell.

"Mrow?" he whimpered.

Rebecca and Jerome looked down into the black. They couldn't see anything.

Seconds later, they heard it. The moaning . . . and it had gotten louder. It was close. Very close.

Finn took a few steps back as more moans started to form.

"Shit," Jerome cursed.

"Uh . . . yeah. Shit. Shit. Shit!" Rebecca said, grabbing Finn as they all ran to safety.

The Bastards were right under them. And they were climbing.

NINETEEN

The three companions darted for the farthest vehicle and hid behind it. Rebecca peeked out and scanned the area. *There must be hundreds . . . maybe thousands!*

Finn curled himself back into her vest pocket, shaking. Jerome lifted his head over the hood, and his eyes went wide with fear. They were here.

In the black, a mangled, flesh-flapping hand emerged on the highway. Then another. And another. White milky eyes appeared soon after, followed by frothing mouths of oozing blood and puss. The Bastards crawled and shuffled along the darkened highway, moaning and feverishly trying to satisfy their id.

Jerome and Rebecca quickly ducked back down.

"What the fuck are we going to do!" whispered Rebecca.

"I don't know! There are a ton of them climbing up. Pretty soon, we're going to be overrun!" he whispered back.

She looked around from her vantage point. The only way to go was forward, but that was now blocked by the Bastards that were clawing their way up from the side. They were surrounded and stuck right in the middle.

Rebecca had an idea. It would be risky, but it was all they had to go on.

Tapping Jerome on the shoulder, she signaled him to quickly go to a vehicle that was upright and open the driver's-side rear door.

She also remembered that their lanterns were on and snuffed their lights. This was going to have to be done in complete darkness.

The moans and shuffling grew louder and were getting closer. Jerome understood the instructions though. As quietly as he could, he crept along the asphalted path to the chosen vehicle. He took a glance, and as his eyes adjusted to the darkness, he could see more and more shapes of the Bastards emerge from the side of the highway. He gulped and turned back to the task at hand. *Gotta remain focused! Come on, damn it!*

He grabbed the handle of the door, pushed the button underneath, and gently opened the door. He then took his lantern and flickered the light twice, signaling Rebecca.

She crept down the path and joined Jerome. The Bastards were closing in. Some had fallen, tripping over themselves, but they continued to crawl.

Both of them climbed into the rear and closed the door, locking all the locks. *Please don't see us! Please don't see us!* she thought to herself, hearing the moans getting louder with each passing second. The two lay together, Finn looking out from Rebecca's pouch.

Jerome covered his mouth, as did Rebecca. It was dark, but the damned things could probably still hear. And maybe smell.

They glanced toward the outside. There they were. They had reached them. It was like nothing they had ever seen before. Hundreds upon hundreds of bodies shuffling and gasping for their claim of fresh meat. The Bastards brushed against the frame of the vehicle, their skin flaking off, blood exploding on the rusting sides.

Jerome and Rebecca inhaled deeply as the damned things crashed their bodies against the vehicle. To them it was like hearing an explosion go off right next to them.

Finn started to growl, which turned into a hiss. Rebecca covered the cat's snout with her hand, Finn struggling to break free.

"Shh, Finn! Shh!" she whispered desperately, looking up from where she lay.

Jerome's eyes widened, his breathing becoming wilder, as he saw some of the Bastards pause. Jerome pointed with his index finger. Rebecca looked at the things standing outside. Her eyes widened, her breathing becoming heavier, her heart pounding so fast it felt like it was going to explode out of her chest.

Finn noticed what was happening and calmed down for a moment. He curled back inside her pouch and hid.

It was at that moment the Bastards that paused turned and were facing the inside of the vehicle. They peered into the darkened window, curious to see what was inside.

Hunger . . . Food! Flesh! Flessh!

The two captives inside were in pain. Their hearts were about to burst at any moment.

Rebecca clutched her chest, trying to calm herself down, Jerome following suit. They gritted their teeth, breathing even heavier now, sweat rushing from their pores as they could see the Bastards looking inside.

The Bastards outside leaned their heads back, looking up at the sky. They came crashing down against the door frame, repeatedly bashing their skulls against the door.

Rebecca and Jerome had to literally bite their fingers to keep themselves from screaming and alerting the horde outside of their presence.

Oh God! Oh God! We're fucked! We're so fucked! Rebecca thought.

The Bastards kept banging their skulls against the door, eventually breaking open their skulls. Brains, blood, and black ooze were smeared all over the window. The other Bastards didn't seem to notice.

The banging continued, when finally, the Bastards' heads exploded with one final blow to the door. Jerome and Rebecca gasped as they saw chunks of brain matter and blood smear across the window as the Bastards' bodies slumped to the floor, twitching and then slowly becoming still.

Closing her eyes, Rebecca buried herself in Jerome's chest, hoping against all hope that this blasted nightmare would soon be over and they would be free to continue their search. *This is total bullshit!* It was, and they still had no food for their growling stomachs. What's more, her mind still asked the question about Finn. Just how did he survive all alone down here? And where was he getting his food?

TWENTY

Hours passed and the Bastards' moans seemed to finally die out. There were faint groans that leered in the distance, but Jerome and Rebecca were able to fall asleep in each other's arms.

Finn was still curled up inside her vest pocket; his eyes, however, remained open, scanning the outside and making sure his masters were safe and no other threats were looming around them.

He stretched his body and nuzzled Rebecca and then Jerome. They were both still asleep and wrapped their arms around each other, keeping warm. The cat circled between them and curled into a ball, his tail covering his eyes. He didn't mind the quiet, or stillness. Or even the current predicament they were in. He was with people that loved him and weren't trying to kill him . . . like the monsters lurking outside. His tiny stomach grumbled. It was time to eat. Using his nose, he pressed it against Rebecca's cheek and gave a low meow. Nothing. He put his paw on her nose, giving it a slight bop. Her head moved and she groaned. Finn's tail wagged back and forth, thinking he had finally gotten her attention. He tilted his head to the side when her eyes didn't open. *Other one.*

He trotted over to Jerome and patted his face. He saw Jerome's face stir, and he opened his eyes.

Eyes opened, he adjusted his line of sight and could see Finn close to him, staring directly at him. Finn "smiled" and purred, nuzzling Jerome's face as he felt his master's fingers run down his head and across his back.

"Hey, little buddy," he whispered.

"Mrow! Mrow!"

"Shh. We don't want to wake her up," he whispered, looking at Rebecca. She was beautiful. Never in a million years would he have thought he would be in a relationship with such a smart, bright, pure of heart woman. *Life is a twisting and winding road.*

He brushed her hair and kissed her forehead lightly. Finn nuzzled Rebecca again, purring as his paws touched her cheeks. He felt Jerome's hand wrap around his stomach.

"Mroow," he said in a sorrowful tone, not wanting to leave her side. He was now in the air, his front and rear paws wiggling; his body squirming, trying to break free. Jerome put him down on his chest, smiling.

"You are an oddball, little one," he whispered.

"Mrow," Finn replied.

"You whisper any louder, they're going to hear you," said Rebecca, opening her eyes.

Jerome looked at her and asked, "How long have you been awake?"

"Long enough," she said, watching Finn's tail wag excitingly. "And *you* woke me up."

"Mrow!" he said cheerfully.

"You say that, and I say I need more sleep," she declared, scratching his head softly.

It was true, she needed sleep. A lot more. Her body ached and groaned as she re-positioned herself. She had lost a man that she grew up loving and respecting immensely. And she was scared, fearful for her life. She didn't show it though. Rebecca had to be strong. For everyone.

The rest that she did get felt like seconds of her life passing by, not hours. That was the hard part. Her mind insisted, being alert, that she had only rested for a small amount of time, but she knew it wasn't true. Not in the slightest. Her body was telling her to stay put; it needed to heal. And it also needed nourishment. Her stomach growled too, from hunger and thirst. *Shit. How long's it been since I ate? A day? Two, maybe? I can't remember.*

Finn looked at her stomach and sniffed, patting it with his paw.

"Yeah, I'm hungry too," she said, rubbing his chin.

Jerome looked up and slowly adjusted his body as Rebecca and Finn did the same.

"See anything?" she asked.

"Nothing," he replied. "I don't see any of them—Wait. Okay, yeah. There are a few to the south of us. And a few . . . to the east."

"Crap," Rebecca said.

"Yeah, my thoughts exactly."

They could stay inside and wait it out, but they would probably kill each other from hunger. It was time to get a move on. They just had to be careful. Extra careful. Along with Finn.

Rebecca scooped the feline up and placed him in her vest pocket.

"Time to make a decision," she said.

"Yeah . . . time to go," he said, watching the stragglers outside wander around. *Why didn't the others notice we were in here? Makes no damned sense.*

He shook the thoughts from his head, but made a mental note to find the answers somehow, if there were any. Now, it was time to survive and find some goddamn food.

Slowly, he put his hand on the handle and carefully opened the door, just a crack, making sure the coast was clear.

The moans were there, but far away. He blinked and paused. He pushed the door open. As he pushed, it creaked, and his heart dropped to his stomach. His eyes widened. He wanted to be as silent as possible. Unfortunately, that wasn't going to be the case.

Shit! Slow . . . careful.

He focused his attention to his hearing and listened. No Bastards were alerted by the noise. That was a very good sign. So far.

Jerome turned around and faced Rebecca, grabbing her shoulder, signaling it was clear for them to move. She tapped his forearm signaling she was ready. She thought about using her lantern, but quickly put that idea to bed. *Bad idea, girl.* They would have to move in the cover of darkness, and complete silence.

They crawled out of the vehicle and were on their haunches. The two companions, along with Finn, surveyed the area around them one more time, just to be sure. Still no signs of any Bastards. With the first step, they made their way up the highway in the cover of the darkened night and the armor of the silent vehicles. There was not time to search each one like before. They had to put as much distance between them and the horde as possible.

Gotta move. Gotta keep moving. Jerome thought to himself. He too missed the daylight. The feeling of the hot sun on his skin and the home he once had. *Kira.*

An image of his sister exploded in his mind. It had been months ago, but the pain was still evident. In some sick and twisted way, he was glad his sister was dead. *Thank the gods you aren't alive to see this.*

She had escaped an uncertain kind of hell. And to him that was comforting.

"Hey. You okay?" Rebecca asked.

Jerome popped back into reality. "I'm fine. Just thinking about something." He smiled, and his hands clasped hers in reassurance.

Rebecca still had a look of concern. "You sure?"

Jerome slightly squeezed her hand. "Yeah, I am. Just thought of someone I had almost forgotten about."

"Kira?"

"Yeah. I'm glad she's not here to witness any of this, you know?"

She stopped and faced her friend. She took his other hand in hers. "I think . . . she's very proud of the person you've become. I know I am."

He smiled and saw her stand. He did the same and put his arms around her and kissed her lips. It was a fantastic feeling knowing they could count on each other. They were there for one another.

Finn looked up and raised his paw, gently tapping both of their cheeks, followed by a soft whimper.

Jerome and Rebecca giggled and looked down at him.

"Romance killer," Jerome said.

TWENTY-ONE

Hunger. That was a word they weren't used to. The smell of fresh meat. The searing pleasure of chomping down on a big, juicy piece of tendon. Then there was the heart and the other internal organs. Yes, those were the best parts. It was the mouth-watering, make-your-teeth-tingle kind of meal that they craved. A delicacy, to be sure!

An arm! Yes, that's it. Just the feeling of biting into a bicep was exhilarating. Seeing the veins dangle as blood and tissue exploded onto their rotted faces, their hands holding as much of the dead carcass as they could.

But, the best part was before. It wasn't the chase; no, it was the overtaking of the food itself. The screams. The fear that the meal was displaying in its eyes. Then there was the twitching of the body. The dying thing looking at itself being *eaten alive*.

This is how the world really is. No one giving two shits about anyone else. The eaters getting eaten.

This is what the Bastards yearned for. Nourishment. Survival. It was a long time coming, and they were going to have their retribution.

There's plenty to go around. Another organ. Some brain. An eye. The Bastards were like giant swarms of locusts. Going from one spot to the next, never having their fill, but always searching for that next big score.

One of the things lifted its head, and a piece of lower intestine dangled from his teeth and lips. He slowly slurped it up into his mouth. With what was left of his nostrils, he wheezily sniffed the air.

Fooooooood . . .

He turned his head back to his meal. It wasn't a living person he was dining on. It was a Bastard.

TWENTY-TWO

In the distance, moans were heard. Finn focused his eyes in the direction of the sounds and whimpered as Rebecca and Jerome made their way down the edge of the highway.

The two had walked for a mile and a half before reaching the edge of the twisting road. New Mombasa had been torn from the rest of the highway. There was no way for them to cross.

"Can we find another way?" Rebecca asked. "Maybe another road?"

Jerome shook his head and said, "Doesn't look like it, babe. We are officially cut off." He thought to himself for a moment. "Well, we've got only one choice, it looks like."

He looked around to make sure no Bastards were tailing them. He was getting tired of having to look over his shoulder in order to make a decision or prevent himself from being attacked.

He cranked his handle a few times, and the lantern ignited. He put it on a low setting. Kneeling, he tried to see how big of a drop the edge was. But most importantly, he wanted to make sure there weren't any of those damned things waiting for them at the bottom, waiting for an easy meal.

"See anything?" Rebecca whispered.

Jerome lifted his finger. "Hold on."

He turned his ear to the ground, focusing on any kind of sound that was coming from below. A few minutes elapsed, and he turned his attention to Rebecca and Finn.

"Nothing from below that I could hear."

"Well, that's good. Right?" she asked, leaning over his shoulder, looking down into the unknown, holding Finn steady in her vest.

"Mrow . . ."

"Yeah, my thoughts exactly," said Rebecca. "How are we going to get down? Were screwed on the rope plan."

Jerome raised the brightness of his lantern and lowered it deeper into the black. He found a rebar wire that was faintly noticeable a few feet below. It resembled a ladder.

"We could use that," he said, pointing to the ladder.

Rebecca focused on where he was pointing. "Do you think it's safe? Like it won't let loose when we climb down?"

Jerome looked at her. "Don't know. Only one way to find out, right?"

"Yeah . . ." she trailed off. "Still, seems like a long way down."

"You got that right, girl. But I've got you," he said, kissing her on the cheek. She smiled and blushed in the faint light.

This was new to her. It was both exhilarating and scary. She knew she could trust him, and she loved him, as he did her. But she was still uncertain about it all. Would it work? Would they be able to stand each other after everything was said and done? *Let's try and get out of here alive first, shall we?*

A thought had popped into her head as she went down first, and she said, "If we get out of here, I'm so getting laid." She gingerly placed her hands and feet on the edge and slowly climbed down to the ladder and descended.

Jerome smiled. "Well then, let's get out of here!"

She laughed and continued downward, putting her lantern on a higher setting and attaching it to her vest, as did Jerome.

The bars themselves were full of a copious amount of dust, grime, and *blood.* It was dried, and there was something else. Rebecca looked at the palm of her hand. It was a dried, flaky substance. *Skin. Fucking dried, torn-up skin. Shit.*

She lifted her head and looked at Jerome. "Hey, you see this?" she asked.

"What is it?" he asked.

"Skin. And blood."

Jerome rubbed his fingers together, grossing out. He looked up toward the surface. "What do you think happened?"

"I don't even want to know," she replied.

Finn curiously looked at the falling flakes and began to paw at them.

"No, no, baby! Not food! Definitely not food!" she scolded him.

The cat gave a grumble and looked up at his master, meowing again.

"I know. We're hurrying as fast as we can."

Finn curled into Jerome's vest, but decided to poke his head out and look down. Big mistake. His eyes widened, and he was scared that he couldn't "see" usable ground.

Rebecca gently rubbed his head, and he, while shaking, went back inside his pocket. "We'll let you know if we reach ground, okay?"

Finn moaned and continued to shake, but he was purring at the same time because of Rebecca's soft touch. He loved that the most. The feel of her fingers and nails running through his scalp, padding his ears. It had been a long time since he had felt that kind of affection . . .

The two companions slowly made their way down. Rebecca put her foot down thinking there was another foothold, but all she felt was open space. It caught her by surprise. *Oh, you've gotta be kidding me!*

"Uh . . . we've got a bit of a problem."

Jerome stopped and looked down at her. "What is it?"

"We've got no more ladder, sweetie."

"Seriously?"

"Yeah, seriously. Climb back up? Think of a plan B?"

Shit! Shit!

"Yeah, c'mon, let's go back up. We'll think of something else."

He froze in his tracks. He heard something in the distance. Rebecca heard it too. She looked in the direction of the sound, and her eyes widened, along with Jerome's.

"No . . ." she whispered to herself.

It was an earth-shake.

TWENTY-THREE

The earth rumbled. The rock-covered walls shook violently and without mercy. And Jerome, with Rebecca, was holding on for dear life. It was one thing to be above on the surface out in the great, wide open. But it was an entirely different experience to be right in the middle of the chaos.

Jerome closed his eyes and wrapped his arms around a piece of scaffolding. He looked down at Rebecca and shouted, "We've gotta climb!"

Rebecca looked up and nodded a yes.

As fast as they could, they climbed back up to the highway's ledge. Another earth-shake, this one was much more intense.

The rebar scaffolding shook as the two friends could feel the chips of cement rain down on their heads, along with bits of rock and dust.

Rebecca closed her eyes, and another violent shake erupted around her. Finn was still curled up inside her pocket but was shaking and panting frantically.

"Mrow."

Rebecca pulled her vest close to her breast, trying her best to comfort the scared feline. With one hand, she grabbed another piece of metallic structure and continued climbing up.

Jerome didn't look down. Just up. That was his folly. *Go! Go! Go! Faster, damn it!*

One by one he gripped another wire. *Almost there! Pick it up, asshole!*

Another earth-shake. This time more violent.

"Keep going, Becky; focus!" he called out to her, continuing on.

She exhaled and climbed faster. *What the fuck do you think I'm doing!*

"Yeah . . . no problem!" she shouted back, grabbing another foothold. This was utter bullshit. Why did this have to happen now? Of all the times, this was the most inconvenient one!

The scaffolding continued to sway with each thunderous shake. They had never experienced earth-shakes like this before. These were assaulting them repeatedly.

The shakes finally stopped, and Jerome and Rebecca made their way to the ledge. Jerome was able to reach the edge of the highway. *There it is!*

With his right hand, he reached up, aiming for the ledge. But something was wrong. He could hear it—a shuffling of rebar. The ledge was now farther from his grasp. The ladder had come loose, out of its holdings. They were now falling.

Oh fuck! Oh fuck! No! No! No!

"Shhhit," Jerome said as he felt himself being pulled down by gravity. "HANG ON!"

"Ah, shit!" Rebecca shouted, holding onto the ladder with all of her strength. She pulled the ladder closer to her vest, careful not to crush Finn. She felt his sharp claws dig into her vest, pinching her side as he feared for his life.

They fell, the air in their lungs evaporating. It was hard to breathe. Their chests tightened as they tried to inhale once more.

Jerome had his eyes shut tightly, his teeth gritted, his body pressed firmly against the metallic ladder, his arms and legs wrapped around the holdings. He risked a peek through. He had to make sure Rebecca was doing okay and was still holding on. He slowly opened his eyes, tears streaming from their sockets as the wind cut into them. He could see she was firmly pressed against the ladder as well; Finn had his eyes also closed. *Hang on, baby. Hang on.*

The scaffolding fell faster. Both were still holding tightly, wondering when the hell they were going to land. And if they were going to survive.

Finn meowed, still grappling to Rebecca. This was not a fun ride, and he wanted to be on the ground. Immediately his stomach heaved, but he held on. There was no way he was letting go. "Meow."

They finally came to a stop. The structure slammed into the hard ground with a loud thud. It didn't fall and stayed vertical.

Both of the friends were breathing heavily, trying to catch their breath. Then they heard it, that creaking sound. The structure began to lean and make its entrance onto the ground. They leaped off and made their way to the side as they heard the thunderous crash of metal against the ground. Dimly lit dust exploded from the crash, enveloping their lungs as they covered their faces as best they could. Rebecca covered her vest pocket, making sure Finn wouldn't be breathing in any of it.

Jerome coughed and wheezed, closing his eyes as dust particles entered his eyes, nose, and mouth. Rebecca knelt down on the ground, trying to remain calm, but the agony of trying to breath was a real bitch.

Moments passed, and the dust finally settled. The pair regained their breathing and were able to open their eyes again. Rebecca checked on Finn. He looked up at her and outstretched his paw, lightly coughing in tiny squeaks. She smiled and took his paw and kissed it.

"Mrow."

"Are you okay?" she whispered.

"Mrow!" he replied.

"Well, that's reassuring. Jerome, you okay?" she asked.

Jerome inhaled. "Yeah, yeah. I'm good. You? Finn?"

"We're both fine. Just a little rattled."

Jerome inhaled. "Yeah, no shit. One hell of a ride though."

"Not funny," Rebecca shot back, now standing next to him. She checked her lantern. She turned it over and examined it. No cracks on the exterior. She opened the compartment housing the ignitor. *Well I'll be. Still working.*

Jerome checked over his lantern as well. There was a small hairline crack on the glass shaft, but the handle still cranked perfectly and the inside was complete. With all that had happened to them in the past few hours, that small miracle gave him a tiny ray of hope.

They cranked their lanterns and ignited their flames to discover where they had fallen. The ground, from what could be seen in the dim light, was filled with dust, but now it was a mixture of hard rock and soil.

The two lifted their lanterns and looked up. They could see the outline of the highway and the support beams high overhead. And they could also feel something. *Water.*

They opened their mouths and stuck their tongues out, feeling the wet liquid permeating their senses and taste buds. Immediately they turned around, desperately looking for the sources. What their lanterns showed, however, was ore-rock-faced cliffsides rising in the darkness.

They made their way through the vortex maze that was the deep below. To the left towered the cliffside, with streams of water trickling down. To the right was black and bleak. From what they could tell, points of light hit certain spots of the rocks that were in the distance. Finn poked his head out and looked. He raised his head fully and looked at Rebecca and whispered a soft, "Meow."

"Yeah, you can say that again."

Jerome crouched down, Rebecca following his lead once more. There was a giant slanted beam blocking their way. He signaled her to be careful and mind her head. She understood. The "beam" was protruding from the wall itself. Upon closer inspection, it was a remnant of the ancient city. It wasn't made of rock. This was concrete that had dried mud and bits of grass encasing it. There was more to it, but their lanterns only proved so useful. Corpses lay inside the building, as well as outside.

Jerome had made it through and helped her through, grabbing her hand. It was soft and reassuring. And it was nice to feel her skin. It made him think that just maybe, there was a sliver of hope for the two of them.

Rebecca and Jerome both walked down a narrow path, both sides now enclosed by looming rock walls. It was a weird feeling, but it was also reassuring that they were enclosed. It felt safe, and it was nice there were no Bastards on their tail. Still, the towering cliffsides did put them on edge some. They knew they weren't out of the woods yet. Both lifted their lanterns overhead and made their flames brighter as they came around to a rock-covered cul-de-sac. Then they heard it. A sound that their ears and lips yearned for.

Water.

Finn peeked out of his pocket and climbed out, rushing to the pool of fresh liquid. He put his nose to the surface and sniffed. *Clean. Good.* With a flick of his tongue, he began to drink.

Both couldn't believe their fortune. Finally, some luck was going their way. They could refill their canisters and clean themselves, and what they needed the most—a break.

How has the earth-shake not destroyed this place? Or did it just happen when we were hanging for our lives? Rebecca thought. Whatever happened, she was just glad there was a fresh supply of water.

They ran to the large pool, dropped to their knees, and cupped their hands, immersing them in its cool aura.

Jerome took his lantern as an afterthought and hovered it over the liquid. *Gotta check. Gotta make sure.*

The water was not murky or contaminated from what he could see. It was clean. Rebecca looked at him curiously.

"Had to make sure . . ." Jerome said.

She had a mouth full of water and slowly spat it out. "Make sure of what . . . exactly?"

"Make sure it was safe," he said.

Finn stopped drinking and looked at both of his masters.

Jerome smiled. "Don't worry. It is."

Finn immediately went back to taking sips, as did the two humans.

Minutes had passed, and Jerome began to undress. Rebecca looked and decided to do the same. It felt refreshing to take off their uniforms. They felt free.

Jerome untied his shoes first, slowly taking them off, letting his toes feel the air rush to his skin. His toes were chapped and dry, but he was able to stretch them. It was a feeling he had almost forgotten, like some faint memory in the back of his mind.

The cracking and instant relief of cartilage loosening was a reminder that he was still alive. He took off his vest and finally his pants. He looked down at the ground at his crumpled-up uniform and then at his own body. He felt revitalized being naked. *Free.*

Rebecca glanced at him and smiled. She undressed herself next. The uniform's insulation proved useful, but still sweated as she took it off. She looked at herself. There were bruises and indents that would go away over time. Before she knew it, Jerome was in front of her. He tenderly took her chin in his hands and lifted her head up. Her eyes nervously stared back into his. *It's really happening.*

Their lips locked, tongues gently touching one-another, coaxing the kiss even more. (Finn was off in a corner, asleep). She felt his hands run from the back of her neck, slowly down her back and grasp her buttocks, making her body thrust upward.

“Mmm!” she moaned, wrapping her arms around his neck, bringing him in closer. She could feel it next to her, touching her ever so lightly. She pulled away from the kiss and smiled, looking deep into his soft-glowing eyes.

“What?” he asked, smiling.

She put her fingers to his lips, and kissed his neck, then moved her way down his chest, feeling every part of his upper frame. It wasn’t that muscular, but she didn’t care. She licked his stomach, kissing it all over, making her way down even more. *There it is*. With her left hand on his thigh, her right one took him into her mouth. This was instinct, she thought. It had to be.

Jerome moaned as he slowly thrust his pelvic region back and forth, feeling invigorated by her mouth. His eyes closed and quickly fluttered as the sensation became faster and *deeper*. Animal instinct took over as he looked down at her. With both hands he took hold of the back of her head and pushed it her further onto him. He began to growl; the pleasure was intoxicating. He smiled as she continued to perform on him. He put his hands on her cheeks, and gently exited her mouth, her tongue quickly getting the last lick.

Jerome took her hand and stood her up, turned her around, and began kissing her neck. His hands feeling her breasts, caressing them, and slightly pinching her perked-up nipples, making her quiver.

For a split second, Rebecca thought this was a dream. It wasn’t. This passion was real. She felt his slender hand slide down her body, his touch soothing and gentle as he kissed her shoulder, his breath touching her ear. She looked down and gasped as she noticed his fingers going inside of her. She closed her eyes and moaned as the pleasure increased from the vibrations and pulse of his fingers caressing inside her. She bit her lower lip as her thighs began to shake.

“Ohh . . .,” she exhaled as her hand began to stroke him.

Her breathing became heavier as his fingers went faster. She realized that she too was motioning faster and faster on him.

Moments later she found herself bent down, but she didn't enjoy that position. She opted for something that was more comfortable. She quickly took both of their shirts and placed them on the ground. With her knees bent, she placed her hands on the ground, her buttocks raised in the air.

Jerome smiled and began to tenderly rub her cheek.

She turned her head around and looked at him and said, "Go ahead. It's okay." Her ass shook seductively.

Jerome grabbed her waist and inserted himself into her. The sensation of being penetrated was both surprising and exhilarating. She opened her mouth and closed her eyes as she felt him thrust inside of her, going faster and harder.

Rebecca felt his hands grasp her slender hips, pulling her closer to his pelvic region. She slammed her buttocks against him to keep up with the steady momentum. She was in pure ecstasy, having such an amazing man with her. She looked back at him, and his face said it all. It drove her wild. The sexual pleasure became even more intense.

Jerome removed his hands from her waist and repositioned himself. He bent himself over her backside while still being inside of her and grabbed hold of her ample breasts, squeezing them as he mounted her more aggressively, thrusting into her with even more ferocity. He had unleashed his full animal tendencies. There was no turning back. And he didn't want to.

"Uhh . . . Becky," he moaned, slapping her breasts, going faster inside her.

She smiled and exhaled. "Yeah . . . harder. Deeper . . . Fuck me! Fuck me, hard!" she said, thrusting herself as hard as she could into him. They were one. It was like they knew each other's thoughts.

With all of his strength, he gave Rebecca a giant thrust, making her entire body shake and convulse, and finally, she collapsed on the ground.

While still inside her, he gently flipped her onto her back and began to grind himself on her. They stared into each other's eyes passionately. Rebecca spread her legs more, and Jerome tenderly licked her inner thighs, kissing them softly. She loved that. He had a gentle touch that she found invigorating.

Rebecca lifted herself upward and kissed him passionately, running her hands all over his back, down to his buttocks. She signaled that she wanted to change positions, and slowly pushed him onto his back, spreading his legs apart, just ever so. He laughed as she hovered over him and gingerly lowered herself down onto him, placing him at just the right angle.

Now straddling him, she began to grind on him, eventually bouncing at a quickened pace, her hands now on his chest, feeling his fast-paced heartbeat. She quickened her pace, feeling his hands grasp her buttocks, squeezing them as he thrust harder inside of her.

Rebecca bent down closer to him, her nipples lightly touching Jerome's chest as she kissed him once more. They separated their lips from one another, and Jerome buried his head between her bosom, making her moan with a hot, fiery passion. He looked at her again and started to suck her right nipple while squeezing and massaging the other. She closed her eyes and moaned again.

"Yes . . . suck them. Suck them. Mmm . . ." she whispered.

Jerome lightly licked her nipple, gently biting it, teasing her. He let out one last thrust from his hips, exploding inside of her.

"Ahh!" she gasped, feeling what Jerome had just done. In response, she too exploded, dripping down him. She feverishly panted, moaning in erotic pleasure and satisfaction. She laid her head on his chest, catching her breath and giggling along with him. He caressed her hair and kissed her sweaty, blood-boiling lips and put his arms around her. The whole experience had been electrifying.

An hour passed, maybe it was more. The two lovers couldn't tell. They were bathing the sweat and dirt off of their bodies. Time did pass, but they didn't care. To them, this was a little bit of paradise.

Rebecca looked at him with concern written all over her face.

"Jerome . . . ," she said.

He saw it as well. "Finn, buddy, what happened?"

Finn was dripping blood from his chin.

TWENTY-FOUR

"Mrow."

"Poor baby, let's get you cleaned up," Rebecca said, scooping up a handful of water. *He was sleeping. How could blood just appear on his chin? What the hell did he eat?*

She gently rubbed the feline's chin. It was clean, for the most part. A stain could be seen, soaked through his fur.

"Well, that's the best I can do. We'll have to get a towel or something and see if we can get that out."

Moments later, more blood dripped down the cat's chin.

"What the hell!" she exclaimed. It wasn't stopping.

Jerome looked worried as the blood continued to pour down Finn's chin.

"Finn . . . ?" he asked.

As he said the cat's name, they heard it. That sound. The Bastards had found them. And they were closing in.

"Not now!" Jerome said, quickly getting out of the pool. Rebecca did the same.

The two hurriedly suited up, double-checking that they had everything on correctly.

Finn just looked at them with curiosity, questioning why they were in such a hurry. He wanted to stay in the makeshift cove. But, he also knew that wherever his masters would go, he'd follow.

Finn arched his back, his tail in an array of fur. He was ready to attack.

Rebecca grabbed Finn, and with Jerome, lanterns attached to their vests, they made their way toward the entrance. They had only taken six steps when they saw the mangled, decayed gelatinous hand. It grasped the rock and revealed itself to the group. Its eyes, blackened holes; its skin, rotten, and also filleted, like someone had used a jagged piece of glass and sliced it, layer by layer. It opened its mouth and spewed black ooze as it slowly lurched forward, clawed hands desperately trying to reach for the new form of nourishment.

Food. Yess . . . Flessh . . . Tasty . . . Eat them! Eat them!

It took a giant step forward and lost its balance. The damn thing had realized what was happening and corrected itself, trying to shift its center of gravity with its decaying legs. It had worked. The Bastard regained its balance and continued forward. It moaned, like it was gasping for air.

Does this thing even breathe? thought Jerome, taking Rebecca's arm and carefully backing away.

Another gasp. And another moan. Only it didn't come from the Bastard in front of them. The sound came from around the corner.

Two more of them! Shit!

Soon the other two decayed monstrosities came into the low-lit view, completely blocking the way out.

Finn squirmed and kicked in Rebecca's arms.

"Mrow!" he let out.

"No, baby! Stay still!" Rebecca ordered, trying to keep him calm. It was no use.

Finn leapt from her arms and landed on the ground. His tail poofed as he growled and hissed at the three Bastards. His chin was bleeding even more. Rebecca and Jerome clearly saw what happened next, their faces shocked.

Finn's jaw *split* open. Bone crunched and cracked. Tiny bits of muscle and tissue ripped and tore apart. Finn's jaw had now become two mandibles with sharp teeth extruding from both sides. His back arched, tail furled, ready to kill those that wanted to harm him and his masters.

"Holy—" Jerome started to say.

"Shit!" Rebecca said, finishing the thought.

Finn growled even louder, his mandibles spreading farther outward.

The two friends tried racking their brains at what was happening, trying to find the right words. None came to mind. Though they saw what was happening on the exterior, they didn't see what was happening on the inside.

In the back of Finn's mouth, two milky-white orbs sprouted forth from his gumline. Then in a flash, they shot out, attached to vein-like whips. The two whips lashed out wildly and made their way to the closest Bastard. They wrapped themselves around the damned thing and with a jolting tug, thrashed the Bastard in every possible direction.

The Bastard knew something was wrong, but couldn't do anything. He just felt an immense amount of pain as his brittle body was getting squeezed tighter and tighter, bones cracking and shattering.

After one final slam onto the rocky ground, a vine loosened and inserted itself through a decayed fleshy hole on the Bastard's face. Suddenly a gasp and a long-winded moan escaped its rotten mouth. It then fell to the ground, lying motionless and dead.

The vine that was wrapped around the body loosened. The orb flowered open and grew as big as an average adult hand. The newly formed "flower" placed itself on the top of the Bastard's skull and pulled. Hard. The skull detached from the body, and the vines retracted, reeling the head closer to the opened maw of Finn.

Inching closer, Finn's mandibles elongated, now scooping the body part into its mouth. The top incisors grew and in one motion, broke the rotted skull into smaller pieces and consumed them. Brain matter and sickly flesh erupted from Finn's mouth as he chewed. Seconds later, his mouth had returned to normal, his mandibles fusing back together to form his jaw, and his top incisors shrinking back down. He licked his snout and looked at his masters.

"Mrow!" he exclaimed gleefully.

The two Bastards that were left began to close in, stretching out their quivering fingers, hungrily wanting to grasp at the fresh meat that was in front of them. Rebecca hesitantly picked up Finn and put him back in her vest pocket. He licked his lips and "smiled" at her.

A Bastard swayed his body backward and took a giant lunge at Jerome. Quickly, he countered the advance by putting his hands up and grabbing the thing by its wrists. It tried desperately to claw at him, bending its wrists as far inward as possible, attempting to get a mere scratch of his skin.

Its lips quivered as it was mere inches from touching Jerome's skin. Jerome could sense that the thing's nails, elongated as they were, were almost able to puncture his skin. He gritted his teeth and pushed the lengthy arms away from him. He pushed with all of his strength, and the Bastard toppled backward, falling onto its back. Upon impact, it dislocated its left shoulder, and its ribs protruded out from its dead skin. As it "breathed," Jerome could see its chest heave outward as its dead lungs fought for air.

Jerome rushed beside the downed Bastard and lifted his boot, stomping on the exposed rotting chest. The Bastard lifted its head and moaned, as it could feel the boot crash down on its chest, breaking the rib cage. Jerome felt the fingers claw at his boot, the nails breaking off, blood spurting out from its newly formed wounds. The son of a bitch was trying to pull the boot from its chest. It was no use. Jerome lifted his boot. A final blow. It came down with thunderous impact, obliterating the rib cage and exploding the deadening lungs and heart.

He then took a piece of broken rib and jammed it directly into the head. It died instantly. He looked for Rebecca. She was having troubles of her own. The other Bastard grabbed ahold of her vest and dug its fingers through the material. Finn swatted at the decayed arm, hissing furiously at the dead thing.

Rebecca felt the nails pinch her left breast. She shrieked in fear and balled her hand into a fist and repeatedly punched the creature in the head.

Jerome rushed to her aid and grabbed it by the waist, pulling it off of her. In doing so, he also tore the Bastard's waist from its torso. Entrails and what looked like a stomach were dangling as blood and ooze dripped, washing the ground in its grime-filled mess.

He threw the torso to the side. It crashed into the rocks with a thud, but it wasn't dead. Using its remaining strength, it rolled itself over onto its chest and crawled toward the two.

Jerome looked at Rebecca. "You okay? You alright?"

"Yeah," she replied. "Yeah, I'm good." As she said this, she saw the glistening milk-white eyes as it hungrily crawled toward them. It reached for the ground, digging its fingers deep into the hard-covered dirt, pulling itself closer to the prey. The jaw opened, and it let out a raspy howl. It was that of an unquestionable appetite. It needed to feed, to regain some of its energy. Most importantly, it wanted to stop the pain. Its stomach (what was left of it), churned and vibrated as acidic juices gushed outward from a torn hole in the rotting sack.

As it lifted its head and let out another raspy howl, its rib cage came into the dim view. The heart. The damned thing was *still* beating somehow. It was like a paper bag being inhaled and then exhaled slowly. The world seemed to pass by slowly with each exasperated beat. Its ribs petaled and outstretched wider, though they were cracked and broken down the middle.

Rebecca quickly made her way to the decaying monstrosity and, glaring down at it, slammed her boot on the back of its neck, applying the ever-slightest pressure, making sure she didn't break the spine. Not yet, anyway. She wanted it to suffer. She was pissed, frightened, and confused. Her boot weighed down even more on the bones. Using its clawed fingers, it grasped at her boot and leg. It wanted to be free and even tried using its feeble strength to propel itself upward in an attempt to unbalance its dominating foe. With milk-white eyes it looked up at her, letting out what sounded like a mourning moan.

She bent down and looked it straight in its eyes. Jerome wondered what she was doing and stepped forward with one foot. Finn hid in her vest pocket but was hissing all the same.

"Goodbye," she whispered, and stood back up, crushing its neck, the body immediately going limp and crumpling to the ground.

The "Goodbye" wasn't for the Bastard. No, it was for her. This was a change. A major change for her. *No more being scared. No more being fragile. It's time to stand tall.*

"You alright?" Jerome asked in a soft voice. It was like he was a million miles away.

Rebecca slowly turned and faced him, lifting her boot from the creature's neck.

Jerome could instantly see a transformation. This was a different Rebecca, and she was determined to let nothing stand in her way.

"I'm fine."

TWENTY-FIVE

NIROBI - ELEVEN YEARS AGO

"Kira! That's not funny!" shouted Jerome, wiping the mud from his face.

"Don't be such a baby! You look better with mud on you! Ha ha!" she said.

Her voice was that of an angel. It was serene and loving. Kira's hair, braided as best she could, whispered in the cool breeze, which was a rare and refreshing surprise. The touch of wind cooled her chapping lips and reddish sun-soaked burned skin. They had been outside playing all day. Their parents giving them some time off from doing their morning chores.

Jerome wiped his face. The mud continued to drip from his lip and chin, making its way onto his school uniform.

"Great. Because of you, I have a ruined shirt. Teacher will not be pleased!" he said, trying to get the excess mud off of his shirt as best he could. The teacher. He ran the classroom like a boot camp. It was a well-oiled machine, and it taught Jerome about respect, honor, and most importantly, how to listen and survive.

The school was not at all cheap. Nor was it all too expensive. Their parents had played the stocks, invested wisely, and were able to give their children a modest home and a good life. That didn't mean, however, there were no boundaries. Chores still had to be done, and help around the house was necessary. Jerome and Kira's parents still remembered what it meant to work hard, something they instilled in their children when they were old enough to understand, and continued to drill it into their heads every day. That was one of the reasons why they also refused any sort of butler or maid of any kind. How else was one supposed to learn, if not by doing?

Kira giggled and smiled. Her brother's uniform wasn't a total loss. He would have a green stain, but it could have been worse.

Yeah, it could have been much worse. But still! He thought to himself as he straightened his clothing out and fiendishly smiled at his sister. It was time for some payback.

He sprinted toward her, and as he did, he picked up a glob of mud and chased her down. She ran and screamed at the top of her lungs, "Jerome! Get away! Get away! Don't you dare!"

He didn't listen. He arched his arm back, aimed, and flung the liquid gray substance at his sibling. At the last second, she darted the opposite direction.

"You are so dead, Jerome!" she shouted, racing toward their house. She ran faster, heading to that wooden door under the archway. A quick glance, and she noted that their parents were home. They were supposed to be at the market. (Their father had always insisted on getting the freshest vegetables possible, and that meant going shopping early in the morning.)

Maybe they forgot something. She thought.

The car, a Chrysler from the 1980s, was parked diagonally and not parallel. Their father loved old, classic cars. It was one of his hobbies.

Kira burst through the side entrance, quickly slamming it shut and locking it, just as Jerome reached for the handle. She heard his fist pound against the wooden frame in frustration.

Running into the living room, she saw her parents stare intently at the TV screen. Looks of shock were running down their faces. Kira was confused, and before she could ask what was going on, Jerome dashed in behind her, grabbing her.

"Got you, you little cretin!" he shouted. "Mom! Look what Kira did to my uniform! It's ruined!"

"Shh. Not now, Jerome," she said, waving him away. She sighed and took a quick look at her son. "That's not a big deal. Go and clean it in the wash."

Jerome groaned and began to take his dirty uniform off. He had another shirt, but it was a long sleeve, and he didn't want to wear that when he was going to be in such high temperatures. *Going to be one of those days, I guess.*

He paused and noticed that his parents and his sister were glued to the TV. He decided to keep his dirty clothes on for a little while longer. Curiosity had gotten the best of him. He decided to see what was so important. He slowly walked over to the couch and sat down, his parents wrapping their arms around their children. They watched attentively:

> *Evacuations continue throughout the southern*
> *border state of the country as more and more*
> *residents flee from the dangers of the countless*
> *number of attacks. The body count continues to*
> *rise as more and more civilians from around*
> *the country, and the rest of the world, try*
> *to escape what has happened.*
> *Representatives from all over the world*
> *will be meeting at UN Headquarters to*
> *discuss what the best solution*

is for this global catastrophe.
For your safety, and the safety
of those around you, we ask
that you stay in your homes, lock
your doors, and protect yourselves
and your loved ones.
And may God or whatever deity
you worship, if any, protect you.
This is Sasha Mann—

ZAP!

"Enough of that," said father. The TV had turned off. Jerome looked at the old man, and then at his mother. "Not the time to think of such things."

Kira looked to her father, eyes wide and frightened, and asked, "Daddy, are we going to have to move?"

Father stood up and tossed the remote to the side. He looked at his family with a stern expression. "There is no way we are moving from this spot!"

TWENTY-SIX

"Here! Mirim, in here! Quickly!"

A flimsy hand opened the hard-plastic lid. Mirim gently placed a nest of blankets down into the sickening, bile-infested garbage bin. She could barely stand the smell, and neither could her husband, Christopher.

The two had only been parents for five months.

FIVE MONTHS EARLIER

"YARRRGGH!!" Mirim screamed as she held onto Chris's hand for dear life. "God! Oh fuck! Holy shit!"

Her forehead sweated profusely, veins throbbing as she screamed out in pain again.

"Another push, Mirim. Almost done!" said the doctor.

She and Chris had been trying to conceive for years. They even went as far as getting the next, best organic miracle drug. Nothing helped.

He had a high sperm count. The doctors confirmed it. But for whatever reason, they kept giving up halfway through their journey.

It was the most bizarre medical case their physician had come across. They secretly called her vagina the "Bermuda Triangle." A man with a high count should have been able to pop out a child nine months down the road. The doctors didn't know what to do. Diagrams. Different sexual positions. Remedies. Nothing. The pair were about to give up hope on having any biological children of their own. A secondary plan came to fruition though. If they weren't able to conceive, they could always *adopt*. They wrestled with the idea. It wouldn't be theirs biologically, but it was better than having no children at all. They needed that innocent laughter in their lives, especially in such shit-infested times.

It was like the entire world just gave up and all the good up and left. Now, murders were happening all over the world. Society had been royally screwed. Various reports indicated citizens had been killing each other. Some used knives. Some used guns. And some . . . used teeth. The world was slowly rotting and becoming even sicker.

"AAHHHGH!" she screamed again. Another push. *C'mon! Out with it, already!* She had been in labor for almost fourteen hours. They almost didn't make it. Traffic had been diverted. The road had sunken in and closed off.

The police diverted the traffic east and west. Luckily the hospital wasn't that far away. The city was still growing, but from the looks of it, one could already see that it had quickly established itself on the map as a major contender, even though it was rotting.

Chris made a left on Baroque Street and was detoured to a residential area. The car sped through as the sun had finished setting. The two didn't know the sex of the child. They didn't want to, not until it was born. Mirim was irked by the pain. Another contraction. She glanced out the window a quick second and recognized where they were.

"Go down Nala Avenue!" she ordered, trying to keep her breathing constant and stable.

Chris followed her directions without question. That's the thing she loved most about him. In times of crisis, he followed her to a T. No questions. They trusted each other with everything, as a couple should.

The neighborhood on Nala wasn't the best. Crime had gone up, and homeowners had started putting bars on their doors and windows.

It may not have been the nicest of areas, but it was a shortcut to the hospital. A ten-minute drive had turned into twenty with the detour. If they had gone all the way around, it would have been forty.

The car was an old Model-C Volkswagen, and it pulled up to the Emergency Room entrance. Chris blared on the horn for help. Two nurses came rushing out, wheelchair in tow, as Mirim stumbled, carrying her stomach with both hands, trying her damnedest to keep the baby inside and not have it pop out. Then it came. An earth-shake. She toppled over! Chris rushed to her side and grabbed her by the waist and placed her haphazardly into the wheelchair, the nurses rushing to get back inside as the whole place shook. It wasn't a major event, thankfully. The earth-shakes were just a giant pain in the ass, and it didn't seem they would stop anytime soon. The hospital got wise, as did the rest of the city, and doubled up on earthquake protection.

Chris chuckled for a moment. In a twisted sense, he found it amusing that these earth-shakes only started about nine years ago . . .

"GET IT OUT OF ME ALREADY! ARRRH!" Mirim screamed, clenching her teeth, holding onto Chris's hand. This was the worst pain she had ever felt. "HURRY UP!"

The doctor looked under the towel. "It's beginning to crown. And . . . push!"

"AHH, FUCKING HELL!" she screamed, being patted down with a damp hospital rag, her face bright red.

"Okay, Mirim—" the doctor started.

"STOP SAYING OKAY! IT IS *NOT* OKAY!"

The doctor stared at her for a beat and continued to monitor the delivery. Cautiously, he said, "I understand you're in a lot of pain, but it's almost over. You're almost done."

Chris looked at his bride. "Honey," he piped up, "um . . . you're hurting my hand. Honey?"

Mirim slowly turned her head to him. It was like a full five minutes passed.

"YOU'RE LUCKY THAT'S THE ONLY THING I'M HURTING OF YOURS, BUSTER! I swear to God after this baby is born, I'm getting tied! I swear to God and the devil himself!"

"It's not nice to swear to the devil, dear—" Chris said nervously.

"OH, SHUT UP! YOU'RE NOT HELPING!" Another contraction. "YYEARRRGH! It's coming! It's coming!" she shouted.

"Mirim," said the doctor, placing his hands gently near her vaginal opening. "Big push! C'mon! On three. One. Two. THREE!"

She pushed. Hard. A new noise erupted through the chaos. It was a new life. Mirim inhaled and exhaled deeply as the cries of her newborn baby echoed throughout the room. Nurses gathered the child up and immediately cleaned the blood, shit, and other organic material covering it. They wrapped it in clean linens and handed it back to her.

She and Chris smiled and embraced in a kiss.

"You did amazing, baby. You were awesome!" he whispered in her ear.

"Congratulations. A beautiful baby girl!"

Mirim lovingly looked at her angel and burst out crying, as did Chris. They were finally parents.

Taking off his cap, the doctor asked, "Have you thought of a name?"

"Anna," whispered Mirim.

TWO MONTHS LATER

"Here! Mirim, quickly! In here!" ordered Chris, holding the lid open, eyes frantic.

"But—" Mirim objected, still holding Anna in her arms.

"They're nearly here! Do you want them to get a hold of her and kill her?"

SMACK. And then another smack across the face.

"To hell with you for even thinking such a thing, Christopher Masters! This is our daughter! Our daughter!"

"Which is why we need to leave her in here! It's for her own safety!" He took his wife's face and kissed her lips. "Someone will come and get her. I'm sure of it. If she is to have a chance at living, this is the only way!"

Mirim cried, sobbing uncontrollably. As did Anna.

Hesitantly, Mirim came to terms with the only ultimatum she had. She reluctantly placed Anna in the garbage dumpster. There was some solace in the fact that it wasn't all the way full, though it smelled awful.

They looked one final time at their daughter, and Chris closed the lid, leaving Anna in the dark.

Both parents held each other and ran, Mirim crying.

They ran as fast as their legs would allow them. *Don't look back. Don't you dare look back! Don't do it!* She turned her head and took a glance. Her eyes teared up again as she turned her head quickly around facing forward.

She and Chris turned down a darkened street. Droplets of rain and had begun to take shape, descending from the sky. A light rain began. The two tried to seek shelter under some wooden planks and loose boards.

In five months' time, things had gone from sour to absolute shit. Murders were becoming more rampant, fear had spread and infected the hearts and minds of Chris's co-workers at the plant he had worked for. It was a great job that paid well. Eventually, people stopped showing up to work, so the plant had to shut down. It didn't happen just to him. This gradually spread like a virus. The economy quickly dropped. People lost their jobs, and then the murders. At first it was just local. Weeks and months went by, the number of attacks increasing tenfold. They were thought to be global terrorist attacks, but the way they were happening was *off*. It was no longer a coincidence. Humanity was decreasing drastically. Government organizations like the CIA and NSA were in the dark. Africa, as well as the rest of the world, had fallen to its knees.

Mirim and Chris agreed that waiting for the rain to pass was a fool's gambit. They threw their makeshift shelter to the side and continued on their journey. A turn, and another turn. Barrel fires and crumbling buildings. Through broken gates and dust and dirt. Down various alleyways until finally reaching a graphite-ridden dead end.

"Shit," said Chris, looking for another way out. There were no ladders or stairs to ascend to their getaway. They turned around and started walking back to the entrance of the alley. "Come on."

He held his wife's hand and abruptly stopped. Shadows had appeared in front of them. The sickening sound came next. The sounds of *hunger*.

Chris put his wife behind him for protection. Only two had come forth. Chris pushed Mirim back more and changed his stance, fists up, ready for a fight.

There was something strange about the shadows though. He could see it. They stumbled and swayed as they made their way toward them. *I've got this. Just a couple of drunk assholes.*

"Listen, fellas," he started, raising his hands up.

The two shadows quickened their pace. Chris heard the sounds they made. They were moaning. It was disgusting.

Goddamn pervs.

Closer they advanced, Mirim backing away more.

"Chris . . . ," she said softly, "do something."

He glanced back at her and said, "Don't worry. I'll handle this, babe." He walked up to the shadowed figures. "Now, fellas. Look, we don't want any trouble. So, if my wife and I could just walk by. That'd be great. Just made a wrong turn is all."

One shadow lunged forward and grabbed Chris's arm. Instinct immediately took over, and he punched the shadow in what was to be the face. *Did these guys roll around in shit as well? God, they smell horrible!*

The shadow crumpled to the ground. The other one advanced to Chris and, like the first, lunged at him. Again, Chris punched it square in the face, it crumpling to the ground. He grabbed Mirim's hand and tugged, and as fast she could, they made their way to the entrance. It was futile.

Just as they were about to exit, more and more shadows appeared. Chris and Mirim were trapped.

In an act of desperation, they tried to fight their way through the horde. The moans that were emanating from them were sickening. And the smell was absolutely revolting. It was like someone had mutilated hundreds of livestock and dropped a huge bucket of urine onto it.

Teeth. The shadows had teeth. Chris's neck exploded with blood shooting in every direction as he felt teeth penetrate his skin. He screamed in agony as he tried to break free, holding onto his neck for dear life.

Mirim had her throat gutted as well. She could see her jugular and vocal chords being ripped out as the things ate
them in front of her. The horde then ripped open her abdomen as her body fell to the ground, entrails and acidic juices everywhere. One shadow dug its sharp claws into her breasts and tore them off, clawing its way through her flesh, devouring her organs in a bloody mess.

Chris fell backward. Horrified at what was happening to his wife, he tried one last time to fight them off. The shadows toppled onto him and tore into his meaty flesh. He could feel every bit of it but couldn't do a thing as he, too, saw his own beating heart and entrails being devoured before his eyes. Everything went black. All that would be heard was the moans and crunches of bone and tears of flesh.

FIFTEEN MINUTES LATER

"Bah! Not a looker among 'em!" Lenny Salt said to himself, slamming down the last bit of alcohol in his glass. He wiped his lips and tipped the night's bartender, Bridget. "Tired of this plaacce . . ."

The place was called The FoXXXy Tail. A hole-in-the-wall on the outside. On the inside, a man's paradise. And woman's. Tonight was a slow night. To Lenny, the talent wasn't that impressive. On the other hand, he didn't mind the action. It was a place where he could rest and shut his brain off. He watched though. Tonight's entertainment was named Diamond. That was it. Diamond. She smiled at the asshole in front of her. *Trevor.* An oily-skinned balding loser. And a degenerate of a human being.

"Yeah . . . who's your Uncle Trevor?"

Diamond giggled. She hated this sleaze. But after he had a few drinks in him, he tipped really well. So, she put up with his crap. He looked in his wallet. *Well I'll be . . . only a twenty.* He thought for a minute. The ATM was twenty feet away. He didn't want to have to get up and walk over to grab some quick cash.

"Fuck it. You're worth it, darlin'," he said with a perverted grin.

He threw the twenty on the stage in front of her. Her eyes lit up. She picked it up, putting it between her breasts, bending over, and circling her hips slowly. She blew him a kiss and sat down, spread eagle. She was the stuff dreams were made of. Perky nipples on beautiful breasts. She was Trevor's favorite dancer. Black hair that shone in the light as her doll-face eyes seductively teased him and the rest of the patrons.

CLAP

She clapped her stilettos loudly and smiled again, nibbling on the twenty. Diamond folded it in half and put it in her bikini string. The song ended, and she picked up her tips from the stage and walked off, blowing a kiss to everyone watching.

Trevor leaned back into his seat and closed his eyes. The drink had gotten to him. The announcer—a balding, middle-aged man—came onto the mic.

"Fellas! Give it up for Diamond!"

A few claps here and there. Lenny tapped his glass.

"Fellas! You had better not be beating the bishop for our next dancer, because she will find out and give you one hell of a spanking! Up next is a girl that was kicked out of the monastery for being too naughty! Give it up for the kinkiest nun . . . Sapphire!"

There she was. Stilettos, and robes, strutting herself on the catwalk. She removed her headpiece first, her black hair whipping around as she shook her head, smiling. Next to come off was her robes, which revealed a naughty school-girl uniform.

The best kind of fantasy, I must say, Lenny thought, gulping down more of his drink.

"Well whaddya know . . . there is a God," he said, turning to Bridget and tipping her a ten. "Thanks, love. I'm gonna go up front for a better view."

"No prob, Len. Take it easy," she said, showing that cherry-lipped smile.

Bridget was a sweet girl. A curly brunette, and wicked blue eyes, with a skull tat to match on her wrist. She looked onward at Lenny. He had an accent, which she loved. He had come by the Tail often, so it was only a matter of time before they knew each other's names. He was the kind of customer who was the sweet, nice guy. And a funny as hell drunk. Never caused a problem, and respectful to her and the other dancers. The bouncers enjoyed his company too. He was also tall, which was a plus in her book. But, he was also married. She never pried, but she guessed that the missus was okay with him going to a kind of place like the Tail . . . or his wife had no idea at all.

It didn't matter though. Bridget's rule was no dating customers. Just give them the fantasy, flirt a bit, and make the money. But, she thought, if things had been different, she'd give Lenny a shot. Go out on a simple date, get to know him better. *Could be a classy guy.*

Lenny stumbled into his chair up front and plopped down. This dancer was new. He hadn't seen her before, and he was mesmerized. If only he wasn't married. Bridget rolled her eyes. *Men.*

Sapphire saw Lenny and winked, smiling that sweet smile at him. Her hips slowly moved from side to side as her hands went up her stomach, grabbing her breasts, and every so slowly, taking off her buttoned-up blouse.

Lenny took out his glasses and put them on, eyes widening at the vision before him. He noticed that he had the biggest drunken smile on his face, and didn't care.

Sapphire bent down, her chest mere inches away from his mouth. She smiled again, and before he knew it, she had his glasses twirling in her hand.

Specs in hand, she slowly lowered them to her waist, rubbing them against her pierced navel. She removed her miniskirt. No panties. Sapphire brought the glasses back to her cherry lip-glossed lips and lightly bit the earpiece and then brought it down to her hips. She was now on her knees, swaying her hips from side to side.

She folded the earpieces and began rubbing them on her clit, lightly inserting them, devilishly smiling at Lenny, who was in complete awe. She unfolded them and carefully put them back on his face.

Lenny smiled again as Sapphire grabbed her tips. Lenny had almost forgotten that he needed to tip her. He reached into his wallet quickly, pulled out about thirty dollars in one-dollar bills, and threw them on the stage. "Bravo! Simply bravo!" he shouted, clapping his hands. Sapphire blew him a kiss and waved good-bye as she walked offstage.

Trevor awoke and looked at Lenny. "What'd I miss?"

Lenny fell back into his seat and rubbed his hands over his eyes and headed back to the bar. He took a seat and said, "Bridget, darling, can ya pass an old timer a glass of water?"

"Sure, hun," she replied, pouring his glass.

He took the glass and downed it in one fell swoop. He held the glass with two hands, his attention focused on Bridget. It was his routine. It was his way of sobering up. She never got tired of it though; she was just happy there was one responsible adult in that crap hole of an establishment.

Bridget poured herself a glass of water and held it up high as they both toasted.

"To friendships and other shit."

"I'll drink to that, love! May our bond grow strong and our hearts never waver!"

"Cheers," she said as they both downed their drinks, smiling at each other.

TWO HOURS LATER

"C'mon, I'll walk you to your car. Least I can do," suggested Lenny.

"Alright," Bridget said. "Lemme close up here and I'll meet you out back."

"Deal."

Lenny got up from his seat, rolling his body out slowly as he did most nights during closing. He and Bridget just talked, enjoying each other's company. It was nice . . . relaxing.

He strolled out the entrance and went around back. Trash bins adorned the back alleyway as a cool mist surrounded the Tail. It was comforting. The exit door, graffitied beyond anything, swung open, and Bridget walked out. She had changed her clothes. Tennis shoes, jeans, a Ramones shirt, along with a leather jacket.

They walked down the alley; the cool night air hit their faces as they talked some more—kids, family, etc. They took a right down the street. Her jeep, a Nova Class-B from Cherokee, was parked a block down. She was glad to have Lenny as company. Usually she'd walk with one of the bouncers.

The street was lit up with neon signs of semi-sin. A sleazy motel here, a marijuana lab there. Various homeless covering themselves in shadows. It wasn't safe for a woman to go walking by herself. *Let's not forget about all those crazy assholes killing one another. Now that's fucking scary. Being snuffed out like that. Jesus Christ.*

They reached her car.

"Thanks for walking me. It was nice."

"No problem at all! Just be safe getting home."

Bridget looked down, thinking to herself. She puckered her lips and kissed him on the cheek. "You're a swell guy, Len. A good guy. Your wife's lucky to have you."

Lenny Salt smiled and gave her a six-foot-four hug. It felt relaxing and calm. And most important, it was safe.

"You need a ride?" she asked, pressing her thumb on the fingerprint ID scanner. It hummed a red glow and then chirped a green acknowledgment. "I can take you to your car, or drop you off somewhere . . ."

Lenny took out his phone a scrolled through his Contacts list. "Oh, thank you, love. But I'm going to take an Uber home. Th' missus is using the car. Girl's night out an' all that."

He adjusted his grip on the phone and slightly lost his balance. The phone left his hand, dropping and hitting the concrete at an angle. The screen was cracked, and completely black. Nothing was coming up. "Shit! Blimey. Butterfingers again, Lenny!" he said to himself.

"Here, use mine," she said, taking the device out but quickly putting it back into her pocket. "Wait. Never mind. I'll give you a ride. It's the least I can do, and you need the cool air. It'll help you sober up much more quickly."

He let out a sigh. He felt like he was imposing. But he liked Bridget. She was good company. He picked his broken phone up off the ground and agreed, "Alright, alright. You've talked me into it, you have."

She smiled and giggled, "Hop in."

He opened the door and at the last moment, avoided the overhead bar colliding with his head.

She pressed the ignition button and the vehicle hummed to life. Then it let out a mechanical roar. She took hold of the shift knob—covered with a picture of a middle finger—and shifted the jeep into gear, giving a jolt.

"Um . . . forgive me for being nosy, but did you have work done on this thing? I thought they were supposed to be silent starting? Some vehicle-act you Americans have had for the past five years or so . . ." he trailed off.

Bridget shifted the knob and switched gears. "Yeah, I did. A jeep isn't supposed to sound like a pussy. It's supposed to have some fucking balls. So, I took steps and got ol' Sean here an upgrade of sorts." She patted the dash, and shifted gears again, the cool wind blowing in her hair.

"Sean. You named your jeep, Sean?"

"Damn right I did! Named after Sir Sean Connery!"

"The actor?"

"Yep! He was the sexiest man on the planet!"

"*Was* being the operative word, I'm assuming."

"Yeah, but man, if he was alive, I'd still try and fuck him. Liver spots and all! And that accent! Holy shit! Just thinking about it makes me all tingly!"

Lenny stared at her in disbelief. "You Americans and your celebrity crushes . . ."

"Oh, stop with that shit! C'mon! You can't sit there and tell me you never crushed on some actress!"

"No—"

"Bullshit, Lenny! That's fucking shit!"

Lenny rolled his eyes and sighed. "Okay, there was one. But she's been dead for about God knows how long . . . This is morbid, and weird. You know that, right?"

"Spill. Who was she?"

". . . Audrey Hepburn. Was a phase, really. Before I met the missus."

"God damn! She's ancient! Like, fuck, dude. Dust!"

Bridget laughed. Lenny turned red feeling the sting of embarrassment.

"Hey, hey, you want to fuck Sean Connery!"

"It's funny, Len. Look, I'm sorry. Just a bit of fun is all. Where to?"

She turned the jeep.

"Go up Myst Street, make a left on Flowerpark. Then you're there."

"Got it."

The jeep sped down MacAurther Avenue and headed toward Myst Street. Lenny felt it. The lurch. *You've gotta be kidding me!*

"Bridget, pull over, hun. I'm gonna heave up bits and bops soon."

"Yeah, yeah, no problem. Want me to hold your hair—wait. Never mind."

Lenny threw open the door as she stopped the vehicle. "Really? A bald joke?"

"Sorry, force of habit. Did I mention I was a sarcastic bitch?"

Lenny staggered to a nearby dumpster and bent down, holding his knees, trying to keep his balance. He prepared for the inevitable. *Last time I drink! I swear!*

It flowed from his stomach all the way out of his mouth. The disgusting liquid of alcohol and stomach acid. *Fucking hell!* It stung.

"Hey, you okay?" Brigette asked.

Lenny waved her off, and then his ears perked.

"Len?"

"Shh. I heard something."

He listened intently. There was a whine. A cry. His eyes went wide. "Bridget! Here! *Now!*

She jumped out of the jeep and raced to Lenny, who lifted the plastic, thin lid as she did.

Setting the light icon on her phone to On, she shone it inside.

"Holy—"

"Fuck."

A baby. A female baby, wrapped in a cloth and towels, just lying inside. Bridget picked it up and cradled it in her arms.

"Lenny, help me with my coat."

"Right. Right."

He took the baby and held it as she took off her leather coat and wrapped it around the child.

"Who could've . . . ?"

"You got me, love."

Another cry from the infant, this time more intense.

"God, she must be starving!" she said, taking off her shirt and bra, pressing the baby to suckle her teat. "Whoa, okay, okay, hun. Easy. Easy . . . there we go."

She looked at Lenny. "In my trunk there's some provisions. Get them."

Lenny nodded and seconds later returned with a plastic box.

"Open it."

He nodded and took out wipes and patted the child's face, getting the grime off the child's face. "We need to get her to a hospital."

"Yeah, I know. Nearest one is back that away," she said looking down the road.

It was already getting late. And they didn't have the correct provisions or equipment to care for her. Bridget slowly pulled the child away from her nipple, milk dribbling down her breast, and handed the baby to Lenny, who cradled it in his arms. The whining had subsided for now.

Bridget put her bra and shirt back on. She and Lenny both hopped in her jeep and headed to the hospital.

"I can stay with her. You can take my jeep and get home."

"What? No, no. I'll stay. It's no problem."

"What about the missus?"

"I'll call the house and leave a message. No fuss."

"Okay . . ."

They pulled into the entrance and looked for the maternity ward. They told the nurses and physicians what happened, and they got to work right away.

Bridget and Lenny stayed in the waiting quarters. They both exhaled a sigh of relief. The hospital wasn't that busy, thankfully. Patients were asleep, and the graveyard shift had just arrived on duty.

Lenny looked around and sighed.

What a night.

TWENTY-SEVEN

"You found a baby . . ."

"Yeah."

"In a dumpster."

"Yeah, love. That's right. I'm at th' hospital with Bridget."

"*Who* is Bridget?" The missus. Her voice was stern and calculating over the receiver of the phone.

"She's an acquaintance. She works at the club," he said, rubbing his dry mouth. His lips were dry, and he was dehydrated and tired. "Look, I'm here at the hospital waiting on the baby's status. Call this number if you need me. Celli's broke. I'm gonna take an Uber back to the flat later."

There was a slight pause in the conversation.

"Okay. What 'bout Bridget?"

"She's taking her jeep back home after we see about the baby."

Another pause.

"It's a girl," he said with a slightly optimistic tone. "She's beautiful."

The missus had delivered three boys. She loved them like crazy, but she had secretly always wanted a girl in the family.

"I'll see you later."

CLICK

Lenny hung up the phone. He turned around and saw Bridget standing behind him.

"You in trouble with the wife?"

"Dunno," he said, now slumped down in the chair next to the pay phone. "We'll chat it out."

The waiting took forever. Nurses and doctors were now rushing in and out, and around.

Lenny and Bridget hung their heads down low. A police officer had come in. Lenny looked up, the cop approaching them. A doctor was alongside the officer.

The officer, a young female, early to mid-twenties at best guess, asked the pair numerous questions. The questioning seemed to go on forever. All Lenny and Bridget wanted was a damned update on the baby.

When asked what was with all the questions, the officer simply stated that *it was for her report*. Sure it was. To Lenny, that was lingo for, "*I'm probing and trying to see if you two are batshit crazy*."

"Look, we just want to know how the baby is doing," Bridget piped up.

"A little malnourished, but she's resting comfortably. We have her on fluid," commented the doctor, who was Asian, late thirties, give or take. "If you'd like you can see her yourselves in a bit. You'll have to wear visitor passes and get your thumbprint scanned."

They both nodded a resounding yes.

Thumbprint scanning was a safety precaution. A few years back some asshole got the bright idea to walk into a hospital and shoot up the place. The thumbprint ID tells your criminal history, if any, to the security desk up front, and to local law enforcement. The police had a division made up of dispatchers that handled those kinds of cases. The front desk would notify dispatch with the history of the visitor, and dispatch would then notify the front desk if they were all clear to proceed with visitation.

In the extreme cases, however, the police were immediately notified, and took action. But those were quite rare nowadays.

The doctor nodded and went to fetch the tags and scanner.

Bridget closed her eyes.

Great. More waiting.

She wanted to go home and sleep. Lenny had been awake for almost twenty-nine hours. He, as well as she, was running purely on adrenaline.

The police officer was still standing with them. Making sure the two didn't try anything. Finding a baby was a serious case, and the officer didn't want to take any chances.

Five minutes passed, and the doctor, Catherine Choi, brought the ID tags and the scanner in hand. She held onto the tags and opened the scanner—a small unit the size of one's thumb.

"Please place your thumb on the sensor," she said.

Lenny did as he was asked. A few beeps later his entire record was sent to security. Moments later, a green light lit up and a robotic signal that said "Access Granted" chimed in. Dr. Choi motioned for Bridget to place her thumb next. The same thing happened, except a yellow light lit up the screen. Lenny chuckled, "Ohh, naughty girl!"

She rolled her eyes. "I was fifteen."

The automated voice chimed in: "Access granted—level Zeta."

Level Zeta wasn't bad. The status just meant security was going to keep an eye on you, and an orange sticker was to be placed on your ID tag. One still had access, but Zeta was more of a precautionary status more than anything.

Dr. Choi slapped the sticker on Bridget's ID tag. A bold Z emblazoned it. Choi smiled as she handed the tags to Lenny and Bridget. Both clipped them onto their shirts, and Choi did an about-face and said, "Follow me, please."

Choi led them down the hallway, to two double doors. Lenny looked up and saw that there was a sign that read

He looked across the hall and saw an entrance to the Burn Ward. The doors opened, and he could see a child with second- and third-degree burns covering his face. New bandages were being placed on his face and arms. The little boy saw that Lenny was staring, and gave him a big smile. Lenny smiled back and gave him a thumbs-up. The little boy reprobated the thumbs-up back, his smile growing even bigger. The doors closed as more nurses entered the ward, blocking Lenny's view of the child.

"Lenny?"

Bridget and Doc Choi were partially in the doorway, waiting for him.

"Yeah . . . coming."

He caught up with the two women and entered the double doors into the Maternity wing. Glass windows were to the right side of the hallway as they saw AI helper robots assist the nurses inside. Humanity had a boom in population in recent years. People were humping each other faster than Catholic rabbits. Humanity needed a bit of help. So, they decided to have technology go farther and made the simplest of robots to help with the newborn babies.

Now the only problem was, what to do with the dying and dead. The president passed a law decreeing everyone be turned into ashes. That didn't go over so well with the current population. Protests began, and religious riots against the government engulfed almost the entire country. It was bad for a time.

Eventually, things calmed down, and as time went on, people just didn't seem to care anymore. The country was divided on the issue.

Lenny shook the memories from his head, wiping his eyes. He was over-exhausted. His mind was running every which way.

Almost there. Don't worry. Not far to go.

They entered through two more double doors, though this time, a single rectangular glass barrier was to their right. Dr. Choi stopped, turned around, and smiled.

"And here we are. There she is!"

There were a lot of babies. Each in their own individual incubated cribs—color coded. The classic pink for girls, and blue for boys.

Choi pressed a button on the wall, and a panel slid open and she input a series of numbers. A green light blinked, and inside the ward, a robotic aide—bulky and box-shaped with one "eye" sensor, looked up at Dr. Choi and "waved." It scooted itself to the baby, who was sound asleep.

"Care to see her up close?"

Bridget and Lenny nodded. They were finally going to see the little miracle.

The aide, with a nurse's careful observation, gently picked up the baby and slowly rolled toward the window where the three humans were standing. The robot cradled the infant in its arms. She was still fast asleep.

Lenny and Bridget beamed with joy. Sure, it wasn't theirs, but they were ecstatic that the child was alive and was nourished. She even sported a pink beanie with a tag attached to it that read—JANE DOE.

"There she is! Hi, sweetie!" said the doctor.

"Jane Doe?" asked Lenny, puzzled.

"For now. We're trying to find the parents or any record of her. That's why it was a bit of a wait. I apologize."

"No problem," Lenny said. "How long does it usually take for a baby to be identified with parents?"

"Well, it depends on the parents. I've seen cases where no one claimed the child. Others, though, were more positive experiences."

"Positive how?" asked Bridget. "The parents were reunited with the child?"

"No. In a case like this, we give them good foster homes with the help of a foster care agency. But we also give the parents a month or so to come forward and claim the child. Of course, fingerprint identification, blood type, birth certificates, etc. must be presented and scanned and proven."

"Of course," Lenny replied, looking at the baby, who was now yawning. He suddenly had a thought enter his mind. "Doctor . . . how long does the adoption process take?"

"It depends. It could take up to a few months to a year. Give or take, sometimes longer. Why?"

TWENTY-EIGHT

The missus. A kind-hearted woman, who was overprotective of the things and people she loved the most. She always made certain that her family left the house with full bellies and a smile on their faces. After her sons were born, there had been talk of having another child, but she ultimately decided she didn't want any more children.

So, one day she went to the hospital and got her tubes tied. It was not as an act of protest, no. It was because three boys were a handful. Four, if she counted Lenny, which at times she did.

In solidarity with his wife, Lenny had gotten snipped a week later. He was happy with two children and didn't think of the matter after he had gotten cut. He hadn't expected to find a baby in a dumpster though.

"Are you serious right now? Oi! You're pulling me arm, Len. Havin' a laugh, right?" the missus asked, drink in hand. She was upset. More upset than she had ever been, and Lenny knew it.

"Why not? You've always wanted a girl! I seen it in yer eyes!"

"But another baby, Len? We're too old, we are! The boys are off to college, and this is supposed to be about us! It's why I got tied and you got ya damn berries snipped!"

"Oi! Things change! Feelin's change. Did yeh ever think that maybe this would be a good idea for both o' us?" argued Lenny, his hands gently touching his wife's cheeks as he looked deeply into her eyes. "Look, just think it over. For me."

A pause.

"Fine. Fine! I'll think it over. Just . . . give me a few, alright?"

"Take as long as you need."

". . . Yeah. Right. Now, sod off you. Ya got that DJ job, yeah?"

"Yeah, yeah. I do," he said, turning around and headed to the bathroom to get ready.

Three weeks later

"How's the baby?" asked Lenny, sipping down a fruity beverage. He was hunched over the bar table. Bridget smiled and wiped down the table, removing empty glasses left by another patron, who according to them, had to "release the Kraken" as they always put it.

"She's good. Spry little thing. I got to hold her. Doc Choi kept a watchful eye as always."

"As always," he said, biting down on his straw.

"What about the missus? She made a decision?"

Lenny sighed. "Not yet. It's a big step, and she's in a weird spot. As am I."

"What spot, Len? She still mad about you and I hanging out?"

"No, no. Nothing like that. I'm just wondering if I really want a child again. It's a huge decision!"

"You're getting cold feet, old-timer. But for as long as I've known you, which is only a few months, I can tell you're a great person and a good man."

Bridget put her hand on his, smiling with her bright, arctic-blue eyes.

Lenny squeezed her hand lightly and slipped out from hers. He took another sip from his drink and said, "Ya know, I'm umm . . ."

"It's okay. I know. Unprofessional of me. My mistake," she said, clearing the bar counter, slightly blushing.

"Bridget—"

"No, never mind. It's fine. It's fine, Lenny. Stupid, really."

"It's not stupid. Find it rather flattering, I do."

"It's just . . . you're not like the other jerk-offs that come in and try to get action, you know?"

"I do. Me mum raised me right, I guess you could say."

"An upstanding gentleman."

"And loyal—to a fault," he said, sipping down the last of his drink and paying for it. He set the money down and began to get up, when he began to question something. "Hey, Bridget. Have you, y'know, ever thought about adopting?"

"Ah, no. No, not really. 'Sides, I don't think a lot of people would approve, given my job title and all," she said as she poured him a tall glass of water. "Including my adoptive son or daughter. Wouldn't feel right, y'know? I mean, how do you tell your kids what you do for work? *'Mom, what do you do for a living?' 'Well, Mommy takes off her clothes and dances for complete strangers, and if they pay a bit extra, she sucks their cock.'* Weird, right?"

Lenny sat motionless and stunned. He didn't think about it like that.

"Don't worry; I haven't done that in a long time. Got tired of it. Why I mostly stay behind the bar, and dance."

"You could always tell a fib, just for their young years."

"Nah, not my thing. I'd want to be straight up with my kid. I'd expect it from them."

"Did you ever think of a change of scenery? A new job?"

"Hah!" she scoffed. "Tried that. Went back to school, got my classes canceled without telling me beforehand."

"What were you studying?"

"Physics. And art. I love painting. But that fell through, so, here I am. Back in the seedy party of life. Least the money is good, right?"

"Well, yeah, but don't you feel a bit exploited?"

"Hah! Says the one who comes and visits me and my gals almost every week like clockwork! You're on a roll, Mr. Salt," she said, pouring a shot of whiskey to a customer down the table, sliding it toward them. "Catch!"

The patron caught it and said, "Thanks."

She returned her attention to Lenny. "No, I don't feel exploited. Never did. Think about this. We take off our clothes and give you, the customer, a very good peek at the merch underneath, providing a fantasy. You shell out tons of money because of the services we offer. Now, ask yourself this—who's really exploiting who?"

She was right. Goddamn it, she was right.

"Sonofabitch."

"Right? But change of subject. Let's say the missus agrees to the adoption and it's granted. Do you have a name for her?"

He didn't, come to think of it. He thought intently and came up with an answer.

"Probably something like Rebecca."

TWENTY-NINE

PRESENT DAY

"Babe? You awake?" whispered Jerome.

She was awake. But she was deep in thought. She finally answered, "Yes. Yeah, I'm awake."

Her hand brushed his thigh.

Jerome looked down at her; she was still lying her hand on his lap. Finn was curled up next to her stomach sleeping. She looked down at the cat and caressed the back of his head. He curled even more into a ball, his paws covering his face. Finn was tired. They were all tired. And it also smelled. Dead, rotting flesh and carcasses of Bastards lay at their feet.

TWENTY MINUTES EARLIER

"Mrow!" Finn exclaimed, reaching for Rebecca's vest pocket.

Nervously and very cautiously she picked him up and studied him. With her thumb and index finger, she opened Finn's mouth, and taking her lantern, she looked inside. There were three dots on the top that he must have been born with; the incisors and canines were all intact. His mouth and teeth were completely normal. There were no signs of pre-existing damage or aftereffects from the transformation, which had Rebecca stumped. As well as Jerome.

Animal testing? Accident? What the hell happened to you, pal? Jerome set those questions aside for now. In his heart he knew that he probably would never get the answers he was seeking. *Might be for the best.*

"Mrow."

Finn looked at Jerome as Rebecca finished examining him. He decided to stretch out his paws and began to squirm in Rebecca's arms. She grabbed him by his bottom, balancing him as best she could. "Whoa, okay, okay, you want to go to Jerome. I get it."

Jerome smiled as he took Finn in his arms and cradled him. Finn nuzzled his neck, purring intensely, and closed his eyes, his tail wagging slowly back and forth. He felt Jerome's fingers run through his fur to the back of his neck and down his spine. He arched his buttocks in the air and held onto Jerome's vest tighter, "smiling." He felt Jerome's big hands hold him by his ribs and abdomen and stick him in his vest pocket. With his front paws out, he popped his head out and looked up at his master, and then waved his gaze to Rebecca.

"Traitor," she said, smiling at him and rubbing her fingers under his chin. Playfully, he nipped at her, and then immediately kissed her hand.

An hour passed, and the two companions decided to get back to their task at hand—trying to find an exit.

Jerome was the first to stand, helping Rebecca up, and with a smile, they refilled their canteen. Finn leaped out of Jerome's pouch and took one last drink from the makeshift reservoir. He turned around and jumped back into Jerome's vest pouch, ready to go.

The three made their way around the corner. The smell of decay was ripe in the air. Cranking their handles and igniting the flames, they felt their way along the cliff face. The path was narrow, so they had to put their backs to the jagged wall. Rebecca muttered a silent prayer to herself in hopes that whoever was listening would hear it. So far, it was being answered. No Bastards bursting through the rock.

Unfortunately, there were Bastards. They were the stragglers crawling and quickly dangling from the fallen building they crouched under earlier.

"Shit," she cursed. "Guess the break's over."

They moaned louder and were getting closer.

"We need to move faster. They won't be able to get across . . . I don't think so, anyway," said Jerome.

Not a good sign! Rebecca thought to herself. She glanced down below. Darkness. That's all there was. More darkness, followed by the hungry moans of those damned things.

Feed! Feed! Flesshhh!

Milky-white pupils glowed in the shadowed dark. A rotted nose sniffed the air. The scent was stronger. It was close. So close!

A rotten hand pressed against the rock-scarred surface. The thing felt along the jagged edges as it began to puncture its dead skin, making blood seep out from the wounds. Soon, the surface of the hand looked as if razors had sliced it open.

The Bastard's jaw opened and moved what was left of its tongue to somehow croak out the hunger it was feeling. It hurt to do this; the trachea was still dangling by a loose strand of tissue, it's Adam's apple had long since dissipated. The only thing remaining was a shallow, rotten black hole.

Groans echoed in the dark as their shuffling became quicker. They were like lemmings—a group with one goal on their minds. Well, what was left of them anyway.

Rebecca and Jerome shifted across the ledge. She lifted her lantern and saw the shadows of the Bastards were now silhouetted even more so. She could see a hand, then a foot, and finally a full-figured body as the first one came into perfect view. Her body was in the center point of the ledge, along with Jerome, their backs still pressed firmly against the jagged edges. Their hands were grabbing what they could get ahold of. She gave Jerome a look of anger and determination in her eyes. Her soul was on fire.

"Keep moving!" she ordered, grabbing his arm, steadying his footing. This was indeed no time to be scared.

You've changed, remember. You have to be strong now, for both of you.

For some reason or another, she was curious at the coming horde. She secretly watched to see if they were going to attempt to make it across the ledge.

A fool's errand. Don't wanna get yourself killed.

They stepped across, looking down, making sure their footing was solid and they had good balance.

The Bastards' moans became louder. *Closer.*

Jerome shot a quick glance at them. *Shit! Shit! Shit! Just go away!*

They were just standing there now. A good dozen or so. Jerome stopped mid-step. His heart was beating fast. The panicking was setting in. His chest began to hurt. He could hear it—his breathing was now becoming faster. Beads of sweat dripped from his forehead.

"I guess this is a bad time to say I'm kind of scared of heights."

"It's okay. We're almost there, it looks like," Rebecca said, leaning past his frame. She could faintly see a large platform of dirt and rock. A solid foundation.

They moved closer, inching their way across. Jerome took his lantern and could see the other side. The platform was on the other side, but it was like parts of it had been broken off. That was it. The earth-shake. It had made a giant chasm, and the two were feverishly trying to get to the other part.

Rebecca held onto Jerome's arm, keeping her balance. They shimmied across some more. *Almost there.* She suddenly felt a tingling on the back of her neck. The hairs began to stand up. Slowly turning her head to the opposite direction, she soon found out why.

The Bastards were crossing the chasm.

"Fuck!"

THIRTY

"This is bad, right? Like *really* bad," Jerome said, looking at the onslaught of Bastards making their way toward them. It wasn't enough that he and Becky had the arduous task of crossing the damned ledge, but now they had to deal with those things.

"How in the fuck—?" she replied, trying to keep her balance, looking at the rotten mass. "Never mind, let's keep going!"

She didn't want to try and rack her brain about how these things had the brain power to make a decision of crossing the ledge.

There they were. The fresh meat was on the move. One opened its mouth and moaned, puking out black ooze and blood. It slowly cocked its head to the side, and with one rotten foot, it stepped forward. Another food. Then an arm. And another arm. It then grasped at the rocky surface, slowly stepping as best as it could toward the meat bags. *Closer. Clossser. Yess. Meat! Hunger! Flesh!*

The others had gotten the idea and soon followed. One by one they made their way toward Jerome and Rebecca. Some, however, lost their balance and fell into the chasm below, while others were luckier. By lucky, one could see that they kept their balance, and others were hanging on the edge of the ledge, shimmying toward the duo. Perhaps they thought stealth was a better motive. Whatever the reasoning, it was working. The horde was getting close.

The "leader" decided to lunge for the meat bag closest to it. The thing's abdomen was caved in. No muscle density could be seen. In its place was the complicated wiring of the intestinal tract, and above was the stomach, deflated and dried up.

It opened its jaw and raised its arms, doing its best to get just a feel of Rebecca. Its fingers grasped onto her arm. It wasn't the soft, squishy feeling it was hoping for, but it could sense it was there.

Face! Neck! Neckkkkk!

The Bastard didn't taste the warm meaty nectar of Rebecca's jugular. It didn't drink of her warm blood. Instead, it felt a shove. A hard shove, followed by a fist to its face. It lost its balance, teetering backward. In a desperate attempt, it grabbed ahold of her vest. Its elongated, dehydrated fingers clamped down on the material as hard as it could. In its mind, it figured if it was going down, she was too. But she didn't fall. She was still on the ledge. It sniffed the air and sensed another meat bag. *Two! Two by two!*

With its other hand, it grabbed another piece of her fabric. Behind it, the other Bastards were toppling over one another, racing to get a piece of soft, moist flesh to fuel their appetite. It was like an avalanche of bodies. The moans were growing more desperate. They were jealous of what their leader was trying to accomplish. So, they crawled and shuffled as fast as they could to the finish line that was the two delicacies. Some had fallen off the edge, while others tried their best attempting to feed.

Jerome knocked the Bastard in the head. Finn, holding onto his vest, hissed and snarled at it. The boot crashed against the forehead again, making it jerk violently to the side. With his lantern, he could see its jaw open, its mouth vomiting as it lunged upward.

Rebecca took her hands and began to pry the sickening fingers off. They had a firm grasp, the index and ring fingers hooking around the loops.

"Fuck it!" she said and unhooked herself. The Bastard was now clamoring up her vest, its hands mere inches from her throat. Jerome saw what was happening and as fast as he could, pulled the vest off of her and in one swift motion, kicked the Bastard off of the ledge, sending it hurling into the darkened bottom.

Jerome took her arm, and they shuffled to the opposite side. The Bastards, who were now fewer in number, followed their trail. Some were able to take hold of the cliffside, their hands cut and bruised as they slowly made their way across the chasm wall. Others had fallen simply due to loss of balance and even worse motor skills.

Both Jerome and Rebecca had finally made it to the other side and turned their lanterns low as to not be spotted by the Bastards that were in pursuit on the ledge, though they both thought in reality the Bastards weren't going to survive either way.

"Go!" Jerome ordered Rebecca, making double time in the darkness. The two could still hear the distant moans of the pursuers. The dark was beginning to not feel so terrifying anymore. Rebecca was getting used to it, minus the monsters that were lurking around. She, as well as Jerome, desperately missed the cool night air, their solidified cave, and their pool. That was home to them.

Our true home. Idiot. She had to remind herself of that. *It'd be amazing if there were stairs leading out of this shithole, huh? Not likely, girl. Just keep on moving. Hustle!*

Rebecca nodded, tightening her lips, gaining speed, catching up to Jerome, who was a few meters ahead.

Jerome. He wanted to get out of this hellish nightmare badly. He almost felt sorry for the Bastards. Whatever had happened, it was not a kindness, that was for sure. But he had to keep moving, keep surviving. *How in the fuck are we going to get out of here? Feels like we've been running in damned circles for hours!*

It had been hours, but to him it had felt like days. His mind started to wander, and he began to think about the surfaces. If it was this horrible down below; if the Bastards had found out how to ascend to the surface, there was no telling what could happen to the planet itself. For their home and way of life. As far as he knew, he and Rebecca were the last survivors living on Earth. He was glad to have her by his side. It made him feel sane, and there was also a sense of normalcy. Jerome wondered if she felt the same way. *Probably.*

When Rebecca turned her head to answer him, he knew she was different. And to him, at the same time, it both worried him and for some odd reason, turned him on. He loved a strong woman. And that was Becky. He just hoped he was doing the right thing by letting her do her own thing—going through the motions and keeping an eye on her from the sidelines. Maybe he could coax the conversation.

"Babe?"

Rebecca stopped. "Really?"

"What?"

"Giving me pet names already?"

"Hey, if you don't—"

She started to laugh. "I'm just fucking with you. Calm down." Slowly she approached him and kissed his cheek. They were a good distance from the Bastards. At least she thought so.

The two had now come to a dead end. That's what they had thought anyway. It was, in fact, another large, looming building. This time, however, it wasn't on its side. It was vertical. There were broken concrete slabs, with cracks running like thin-layered vines up the front, back, and sides. Window panes were shattered, beams of cement lay crooked and broken. Both held their lanterns aloft and examined the structure. The front entrance was, for all intents and purposes, destroyed. Jerome squinted; the top was still attached and hadn't been destroyed.

"You ready?" she asked, smiling with sincerity.

“I guess,” he replied. He looked down at Finn, who poked his head out of his vest pocket. “You ready?”

“Mrow . . .”

“Yep. Definitely ready.”

Rebecca took the first step. Jerome followed her lead. She saw cement blockades that created a kind of ramp, and climbed. The ramp led to a second-story windowpane. She grabbed ahold of the pane and looked inside. From what she could see, it had once been some sort of office, or living quarters. She wasn’t sure.

Turning her head side to side, she scoped out the area. The coast was clear. No Bastards, or spiders. She lifted the windowpane and crawled inside, landing on a firm surface. She made a note of what she was standing on. It was wood. A wooden floor that creaked. Jerome entered moments later, being mindful of Finn, still in his pocket. He lifted his lantern, as did Rebecca, and scoured their surroundings.

Dust and broken floorboards. But mainly lots and lots of dust. It was musty, and all three coughed as they made their way around the room. Strange devices were scattered around the floor.

“Let’s each take an area,” Rebecca said.

“Okay.”

Rebecca went straight toward the other end of the room. Jerome went left; he had found an opening. The room hadn’t been obliterated as he had thought. It looked more or less like it had been trampled through.

Lifting her lantern, Rebecca knelt down and examined the first object on the ground that caught her eye. There was something familiar about it. *What did he call it? What was the name of it, Cal?*

“Television.”

Rebecca smirked. A tear escaped her eye as she remembered the old man’s voice. She wished he was here with them.

But for now, it was just her and Jerome. She moved the thought of Caleb to the back of her mind and decided to see if the damned thing still worked. Just for shits and giggles. Kneeling down, she reached for the dial, turning it to the right. It made a loud click. The screen was still blank. She checked to see if it was plugged in. It was. The glass screen was still intact. Nothing was broken on the outside at least. She gave it another try. Click. She leaned back, still on her knees. *Better not try anymore.*

Turning the flame in her lantern a bit higher, she checked the large couch that was behind her. *More dust.*

She turned around and suddenly heard a light tap a foot or so in front of her. She lifted her lantern up high and saw that there was a leak in the roof. An oil-green drop descended and dropped on the wooden floor when it landed. *Gray water . . . piss and shit, probably.*

Another droplet.

Jerome carefully stepped around the area that was the bedroom. He coughed again. More blasted dust. He looked up and saw that the ceiling was exposed. Pipes trickled grime-filled droplets of water. Mold had grown on the walls around him, and it was taller than he. As he crept toward the bed, the wooden boards creaked and groaned under his boots. In the air, what there was, wafted a rotten-fruit type of smell. Jerome took out his oxygen mask and put it on. He turned his arm over and pressed his forearm. His skin opened and revealed his percentage of clean oxygen: 87%. Still good.

"Hey! Put your mask on! There's mold here," he called out to Rebecca.

"Yeah, no problem! What about Finn?"

"I've got him covered. No problem!"

"Okay . . . ," she said.

The air was pungent and made Jerome's nostrils wrinkle, even with the oxygen mask on. *Least it's not a rotting corpse. But you've gotten used to it, right? Sure you have.*

He looked one last time around and decided to rejoin Rebecca.

“Nothing here anyway,” he muttered and lowered his lantern, clipping it to his vest.

Finn gave a disgusted response.

“Yeah, my sentiments exactly.”

Jerome walked into the living room and rejoined Rebecca. She turned around and smiled hopefully. “Anything?”

“Nope! Not a damn thing. Just dust and mold.”

“Oh . . . well the same can be said here. Not a thing.”

“Check the next area?”

“Fine by me! Lead the way!”

“It would be my pleasure, m’lady.”

Rebecca shook her head and giggled. “Just go.”

Jerome put one foot forward toward the exit, a crushed door frame. But it wasn’t so badly destroyed that they couldn’t crouch and crawl through. It was just a matter of wriggling their bodies through.

Another step was taken, but Jerome stopped in his tracks and lifted his head. Finn perked his ears and looked up. Rebecca raised her lantern to the ceiling where she had noticed the dripping gray water. Jerome did the same.

“We aren’t alone,” he said.

THIRTY-ONE

SPLASH.

A waterfall of red poured out from the ceiling and splattered in the area where Rebecca and Jerome were standing. They jumped backward, sprinkles of red covering their boots. The waterfall soon changed into a trickle, and then transformed into tiny droplets. Both of them switched their flames to a higher setting. In the faint light they saw what it was—the remains of a body, but it had turned to liquid, entrails such as jellied intestines could be seen, as well as a skull with patches of skin. Sitting underneath the skull was the thick soupy contents of the rest of the body.

Rebecca gagged and threw up first, dropping to her knees. Jerome was next. They never knew that could happen to a human.

"Fucking hell!" she said, desperately trying to keep the rest of her guts down. Even though they both had oxygen masks, the smell and sight were overpowering. She heaved again. "Goddamn it."

Using her sleeve, she wiped her mouth, and spat out the last bit of acidic bile. Her stomach hurt, as did her throat. What was worse was that her lantern began to flicker and went out. "You've gotta be shitting me."

She cranked the handle. No spark. She cranked it again and a spark burst forth. That was great, but it also gave her pause. Her oil might have been running low. And that would only leave them with one working lantern. That was the thought that frightened her. Being stuck in the dark with no light source. She slapped the lantern, making sure the light stayed on. It did.

Both of them stared at the liquefied corpse.

"Look," said Rebecca, signaling to the skull with her lantern. Jerome saw it. There was a small hole, about the size of a penny on the left side, where the temple was. From the hole sprouted jagged cracks and fractures.

"What do you think happened?"

"Don't know," she said, taking a closer look at the skull. She reached to examine it more closely, when she heard a noise. Startled, she dropped the skull. It made a wet sound as it touched the remains. The noise, a tiny squeak, turned into an aspirated growl.

"What the—?"

They saw it. The skull was moving, rolling around on the blood-soaked ground. A prolonged snout, beady black eyes, and a slick tail.

"A rat? We got scared of a fucking rat!" Rebecca asked.

"Must have been the noise I heard."

"Yeah . . ." Rebecca replied, looking up. The rat scurried away as fast as it could, finding the nearest opening to escape the giants. "Want to give me a hand? Try the third floor?"

Jerome smiled. "Sure. Let's go exploring."

THIRTY-TWO

The couch was the easy part. It slid across the wooden floor like an engine trying desperately to start. It gave Rebecca and Jerome the extra height they needed to propel each other to the blood-stained, rotting ceiling. Rebecca was first. Her hands took hold of support beams as she pushed herself up through the ceiling, noting strands of gray tissue hanging from the floorboards and beams themselves. Her hands went to the floor itself where they landed on a thick, wet substance. *Ugh . . . that was probably brain. Yep. Definitely brain.*

She was waist high, when she spotted something in the dimness. She shot herself up in one swift move, rolling onto her side, and reached down to grab Jerome. "We've got another one."

Jerome pushed himself through the hole and followed her.

There was another body, only it was on the other side of the dust-ridden bed. It wasn't like the first one. This body, a female, was intact for the most part. Her face had melted, but the rest of her was complete. No clothing could be seen; she was stark naked, skin like a dry, rubber husk.

Jerome noticed that she, too, had a puncture, but it was in her abdomen. "Look. Same marks as our friend down below."

"Yeah. Think it's connected somehow?"

"Don't know. Can't know."

“Right. Okay. Let’s find a way out of here. Getting claustrophobic with all of the dense air and *that*,” she said, noting the dead woman. Rebecca felt like the walls were closing in around her. She was dehydrated and tired and just wanted to leave. But that bed did look comfortable. Taking a closer look she deduced that the bed must have been owned by someone of importance. Her hand touched the covers. The sensation was soft and extremely smooth, like a ripple of water. Her mind couldn’t stand it any longer, and neither could her body. She began to remove her boots, and soon after her uniform. She was naked, and gingerly she dipped her body under the covers. A smile formed as the sheets kissed her thighs and then her waist, until they were up just past her breasts. She looked at Jerome, who was still standing next to the bed.

“What?”

“There’s a dead body on the ground.”

“Yeah.”

“You’re gonna lie next to a corpse?”

“It’s on the floor. It’s dead. Not moving. Now, come here.”

Jerome rolled his eyes. He too was tired. And the bed did look mighty comfy. *Fuck it.*

He removed his boots and his uniform, climbing in as Rebecca slid over, making room.

“You know these sheets are probably dusty as hell, right?”

She laughed and playfully smacked him on the arm as she rolled onto her side, closing her eyes, and yawned. “Just hold me.”

THIRTY-THREE

Jerome's arms felt safe wrapped around Rebecca's frame. She felt the safest when he was holding her. She opened her eyes and looked down at his hands. They were strong and firm. She squirmed closer to him and kissed his knuckles, moving her way down his fingers. In response, he moved them lightly across her abdomen, his nails tickling her skin as they moved to her breasts, massaging them, then squeezing them, gently pinching her erect nipples. She giggled, "Naughty boy."

"You got that right," he said, kissing her shoulders. "I can move down more, if you want."

"Oh really . . . oh! Mmm . . . you're fast, mister."

"Hey, hey, I'm not *that* fast."

"Mmm . . . mmm . . . this is very true. Faster."

Jerome moved his fingers faster, going deeper as he felt her grab him and motion her hand back and forth, slow at first, and then faster.

"Mmm . . . uhh. Th-this is one way to keep warm. Ah!" she moaned, thrusting her body, quivering as the sensation became overwhelming. A thought came to mind. "W-what about F-Fuu-ckk-kk! Mmm-Finn?"

Jerome sucked on her neck, squeezing her other breast. "He's still in my vest p-pocket . . . ohh yeah, babe."

"Well, we'd better be extra qui—"

"Mrow!"

She let go of Jerome's shaft and smiled, laughing at the feline, who was sitting on the ground, head cocked to the side in a curious-looking manner.

"Meow!" he exclaimed once more.

Jerome pulled his fingers out of Rebecca and sighed as she motioned for Finn to jump on the bed. He understood and did so, walking toward her, whose hand was outstretched, getting ready to cuddle with him. She picked him up and set him down on the edge of the bed, where, in turn, he curled into a ball and looked at his two masters, his tail draped over his eyes. "I'm gonna go wash up," she chimed, kissing Jerome on the cheek. She slid over his waist, her buttocks brushing over the tip of his cock, still under the bed sheets.

As she stood up, Jerome playfully smacked her ass. She gasped and smiled, as did he. "Bad boy! C'mere!"

She leaned over and kissed her partner passionately and looked over at Finn. He was falling asleep again; only his eye slits could be barely seen. She decided to lift the sheets from Jerome's waist, and opened her mouth and went down on him, grasping his shaft as hard as her lips could, and began to suck, causing the hottest sensation he ever felt. He moaned as she continued to suck, his eyes fluttering to the back of his head, and at the same time grabbed the top of her head, forcing her to go further down. She moaned as he exploded in her mouth, hitting the back of her throat.

Smiling, Jerome lifted his hand from the top of her head, while at the same time she slowly released her lips from their grasp and raised herself back up, facing him. Closing her eyes, she leaned inward and kissed him.

"I love you," he whispered, wrapping his arms around her body.

She smiled and bit her lower lip, brushing her hands across his chest. "Yeah, yeah. I know. And don't you ever forget, I finish what I start, mister."

"That, you certainly do."

Rebecca's hand made a fist, and she punched him playfully in the ribs. "Okay, now I'm going to wash up."

"Alright, I'll be there after you."

"You bet your ass you will. I don't need to have you stink the rest of the way," she commented as she closed the door to the bathroom.

Jerome chuckled. He needed a bath. Sure, it had only been a few hours since the cove, but he needed to wash the smell of death off of him. He looked across the bed at Finn, whose eyes were shut, sound asleep. *Never thought I'd have sex in front of a cat.*

He shook his head and wiped his eyes. "What a stupid thing to think," he muttered.

Rebecca illuminated her lantern's light a bit more to get a better view of her surroundings and to see if there was any damn soap lying around, or by a miracle, some water.

She stepped toward the counter where the sink lay. Mold and dust adorned the surface, but the faucet itself looked usable. If the sink didn't work, there was always her canteen, but she didn't want to waste that. Maybe a few splashes couldn't hurt, right? *First thing's first, lady. C'mon.*

Her eyes scanned the counter. Grime-filled toothbrushes, hair combs, and a strange-looking mechanism that looked like a weapon, only, it had a cord attached to it. Caleb never told her what that was, or its use. She took it off its mantle, examining it. She saw that there were buttons that one could press: Cool, Medium, High. Her eyes went down to the end of the chord. It was inserted into the counter. Curiosity filled her mind. *Worth a shot.* Her thumb rested over the Cool option and pressed down. Nothing happened. She tried the Medium setting. Still nothing. "Stupid piece of junk," she muttered, throwing the mechanism on the counter.

She looked around some more and noticed the bathroom was small. Only one person could be in there at a time. Her eyes glanced to the left. There was a contraption. Dust filled to be sure, but as she looked closer she noted that a person could stand inside. Her hand floated over a handle. She grabbed it and turned counterclockwise.

The pipes groaned and hissed. And then they knocked. Loudly. Rebecca perked her ears as the knocking continued. Her hand turned the knob back to its original position in fear of breaking something else. Unfortunately, the handle broke off. Thinking, she tried to screw it back on, but couldn't. A sound came from the faucet head. A few drops trickled out.

"Everything okay?" Jerome called out from the other room.

"Yeah! Everything's . . . great," she replied, looking at the broken head. *Shit.*

She stepped out of the shower station and went back to the sink. Disappointingly, she turned the handle. More creaks and knocks. A few drops coming from the faucet, but nothing sustainable. *Fuck. Soap, anyone?*

Landing her palm on a drawer knob, she opened it. Nothing. Another drawer. Dust. *Okay, one more. Here we go.* Locked. Or . . . was it just stuck? Her fingers clenched the edges like crowbars, trying to pry it open. It wiggled, and very slowly, it started to come loose, until at long last, it was open. She took her lantern in for a better look. There were just plastic-covered casings and hair clippings.

Rebecca exhaled and gritted her teeth in frustration. *Hopeless, this whole damn thing is hopeless!*

She closed her eyes and breathed in deep. "I need you, old man." The long journey was finally getting to her. It hit her all at once, her eyes teared, and memories of the past few hours and days flooded back into her mind. Cal's screams entered now. She remembered it all. She also felt responsible for his death. *No. No, you can't think like that! It wasn't your fault! He ordered you to escape. You were following his orders. And he wanted you both to live.*

"Rebecca!"

"Yeah?"

"Better come out here."

Jeez, what now?

She wiped her tears away and raced out the door into the bedroom, tripping over the female corpse, nearly falling to the ground.

Jerome was standing, looking out the window. Rebecca joined him. Finn, ears perked up, sat erect and alert, looking at his masters. Something was going on, that's for sure.

"Fuck! You've gotta be kidding me," she said.

"See, this is why we can't have nice things."

They stared out into the darkened horizon. Though they could only barely see shadows, they heard the sounds. The Bastards were coming.

THIRTY-FOUR

EIGHT YEARS AGO

"I'm going to teach you a new skill."

"Oh yeah? You really think I need one, Cal?"

"Never hurts to learn something new, Becky. And, yes, you do."

She rolled her eyes and begrudgingly smiled, accepting her mentor's advice.

"Okay, old man. What are you going to teach me today?"

Caleb smiled. "Hope you aren't afraid of heights."

"Wha—?"

The door creaked open, and the bright light of the day washed over her face. As he exited, he could be heard saying, "Lights!"

The voice command prompted the overhead lights in the cave to turn off. Rebecca was left in a momentary quasi-feeling of illusion. Caleb turned around. "You coming?"

She got up and quickly dressed herself, her mind curious as to what he had planned.

She walked outside, and the sun heated her skin, but not enough to cause any serious burns. Taking a brisker step, she caught up to Cal, who was turning around the corner, behind their rocky cavern.

He sat on the ledge, feet dangling, looking out at the horizon, then turned his head to Becky. "Ain't it beautiful?"

She humored him, looking outward. She'd seen it many times beforehand, while either taking a piss or shit off the cliff's edge. One time she was able to get it just right, and it hit the ground below. It was the only time she ever looked down. Vertigo kicked in, and it made her uneasy. *Never look down. Never look down.*

"C'mon, sit for a spell." Cal motioned, patting the ground with his hand. "Gonna teach you a survival skill."

Smirking, Rebecca walked over to him and noticed he had a small satchel on the other side of him.

"I already know how to survive," she said. "You taught me, remember?"

He looked down, fiddling with something in his hands. She couldn't tell exactly what it was at first. Remembering not to look down, she sat next to him, admiring the distant horizon. She finally saw what Cal was fiddling with. It was a hook, and a thinly veiled piece of string.

"You ever hear of fishing?"

"No. Should I?"

"Maybe. I was told a while back that people used to fish out in that great sea over there . . . was higher then. And you could catch things for food."

Rebecca squinted her eyes, trying to make out the sea. She turned her head to Cal. "Maybe someday it'll come back and bring lots of food."

"Possibly. Couldn't hurt. But that's a big maybe."

He finished tying a knot around the small hook. Taking a spindle out of the bag, he cast the line as far as he could.

"So, this is the lesson?" Rebecca asked.

He looked out at the horizon more, squinting as he dangled his feet. "Isn't it beautiful?" he asked again. "The way the colors flow and mix."

Rebecca closed her eyes and smiled, leaning her head on his shoulder. It was relaxing. Peaceful.

“Ya gotta be patient. Lure them in. They’ll come to you. Just gotta be patient,” he said as he wheeled in the line, which, a few seconds later, came to a halt. He gave it to her. She took it and cast it out as far as she could and giggled.

“Maybe we’ll catch some fish today,” he said.

THIRTY-FIVE

The ground was hard, and the cracked earth stabbed their feet. Rocks punctured through the souls of their feet as they shunted forward. The Bastards found their meal. And they were extremely hungry.

Starving and in need of the wet, delicious flesh. The smell was palpable. If their mouths could still produce saliva, their chins would be drenching in it.

Jerome and Rebecca looked out from their window as the Bastards shuffled in full force toward them. Finn hissed and ducked back into his vest pocket. These things were unnatural, and he hated them. Yes, the taste was passable, but he wanted real food.

"Downstairs," ordered Jerome, who was putting on the last of his clothing. "Now. We'll go through the door. Hopefully they won't find us."

"Or we don't find them," Rebecca replied, putting on her shirt. Out of curiosity, she lifted her arm up and pressed her skin. The panel that held her oxygen percentage slid open. The digital readout read 97%. *Huh. Well that's good to see. At least we haven't been inhaling poison.*

The panel slid back into place and closed, her skin solid flesh again.

The two companions gathered the rest of their supplies, which wasn't much by any account, and ran to the opening. Without a thought, they jumped down, landing in the pool of blood and guts. Rebecca went first, nearly slipping when she landed. Jerome went next. His boot came down on the jawless skull, breaking it into two halves.

In the distance, they could hear the moans. They were getting restless. Aggravated.

More of them now. How did they get across? Rebecca thought to herself. As she knelt down and crawled through the narrow opening, Jerome following close behind.

The narrow passageway was easy to get through, albeit a tight squeeze. They could hear the building creak and groan as they moved through the debris.

Rebecca came out and illuminated her lantern. The surface was soft, like a cushion. She turned, Jerome exiting and standing beside her. They were in a long stretch of hallway. On each side were plain white doors with dusty numbers.

"What do you think?" she asked, motioning the lantern toward the first door to her right. "Should we try one?"

"Yeah, sure."

She cautiously made her way to the nearest door. Her lantern lit up the door handle. She reached to grab hold of it, and paused.

"Shit."

"What is it?"

"We need a code," she said, looking down the hall. "We need a code for all of them."

"Fuck!" Jerome said in frustration. "We can't open any of them?"

"What did I just say two fucking seconds ago?"

Jerome bent down to get a closer look at the device. Using his finger, he entered a set of random numeric codes. Nothing happened.

Rebecca sighed. This was not helping. She needed to stay calm and focus.

"Maybe we can break one down?" Jerome said.

"And risk those things hearing us? Or whatever the hell is inside here? No thanks."

Finn popped his head out and squirmed to be free from Jerome's pocket. "Okay, okay, little guy! I get it; you want out!"

He picked Finn up by the collar and set him down on the ground beside them.

All at once, Finn's ears perked up. He sensed something. He quickly trotted down the hallway, being devoured by the darkness.

"Mrow! Mrow! Meow! Mrroow!"

Jerome and Rebecca jogged down the long stretch of corridor. They saw Finn's tail wag impatiently at a door. On his hind legs, he pawed at the door handle, trying to open it himself. He looked at his two masters and meowed softly.

"So you're a dog now?" Jerome asked.

"It's locked, sweetie," Rebecca responded, caressing the top of his head. "We can't get in."

Finn sat down, confused.

The door was locked and bolted tight. But as Rebecca looked closer, she saw cracks below the security lock. She stepped back a space and shone her lantern on the door's frame. There were cracks around the edges as well. Jerome saw this too.

"You know, if we place a well-enforced kick near the weakened parts, we could kick this thing inward and get inside," Jerome said.

"Um . . . what the fuck did I just say a few minutes ago? What about *them*?"

"It's better than turning back. Besides, the exits are probably blocked off."

He was right. Blocks of cement and dirt and boulders were toppled in an orgy in front of the exits and the other half of the hallway. They, however, didn't know that. They were tempted to go the other way, to find a different route.

Screw that. There could be hundreds of those things down the other side, Jerome thought.

The door was their best bet. There was no telling where the Bastards were outside. They could have already made their way inside, or they could be standing outside and just waiting.

Becky raised her leg and mentally aimed at a weakened spot to the lower left. With a powerful thrust, she slammed her boot against the door. But before she could make contact, the door rattled. She froze, her boot inches away from her mark.

Another rattle. Harder this time.

"Mrow . . ."

"Yeah, right," she responded, changing her stance. One ready to fight.

The door rattled again. Finn jumped back, tilting his head to the side, wondering what was behind the structure. He licked his snout, ready to pounce.

Jerome put out his hand and eased Rebecca back. "Let me go first." He lifted his leg and began to break down the weakened door. Rebecca followed, and together they had the door open, hanging on its hinges. Jerome brightened his lantern, hoping to get a visual of whatever or whoever was doing the knocking. He peered inside. Nothing could be seen that was out of the ordinary. Just a floor that was in need of a serious cleaning. "What the hell?"

Rebecca came to his side, Finn in her hands. "There's nothing here."

"Yeah . . . maybe it was the rat from before?"

"Maybe," she said. She hated hearing about them from Caleb. To her, they were the things of nightmares. Now, this was entirely different.

The trio made their way into the room. From what they could see, it was very lavish, save for the mounds of dust and broken utilities. The entranceway felt like it went on forever, but it opened to a living room with a large flat-screen television to their left, which was cracked, showing its technical guts. Below was a counter, adorned in cobwebs and dust at the top. Jerome could see a handle. He gripped it with his fingers and pulled. There was a groaning creak as the drawer slid outward. He took a glance inside. *Junk.*

Fine wine glasses, and various sized glasses. He closed the drawer. Below, there was another drawer. He reached and pulled outward. *Hello.*

Food. There was food. Packages of different candies and assorted dried meats with cheeses. Lying next to them, in a separate container, was a large bottle of expensive-looking wine. Jerome picked it up and examined it. It was in another language. He even tried to pronounce it, sound it out, but it was to no avail. He did, however, see a date: 1996. *I'd say that was a good year.*

"Find anything?" asked Rebecca.

"Oh yeah," he replied, holding the bottle and food, smiling.

Holy shit.

Her stomach growled and grumbled. It reminded her that they hadn't eaten in a very long time. It wasn't much, but it would be able to push them onward. She looked at the door frame. It was still on its hinges. And they couldn't afford to take any breaks. They'd be easy pickings for the horde outside. Or in.

"Let's pack this up as best we can. We can ration it as we move onward," she said.

"Won't they smell it?"

"I don't think so. It's still in the wrappers, so as long as they remain intact and, in our pouches,, we should be fine."

"What about this?" he asked, signaling the wine. "We really can't carry it with us."

Damn, he's right.

"Okay. Pop that sucker open. Carefully and as quietly as possible. And open up one of those packages. I'm starving."

THIRTY-SIX

Eating and running is good, right? Right. You'd die without food. And you're starving. He's starving. And even he's starving. Everyone is fucking starving.

Finn popped his head out at the sound of crinkling plastic wrappers and the subsequent pop they made. He licked his snout and stretched his tiny paws. The meat was savory, and his canines tingled as his throat filled with saliva. Bastards were not healthy. And it was nice to have something different in his stomach.

Jerome took a piece of dried meat and fed Finn, who eagerly grasped it in his paws and wolfed it down. He had another piece and just as before, inhaled it in his stomach. He licked his snout once more, cleaning his teeth with his tongue.

"Better than those things out there, huh, little man?" Jerome asked, petting the cat's head.

"Mrow!"

Jerome took his knife out and screwed it into the cork of the bottle. As careful as could be, he slowly twisted and pulled it upward. The cork made a pop sound, only it was of a deeper tone.

Rebecca grabbed the wine glasses, and with her hands dusted them off as best as she could. It was a quick break, for they knew they had to move. And move fast.

Jerome poured the liquid into the glasses, and they raised them in the air. "Cheers." With a light clink of their glasses, they sipped. It was slightly bitter in taste, but it was better than nothing. To them, it was like living in royalty, if only for a moment in time.

He offered Finn a piece of cheese. Finn cautiously sniffed, and accepted the gesture of good faith. He wasn't much into dairy, but it was something different and even more, edible. With his tongue, he licked his chops and circled around, nuzzling Jerome's hand, purring. Jerome took out another piece of food. This time it was meat. The package read "Dry Salami." Unsheathing his knife, he cut a small piece off and fed it to Finn. Once again, Finn sniffed the ration and cautiously took it in his mouth. It tasted different. But at the same time, familiar, like a type of food he had a long time ago . . .

Jerome handed the food off to Rebecca, who ate the rations and handed it back to Jerome, who did the same. Rebecca's stomach growled as the food hit her gut. It felt like a weight had dropped inside of her. But it gave her a sense of energy and strength. The only downside was that soon, she would have to go to the bathroom, and she didn't want to drop trough while on the run from those things.

They finished up and packed the rest of the rations, putting as much as they could fit in their pockets, whilst saving one for Finn. But before they could continue, a sound could be heard coming from the bedroom around the corner. It was the cries of a small child.

"No way," Rebecca said, her feet automatically aiming for the room where the sound was coming from. *A survivor. Can't believe it! An actual survivor!*

"Proceed with caution, Beck," whispered Jerome. The two, along with Finn, as silently as possible, crept into the bedroom, lanterns on a medium level of brightness. What was shown could only be described as a natural disaster taking place inside the room. While the entryway and the living room were spared, the bedroom had an entirely different aesthetic altogether.

Rebecca and Jerome scanned the area that lay before them. First of all, they saw the bed. It was blood-ridden, and worst of all, a corpse was chained to the bedpost. It was a male, castrated and dried up. Perfectly preserved. And then there was that awful smell. That disgusting, putrid odor of decay. There was also something else to the man. His stomach moved. It was on the inside.

The two moved forward to get a closer look. They saw something that shifted inside. Rebecca arched her lantern over the corpse's face. A sunken expression washed over it, the mouth opens wide, but there was something stuffed inside.

Begrudgingly, Rebecca carefully reached into the mouth and pulled the object out. She shone the light closer and examined it. Red lace panties. *Kinky, I guess.*

"Someone was having one hell of a party," Jerome said.

"Yep," she replied, and tossed them aside, further examining the body. His eyes were blank and soulless, the skin pale. With the exception of the nether region, the man was perfectly fine.

Jerome racked his brain trying to figure out how the guy died, while at the same time hoping he wouldn't come back to life and attack them. *That's the last thing we need right now.*

He darted his eyes up toward the ceiling. It was collapsed. He noticed the support beams came down in an almost perfect triangular direction. *Ritual killing?*

His head started to throb, and he rubbed his temples with his fingers. It was time to get his mind back on track.

Finn looked on and then turned his attention to his masters. He gave a somber whimper.

"Yeah. Not a good sight, huh?" Rebecca said. As soon as she finished the sentence, the laughter returned. The two spun around, startled. They raised their lanterns up, trying to find the source of it. It sounded like a little girl. But it was very faint. Muffled. What they saw was just the dust-filled living room.

"What the hell . . .?" Jerome whispered.

"I think we should leave."

"Yeah," he said. "Good idea."

Another squeak of laughter. The two spun around again, trying to pinpoint the source. It sounded like it was coming from every direction.

"This isn't funny!" she whispered.

"Go. Let's just go."

Both she and Jerome headed toward the slanted sliding door, and a cracked and bruised balcony was awaiting them outside.

"We'll have to climb up," said Jerome, readying himself to climb upward. He lowered himself and crept under the slanted archway, Rebecca following his lead. Finn looked down, eyes wide. He was able to see the horizon. He didn't know where they had come from, but they were thousands now. The team looked out in disbelief as the giant horde assembled on *both* sides. It wasn't long. The direction they were facing now was the starting point.

We must have entered through the back, Rebecca thought to herself, putting her boot down on the cement. *Can't think of that now. Gotta climb.*

They turned and looked up. Above there was a balcony, but it was only partial. Bits of dust and chips were falling on them. They didn't care; they just needed to get higher.

The moans and gasps were getting louder. *Closer.* Their hunger pounded itself into what was left of their minds. Their shuffling became faster. Not a pace or jog, but they were definitely picking up pace. Their milky eyes darted up toward Jerome and Rebecca, but obstacles were standing in the way.

Lifting their arms and skeleton-like hands, they placed them upon the fallen debris and began climbing up.

"Shit, shit, shit, shit!" Rebecca cried out, looking down.

Jerome cupped his hands, Rebecca acknowledging the move and putting her boot on his hands. He hoisted her up, and she grabbed onto the edge of the balcony, the skin on her palms getting cut when the jagged edges made contact. It stung, but she ignored it. She had to stay strong and concentrate lifting her ass up and over. She pushed herself up and turned around, immediately offering her hand to Jerome. He jumped up and took it. With the rest of her strength, she held onto his hand with both of hers, gritting her teeth as she pulled him up.

Finn was tucked safely in the pocket of Jerome. He was sure not to move, and trusted his masters' choices. He also hated the Bastards and didn't want to be a snack for their endless hunger. Just that thought made Finn uneasy. He changed his demeanor immediately. There was no way he was going to become a sacrifice for those things. And he always had his backup . . .

Jerome was almost up when he felt a jerk coming from Rebecca.

"Ugh!" she let out. Her hands were now shaking as she was pulling up her friend. A Bastard had burst through the shadows and was strangling her! Its grip was strong, its breath like a shit-stained sandwich, as it opened its jaw, going in for the kill.

In her defense, Rebecca clenched her throat muscles, desperately fighting for her life. Her hands released Jerome, him falling to the lower balcony and hitting his back and head.

She tried prying the skeletal fingers from her jugular. She gritted her teeth again and slammed her head into the thing's nose-repeatedly. After a few solid hits, the Bastard's skull began to crack. Rebecca was suffocating, but she was making progress. She took her hands and tried prying its finger from her throat. It tightened its grip. She could feel her larynx slowly began to crush. *Again! Hit it again!*

With one powerful thrust of her spine, she lunged backward

and hit the thing's skull with a powerful force, cracking its skull, splitting it open. Brain matter, and a mixture of blood and black ooze poured out its neatly formed face-hole. Its grasp loosened from her throat, it "screaming" in agony. *Or whatever the hell those things feel.* She didn't know if those things felt anything at all.

Balling her hands into fists, she used her peripherals and tracked where the opening was and began to punch the temples of its head. It was working. She decided to punch the nearly formed hole. The hole broke into a bigger opening.

Jerome saw Rebecca's feet struggling above. He looked around, trying to find some kind of leverage to get himself and Finn up to her level, but there was none to be found. Suddenly, he felt a sharp pain come from his ankle. The Bastards had reached him.

Rebecca reached behind her and felt for the opening. She found it. Now using both hands, she clawed at the oozing brain, her fingers clasping down onto the muscle's exterior, and with all of her might, she ripped it out, piece by piece. The Bastard's eyes fluttered as it moaned, feeling its brain being torn out from its own head. Its tendril-like fingers let go of her throat. She could breathe again.

Air!

She turned around and began to tug, pulling the rest of the brain out. Along with part of the spinal cord. The Bastard withered and died, its head hanging low. She tossed the remaining elements off to the side and exhaled heavily. She bent over, feeling her throat take in air once more. Her eyes saw that Jerome was in trouble. He was fighting off the horde. And he was losing.

"Take my hand! Hurry!" she said, reaching down as far as she possibly could.

He looked up after punching one of the damn things in the throat, his fist going through all the way and coming out the other end. The Bastard, however, was still putting up a fight. It's slimy jaws snapping like a piranha at Jerome's face, trying to lunge itself at him full force. *Enough!*

Jerome pulled his fist back inside of the thing's throat and lifted up. He could feel the squishy wetness of the organs and the brittleness of decayed bone against his hand. His hand exploded outward from the top of the head. Jerome saw the body clump to the ground, and he could also see that the building was being overrun.

In one swift motion, he pushed an advancing Bastard into a group of oncoming ones and jumped as high as he possibly could, grabbing Rebecca's outstretched arm. He felt himself being pulled up. When he reached the balcony's edge, he pulled himself up the rest of the way. Both of them looked down and then outward. There were too many of them. Way too many.

"We've got to keep moving," he said, wiping the sweat and guts from his brow. She complied with a nod. Moving was their only option at this point. There was no turning back now.

They stood up and hoisted one another, balcony after balcony. If there were none to be found, they shimmied across window sills and shattered door archways. Every now and then, they would glance down, seeing the feeding frenzy that was so desperately after them. They were gathering in greater numbers now. Thousands upon thousands.

Soon, both of them heard it. They were almost to the roof (what was left, anyway). The sound had come out of the blackened distance. It was a howling scream that pierced the windows, shattering them. Both of them had to shut their eyes and tried to cover their faces to protect themselves from the falling shards. Jerome covered Finn's head, burying him in the vest.

"What the hell was that!" Rebecca asked.

"Whatever it is, we don't have time to say hello! Keep on going up!"

They continued to climb as fast as they could. They were almost to the top!

Another shrill scream.

Jerome and Rebecca ignored it and moved at a faster pace.

Without warning, dozens of Bastards emerged from the shadows. Above as well as below. They had no way out.

Their eyes searched everywhere for a possible solution. A sign. Anything that would help them escape. Turning their flames higher, all they could see was the decaying bodies all around them. Heads and arms honed in on where they stood. The entire building looked like it had hundreds of tentacles emerging from inside the building itself.

Another screech. The building shook.

The Bastards, with their long bony fingers, were inches from collapsing on Jerome and Rebecca. They decided to move into a nearby doorway whilst taking a few Bastards out in the process.

The two huddled close to one another, each holding the other's face. They stared into each other's eyes, tears trickling down their cheeks.

Rebecca cracked a smile, as did Jerome.

"One hell of an ending, huh?"

"Yeah . . . one hell of an ending."

The two embraced in a kiss, holding it for as long as they could. The felt the building shake and begin to crumble around them. Outside, Bastards were falling, along with cement and stone. Finn popped his head out and looked up.

"Mrow?"

In an instant they felt weightless. The room fell out from under them. All they could hear was thunder. But they kept their attention on one another. Their bodies hit the ground, but they didn't feel anything, for they had died on impact.

THIRTY-SEVEN

Oh, under the boardwalk, down by the sea, yeah
On a blanket with my baby is where I'll be

(Under the boardwalk) Out of the sun
(Under the boardwalk) We'll be havin' some fun
(Under the boardwalk) People walking above
(Under the boardwalk) We'll be falling in love
Under the board—

"No."

"No?"

"It's too fast. I need something slower."

"I don't think we have anyth—"

"Yeah we do. Look at the records."

"Um . . . let's try this."

"Ah! Good! Good! This is more like it."

Blessed are the Fornicates
May we bend down to be their
whores.
Blessed are the rich,

May we labor, deliver, and more.
Blessed are the envious
Bless the slothful, the wrathful, the vein
May they feast us to famine and war.
What of the pious, the pure of heart, the peaceful?
What of the meek, the mourning, and the merciful?
All doomed.
All doomed.
Doomed are the poor.
Doomed are the peaceful.
Doomed are the meek.
Doomed are the merciful.
For the word is now death.
And the word is now without light.
The new beatitude:
"Fuck the doomed, you're on your own."

"This makes me . . ."

"What?"

"Well, you deserve to be happy, Mrs. Salt."

"I am, Len. I am," she replied, laying her head on his shoulder, breathing in his scent. It was lavender. Her favorite.

"What are we going to do about the problem?" Lenny asked, gently squeezing the missus's buttocks and smiling slyly. "We've had it for three weeks now. Say it's time to rectify it."

The missus giggled. She put her hand on Lenny's crotch, caressing it through his pants. "Oh, I think I have an idea, or five."

"Five?"

"Mhmm. I bought some new tricks to show you."

"Oh!" Lenny exclaimed, eyes wide with curiosity. "And, can ol' Lenny have a hint at what these tricks are?"

"Mmm, nope! But . . . I will say all those times I was going to Yoga . . . those were lies."

"Cheeky girl!"

The missus kissed him on the lips, sucking and nibbling his lower lip. It was his favorite. She pulled away.

"Mmm . . . I guess I *could* give you a hint."

"Oh?"

"Mhmm . . ." she whispered. "Come out!"

A slender, younger woman stepped into view. Reddish hair, freckles, and a devilish smile, adorned with bright blue eyes. She folded her arms and giggled. Lenny looked at her with excitement.

"This is Eve," said the missus.

Lenny smiled and asked, "Darling, how old are you?"

She brushed the hair out of her face. "I just turned eighteen this morning, sir."

Lenny looked back toward the missus. "Oh, you know how to pick 'em!"

"That I do."

"This! This is a fantastic prezzy! Come here, dear!" he insisted. "We both have birthdays today! I just turned twenty-six!"

Eve slowly walked over and massaged Lenny's crotch.

"Mm . . . Best. Birthday. Ever," he said.

Eve leaned in close and asked, "What are we going to do about the *problem*?"

Lenny rolled his eyes. "Oh, yes. *That*." He looked down. There was a baby across from them, eyes full of wonderment and curiosity.

"Hm . . . Eve, dear," said Lenny. "How would you kill that problem?"

"I don't know. Maybe we could try smothering it with a pillow? Break its nose?"

Lenny contemplated the idea. It had some merit, but it wasn't good enough for his taste.

"Bah! Too boring! I need something . . . missus? What say you, honeybunch?"

She thought to herself for a moment. "We could take your Magnum, put it to her temple, and blow her fuckin' head off. Might be a bit bloody."

"No! No! Not in the mood for messy! I need . . . some more thinking music!" Lenny shouted.

The missus knew what he meant. "Searching the records, dear."

"Good," he replied, and turned his spastic attention to Eve, who was still rubbing him. "Now, darling, Daddy needs to think. Go over on that chair, spread those beautiful young legs of yours, and finger yourself. And I want moaning, understand?"

She nodded. "Yes, Daddy." Turning around, she walked over to the chair. It was an ugly mustard yellow. She plopped herself down, noticing the hard cushioning and the beanbag type backing. Spreading her legs, she began to pleasure herself.

"Len, what about this?" the missus asked, handing him a color vinyl record.

"Oh! Yes! Yes! Put this on! Yes!" he said, clapping his hands. She smiled and kissed his cheek. It was an upbeat tempo. Lenny seemed to enjoy it, as he was dancing, taking his wife in his arms, spinning her, as they both locked on Eve, who was moving her hand faster.

"Ah! An idea! A splendid idea!" he said, pushing his wife to the side. He walked toward the infant, towering over it like a giant. The baby began to cry.

"Oh, look! It's crying!" he said to his wife. He lifted his two tree-trunk-like arms and picked the child up into the air, staring at it face to face. "Oh . . . you know what we're gonna do to you? We're gonna drop a goddamn building on you!"

"Lenny, that's a wonderful idea! Eve, isn't that wonderful?"

Eve moaned and nodded in agreement.

"Eve! For Christ sake, finish up!" he yelled, making the baby cry out more. "Oh, it's okay, love. See, I'm a doctor. And we're like clowns, ya see? We poke and prod ya."

The baby continued to cry, fearful for its life.

"What's the matter? Don't ya like clowns? Don't ya like to laugh? AREN'T WE FUCKING FUNNY!"

The baby screamed in terror as Lenny's voice grew louder.

"Len!" said the missus. "Indoor voice, love."

"Bugger off!" he hollered back, then turned his attention back to the baby. "You know why you're about to die? Because you're ugly! UGLY! UGGLLAAAAAY!"

Rubble moved and creaked. A scarred hand slowly emerged, bloody and full of dust. Seconds later, a forearm appeared. As the rubble gave way, another hand surfaced; this one had a dislocated pinky and middle finger.

Holy fuck! Holy fucking fuck!

An eye opened and blinked. There was nothing but darkness. And a blurred, milk-like view. Another blink. More pain shot out. The next instinct was to rise. Lift the head, and then shoulders. *Slow. Go slow.* The concrete shifted and separated as a head rose from underneath the dust-filled tomb. Another pain receptor went off. *Fuck.*

Rebecca lightly touched her nose. *Broken.* She stood up and was electrocuted with pain all over her body. She couldn't distinguish where on her body hurt the most. It was all happening all at once.

She looked around, trying to keep her balance. It was no use. Her legs gave out immediately, and she toppled forward, hitting the rocky bed below her. "Goddamn it!"

"Nngh . . ." came a moan from underneath the rubble, a few feet away from her.

"J-Jerome?"

"Yeah?" he squeaked.

"We're alive, right?"

"Sure," he said, slowly propelling himself upward. "We'll go with that." He looked around his darkened surroundings and realized something was missing. *Finn!* "Finn?"

He checked his vest pockets, fighting through the pain of a dislocated shoulder and three broken ribs. Then he heard it. It was a low, muffled noise.

"Mrow . . ."

Both humans fought their bodies' pain sensors and looked for the feline. No Bastards could be heard, or seen for that matter. They reached for their lanterns to try to get a clearer view of what was around them. All they felt was shattered glass and crushed metal. Their lanterns were destroyed.

"Mrow."

"I know, baby! We're coming! Keep sounding off! C'mon!" Rebecca ordered, furiously searching for her companion.

Jerome lifted a block of concrete and found Finn.

"Mrow."

"Here! He's here!" he exclaimed, blindly picking him up.

Rebecca wadded over and was next to Jerome, who was clearing the rest of the rubble.

Jerome gently picked Finn up; only, he didn't feel fur. It was a wet, slimy sensation. Using his fingers, he felt the texture. It was like he was touching fine strands of rope that were wrapped around Finn's body.

"What the—?" he started to say.

It was Finn's vines.

The vines began to retract. Soon, Jerome and Rebecca could make out the cat's feline features. Fur could now be felt, as the vines were almost done retracting. Finn's jaw was split and elongated as the vines returned to their home in the back of his mouth. With a thwip, the vines finished their return. Finn's jaw returned to normal, and he stared up at his masters, licking his snout and "smiling." He raised his paws up, signaling that he wanted to be picked up. Jerome reached down and grabbed him by the waist, holding him to his shoulder. He nuzzled Jerome's neck and purred intently. Rebecca scratched his forehead, Finn in return, licking her hand. It felt like cardboard, but it was also a sign of reassurance that they were alive, though broken.

"And you didn't tell us about that because . . .?" Jerome joked.

"Meow!"

"Right. Just glad you're okay and have nothing broken. Me, on the other hand—" he said, looking down at his side. He tried to lift his leg. An insurmountable amount of pain surged through. There was a metal pike lodged in his thigh that was sticking out. *Must have been so out of it that I couldn't feel it till now.*

Blood smeared and stained through his pants. He tried moving the injured leg. "Nngh!"

He slowly bent down and, using his two hands, carefully tried to remove the rod from his leg. Blood seeped out even more so. "Ahh! Fucking shit!" he screamed out.

"Let me help!" Rebecca offered.

"No! No! I got this. Just gotta do it nice and easy."

This wasn't like ripping off a Band-Aid. This was a lot worse. *At least I'm still breathing. And it's quiet.* That was a surprise. He stopped and rose up, looking around. It was quiet. No moans. No shuffling of feet or limbs. Nothing.

"What—?" Rebecca started to say.

"Shh!"

They both listened intently. They were alone; no Bastards, just them and the darkness. Finn looked around and slightly murmured to himself, wondering where the enemy was. "Mrow . . ."

Jerome looked down at him and said, "Yeah, my thoughts exactly, little guy. Spooky."

"They're gone. They're all gone."

"Yeah, but where to?" he replied. There were bodies crumpled around on the ground and under the concrete. Besides that, no other Bastard could be seen. *And what was that scream? It was so high-pitched. Thought I was going to go deaf.*

"Don't know. Maybe . . . maybe underground?"

"Who the hell knows," he said. "But, since they aren't trying to kill us right now, we should get a move on."

"What about your leg?"

"That'll get fixed. I can still walk. Just can't put too much pressure on it," he said, looking down at his injury. "And . . . I've gotta find a way to hide the scent." He took out his knife from his ankle sheath and cut his pant leg open.

"You know you're technically out of uniform, soldier."

"Don't remind me."

"You sure you can walk?"

"Yeah, just gotta think of something else. Somehow," he said. He was lucky. It didn't go through the bone, just through his thigh muscle. The wound still bled, but the pike itself was blocking the injury from getting worse and letting out even more blood. He could deal with it. To him, it was an annoyance. A very painful annoyance.

He put his arm around Rebecca, who was trying to balance herself. "Thanks."

"You okay?"

"I'll live."

He fiddled with one of his vest pockets and took out a flashlight. He pressed the indentation, and it lit the area around them. On the console itself, it displayed a percentage: 5%. He lifted the light. It flickered as it reached Rebecca's face.

"Ouch," he said, seeing her broken nose.

"Yeah. Just be gentle, okay?"

"Sure. No problem," he said, cautiously taking her nose, which had signs of blood coming down, and in one quick crack, reset the cartilage. She keeled over and put her head between her legs. The pain was the worst thing she had ever felt. Tears flowed from her eyes and down her cheeks as the fire in her nose was ignited. A moment or two went by, and she set herself erect again. The pain had now turned into a pulsating monster, and she dared not touch it.

Breathing heavily inward, she lifted her hand. Jerome grimaced at the unnatural sight of her fingers.

"You sure—?" he started to say.

"Just do it."

Jerome took her pinkie first. Again, in one quick motion, he put it back into place.

"Nngh!" she cried out. *At least it wasn't as painful.*

He took her middle finger next and repeated the same motion. This one was painful. She landed her head on his shoulder, he, in turn, holding her upright. Slowly she tried closing her hand, wanting to make a fist. She couldn't. She could barely move her fingers. Her head was now spinning. It was a mixture of pain and vertigo. She needed to sit down. Jerome lay her on a flattened piece of fallen rubble. His flashlight flickered and went dead next. Sitting wasn't an option anymore. She was trying her best to catch her breath, her head swimming from the pain.

Peace and quiet for a change. Jerome brushed her hair out of her face. Finn crawled out and slowly approached her, purring; putting his paws on her cheek, nuzzling her at the same time.

"Better?" he asked as he placed his hand in hers. She looked at him and smiled while with her other hand, petting Finn under the chin.

"Yeah. Ju-Just needed to rest. Sorry."

"It's okay. Take your time. I've got the watch. So does Finn."

She giggled. Her eyes closed and body fell still. It felt good to lie down on her back. Jerome's hand was gentle to the touch, but all she really wanted to do was keep moving. The faster they could find a way out of the hellhole they were in, the better off they would be. She lifted her head, and Jerome cradled it as she motioned herself back upright. He bent down and sat next to her, his leg throbbing from the metal pike that was lodged in it. He didn't care, of course. He wanted to make sure she was okay. She was his priority, and he was hers.

She kissed his cheek, and very slowly, they helped each other up. Finn wagged his tail cautiously as he watched his masters stand tall, or as tall as they could. He was worried about them both. They were the only people he had, and he was grateful to both of them for crossing his path.

The two humans carried each other in their arms, shuffling their way from the destruction that crumbled around them.

Finn followed close behind, making his way to the front soon after, scanning the area. It was dark, and humans couldn't see well in the black. But he could.

They hated being in this level of darkness. Sure, back in Eden it was dark, but they were able to see where they were going. This time, however, was a new experience. It was as if they were almost completely blind. *Almost.* They could still see strange shadows and shapes. Not having their lanterns would prove to be difficult, especially when dealing with the Bastards. And whatever, or whoever, made that high-pitched scream.

It was very strange when they awoke; there was no sign of the remaining horde. A miracle. *It could also mean that those things were being called back to their master*, Jerome thought to himself, carrying Rebecca under his arm as they made their way through.

An hour or so passed. Maybe even longer. The two stumbled their way across the dirt surface squinting now and then, trying to get their bearings. They questioned whether or not they were going to be able to get out at all. Doubt crept into their subconscious. It was time to heighten their senses. What their eyes could not pick up, their ears could, now kicked into overdrive. Both, including Finn, perked their ears, trying their best to hear anything around them. It was dead silence, save for the crunching of dirt beneath their boots. Rebecca and Jerome didn't like this feeling. Not one bit. But they kept moving onward.

Rebecca felt a shudder go up her spine, and the hairs on the back of her neck were standing up. She was frightened. On edge. Her good hand motioned for Jerome's and squeezed tightly. *This fucking sucks!*

Jerome smiled. "You sure you're okay?"

"Yeah, can't really see, but I can still feel."

"You got that right."

They walked further along their darkened path, over what seemed like hills, and through narrow crevices and towering canyons. The journey was taking its toll on all of them. Their stomachs began to growl as their bodies became weaker from the lack of a good meal. They still had their rations, but those were easily dwindling down. They stopped for a rest. The pain was too great.

Both of them lay on their backs, looking up into the black void above. Rebecca turned to Jerome and asked, "Do you think the stars are out right now?"

"I dunno. Maybe," he responded.

"I think so," she said. "I miss looking at them."

Jerome exhaled. "Yeah. Same here."

He scratched Finn behind the ears. He could hear his purring getting louder and looked down. "Oh, you like that, huh?"

"Mrow."

Jerome turned to face Rebecca, changing his position to look directly at her. She crawled over to him, laying her head on his chest. Taking a ration from his pouch, he handed it to her.

"But that's yours."

He tapped it on her shoulder. "You need it more." He dropped it on top of her; it slid down, and she was able to catch it with her good hand. She opened the package begrudgingly and ate. She lightly nudged him and offered some. "No thanks. I just want to rest."

She folded the package up and placed it into her vest. There were already rations that were crumbled and crushed. She made due.

Her eyes looked around. She could barely make out the objects in front of her, let alone Jerome and Finn. Finn, who was now curled up next to them, purring, yawned and twitched his ear. His eyes opened, and he crawled on top of her, settling down. She exhaled as the feline purred louder. With her good hand, she scratched his neck and back. He closed his eyes and went to sleep.

Her mind, however, was racing. She tried many times to close her eyes and shut her brain off. She let her mind wander, looking off into the emptiness. She blinked her eyes. Then again. She was dozing off finally. Her mind wanted her to stay awake. *Fine!*

She noticed something in the distance. It was very faint, and she could barely make it out. Her brain was trying to put the piece of the puzzle together. Seconds passed, and it finally clicked. *Fire.*

THIRTY-EIGHT

Her hand motioned for Jerome, nudging his ribs, trying to wake him from his sleep.

"Jerome," she whispered. "Wake up! Wake up!"

"Nngh . . ." he responded. "Wha—?"

"Look!"

Opening his eyes, he turned his head and squinted. His vision was blurred, but he did see *something*. His eyes blinked again, trying to refocus and acknowledge what Rebecca was seeing.

"Tell me you see that."

"Yeah. Yeah, is that—?"

"Fire."

"A city, maybe?"

"Or maybe someone trying to get us killed."

That could have been true. They were alone, and there was no telling if there were any other signs of life—let alone living human life. There was no time to debate. Both knew they had to take the chance. If either felt threatened, each one had each other's back.

It was decided then. Though they were in pain, it was best if they made their way to the faint, glowing light.

Stumbling forward, they made their legs walk to their new destination. It was like a beacon of hope. Each step closer and closer.

Jerome wondered what they would find. He didn't see the light beforehand. *Someone could have lit it. You don't know.* No, he didn't, but he was also cautious. And scared. The hair was standing on his arm, and he glanced over to Rebecca. She was a dark, gray shadow, but he could make out that she, too, was frightened. Finn was hiding in her pouch, his head poking out only halfway.

As they drew closer to the flame, their features started to become more visible. It was nice seeing themselves for once, while at the same time, each noticed the extent of their injuries. The metal rebar, still inserted into Jerome's calf muscle, was an ugly reminder. Rebecca's face didn't fare well either. Her cheek was swelling, bruised, and throbbing.

The light flickered and glowed brighter when they crept closer. Its warm glow was calm, soothing, and very peaceful. There were no signs of wood to make a torch, but there was something. Their eyes wandered away from the glow and saw what it was hiding behind its fiery curtain. Wooden stakes. Thousands of them, soaked in blood, and impaled on them were Bastards.

"Crap."

THIRTY-NINE

"So, this is interesting," said Jerome, looking shocked, as did Rebecca. Their eyes couldn't believe what was in front of them. There they were. Bastards. Impaled on wooden pikes and jagged spikes that seemed rooted up from the ground itself. From their eye level, they couldn't see it, but the bodies formed one giant X. Some were full figured, while others were either decapitated or castrated and mutilated beyond comprehension. It was a giant field of death, and the two could feel the icy chill of its hands enveloped around their skin.

"Do you think, ya know, they could be the ones that were after us?" whispered Rebecca, swallowing her throat.

"Don't think so, hun. I mean, these things look *older.* Like they continued to age after they were killed."

"Human, then?"

"Not anymore. But can't really tell. They're far too decayed to make a judgment call," he replied, putting his hand under his nose, as did Rebecca. The smell of decay had made its way to them. Their brains couldn't comprehend the stench. There was no word that came to mind to define what they were smelling.

Rebecca wanted to throw up, as did Jerome. Their eyes teared, stinging from the acidic wash of dripping flesh and rotting skin. "Let's keep moving."

"Yeah. Right."

Finn put his head into his pocket and let out a whimper. It was disgusting, and he knew none of these looked appetizing. He wanted a challenge.

They carefully squeezed through the mass of flesh. It was like feeling pounds upon pounds of wet grease massaging their skin. Jerome thought he'd easily get used to it, but he was even more scared. The eyes. Those dead, fog-covered sockets staring blankly at him, as if blaming him for their predicament. He knew it was just his imagination playing tricks. But he still couldn't shake the feeling that he and Rebecca were being watched by thousands of eyes. It was nerve-racking. *Just keep going. You're stronger than this.* He began to wade his way through the dead orgy faster, careful not to fall on any of them. There was a feeling that he was disrespecting the dead by trespassing through them. It also felt wrong that he couldn't help to try to find a more peaceful place of rest. *How the hell did this happen? These poor people.*

Rebecca lightly coughed. The smell stung the inside of her nostrils, and she was almost to the point of gagging. Her eyes teared more as she quickened her pace, following Jerome's path. The area around them was darkening. "Now what?"

Jerome looked around, trying to find anything to ignite. He didn't want to use the pikes. It was better just to leave the bodies be. He turned to Rebecca, puzzled.

Moments later, a flame erupted in the distance. Jerome quickly turned around.

"You were saying?" said Jerome.

The two made their way toward the next burning light. It was an endless wave of bodies. Another flame came to life in the distance, near the left "line." Someone was following them. It was time to play catch-up.

They headed toward the newly ignited flame and made their way through the corpses. Rebecca brushed her hand against one. She jumped back. Jerome paused and turned around. "Everything okay?"

Rebecca looked down at the body. "Yeah. Just seeing things." She punched the corpse on the head. Nothing happened. "Thought so." She continued her movement with Jerome toward the faint light.

They finally exited the first giant mesh of bodies. There was now the matter of getting through the other obstacle. It was nice to have an opening. Both didn't like the feeling that they were drowning or being crushed.

Their stomachs growled, but they knew they had to continue. The flame was still ignited, and they had to get closer to it.

Finn popped his head out to see what was happening. His pupils changed when he saw the flame in the distance. Jerome felt bad for him. Cats can see in the dark, but it must have been quite a pain to change focus every few hours. "You okay, bud?"

"Meow."

"Good to hear. Just a little farther."

Finn purred and watched as his masters made their way through the gigantic mound of bodies in front of them.

It didn't get any better. Only worse. Jerome coughed, trying his best to hold back the bile that was yearning to come up from his stomach. Their bodies brushed past what seemed like endless rows of flesh. These were spread out a bit more. But there were still jagged pikes blocking their path that had to be maneuvered around.

Rebecca's heel stepped down on something that made a muted pop. She looked down, trying to see what it was. In her dimmed vision, she finally realized what it was. *An eyeball.* With the retina still attached. It was now a mixture of blood and rotted nerves that looked like tapioca. She lifted her boot to scrape off what was stuck to it in the grooves.

Jerome gently pushed a few heads aside to get through. He could hear cracks and sounds of sloshing—the skin being moved or stretched for the first time in a long while. He looked at one of them. It had a sunken-in face, was bald, and its eyes were up in its head. *Did it just blink at me?*

Minutes passed, and they waded their way to the right and through the second giant mound of corpses. They were closing in. *Only a few more yards*, thought Rebecca. She had hoped it was the last time they would have to move through the rows of corpses. And that the flame would yield some better light.

Jerome staggered faster. His thigh still throbbing, he applied pressure to it. *Maybe if I—ARRGH!* Too much pressure. Blood was seeping out from the wound, droplets that fell like petals to the ground.

He could only ignore the pain for so long. Reality kicked back in. He needed to get the damn thing out.

Together, they hurriedly made their way through the next phase of bodies. Jerome had an idea. The fire was indeed brighter. They stopped for a moment. He needed to get his thoughts together. Rebecca needed to calm her feet, for her ankles ached and she couldn't stand for much longer. She sat down, Jerome cautiously walking to the heated light. He looked down to the ground and saw a broken piece of wood. *Bingo.* He picked it up, tore off a piece of his pant leg as best he could, and ignited it. He smiled, and limped back to Rebecca. "Behold!" he said. "I have mastered the art of fire."

She rolled her eyes. "Whoopee." She was in no mood for his jokes.

Jerome put the torch down next to Rebecca while sitting next to her. She looked at him remorsefully. "Do you need any help?"

"No," he said. "But when I tell you, take that and place it on the wound. It'll stop the bleeding."

"It's going to be painful."

"Oh, I know."

"Okay . . ." she trailed off, readying the torch, looking down at his wound.

With both hands, he slowly started to remove the metal rebar from his calf. He tried his best to mute his screams of pain as he pulled it through more and more. Blood flowed out, and tears streamed down his cheeks. Veins throbbed and pulsed as he continued to pull the blasted thing through. Rebecca watched in front of her, sad that she wasn't able to do anything more to help him.

He was almost done. He kept telling himself to keep his mouth open. Not to scream. He couldn't. His tongue went forward, and his jaw shut down on it. Blood exploded from his mouth as he opened, reeling from the electric surge of pain. He could feel it though—his loosened tongue.

"Shit! Shit! Shit!" she said, hurrying to his aid as he went into the fetal position. Her hand immediately cradled his head, trying to keep him from going into shock. She had to act fast if she was going to save him.

Opening her vest pocket, she removed gauze, a needle, thread, and a tiny pair of scissors. *Hurry!* Taking his mouth and holding his jaw open, she gently pulled out his tongue. It wasn't fully bitten off, but it was showing some raw meat. It continued to bleed, and he put his hand over his mouth, trying to suppress the pain. Rebecca grabbed his hand, pulling it away. He shook his head and tried to put his hand back over his mouth. She pulled his hand away again.

"Stop! This is going to hurt, but it'll stop the bleeding," she said.

He looked at her and nodded in compliance. She took his tongue and wiped away the excess blood, trying to make his tongue dry. It wasn't working very well. *Fuck! Time for plan B.* She threaded the needle and began to sew his tongue. Jerome tried to scream, but he was holding back. He thought that if he did, he would be a beacon for the Bastards. He breathed heavily, tears continuing down his cheeks, eyes bloodshot and stinging. She continued stitching.

"Almost done. I'm almost done."

Moments later, she finished sewing his tongue back together. She snipped the extra stitching and held Jerome in her arms. She could feel the waterfall of sweat pour from his head. Lowering herself, she kissed his forehead, caressing it and trying to calm him down.

"Shh . . ." she whispered. "Shh—it's okay. It's going to be okay."

Jerome outstretched his hand and grabbed hers, squeezing. He looked at her with a fierce determination in his eyes.

She smiled and kissed his hand, putting it on her cheek. She looked off into the murky distance and wondered what was in store for them.

FORTY

Jerome's eyes fluttered and waved. Rebecca could see it. It was in the way his eyelids were behaving. He was dreaming. And in tremendous pain. But she couldn't be sure of which one he was thinking about. It could have been both.

They sat there. Just the two of them. Finn was traumatized by what he had seen. His master was in pain, and he couldn't do anything. Or perhaps there was something. After Rebecca had finished stitching Jerome, Finn cautiously made his way to them, from his hiding away out of fear. He saw her staring off into space. Approaching her, he placed his paw on her leg, letting out a whimper. She looked down at him and smiled. "He's okay. He's finally sleeping."

He climbed on top of Jerome's abdomen, circling around, and laid himself down, purring. He felt the hand of Rebecca caress his head, as he, in turn, buried his snout into his paws, looking at Jerome.

"You two are quite the pair, you know that?" she said. "You can sleep anywhere."

Finn purred louder, stretching his paws, and raised his rear in the air, continuing the stretch like a yoga pose, feeling her gentle fingers on his back.

Jerome stirred and opened his eyes, trying to speak. "Mmm."

"Don't. Lie still. You'll break your stitches," she said, checking him over. His face was battle worn, and he was fighting a light fever. "The bleeding stopped, but I wouldn't try to speak. Not for a very long time. You've lost some blood, so don't get up just yet."

He nodded in agreement. *Great . . . feel like a million bees stung my tongue. This is some ol' bullshit.*

"I gave you something that would help you relax. Wasn't strong enough, I don't think," she said, her lips quivering. She wanted to break down and cry. "We almost lost you, soldier." She looked over to Finn, who was looking at him with worriment in his eyes.

Jerome felt his arm. There was a small-sized bandage on his shoulder. He nodded, understanding. *She saved your ass. You owe her big-time.* He motioned that he wanted to sit up. Rebecca paused and decided to give in. She grabbed him tenderly by the back and helped him sit up. He was light-headed, and nearly collapsed. He caught himself, waving off Rebecca's hands. *Oh yeah. Blood. That's what I need. Steady . . . steady. You're not out of the woods yet. You still have that.* The damn rebar that was still in his calf. Now he remembered. The damn thing was such an annoying bitch. He made up his mind and looked over next to him. The flame on the torch was lower. *Not good, but not terrible either. Think I can still cauterize the wound.* Using his hands, he motioned for Rebecca to back away and ready the torch. Finn jumped down and sat at his side.

Looking at his two hands, Jerome continued to pull the rebar out of his thigh. He remembered not to say anything, no matter how horrible it felt. *Almost. It's almost out.* It was just a bit further now, almost three-fourths of the way now. Blood flowed out with each small tug. *Worry about that later. C'mon! You've got this!*

Rebecca watched as he pulled the remainder of the damn thing from his leg. With one hand he motioned for the torch. She put it to the wound on his right side and paused, looking at him. He nodded. She pressed it firmly against the muscle. It burned like a real son of a bitch. He wanted to growl, scream at the dark abyss, but he couldn't. He closed his eyes tight and held his breath, his mind sending commands to his vocal chords to react to the pain. He motioned for her to start the next side. Same thing. No sound was emitted from his mouth. Just tears falling from his eyes.

She threw the torch to the side and held him in her arms. She smelled of dust and BO, but she was alive and breathing. To Jerome, it was perfection.

"Jackass. What am I gonna do with you?" she asked, brushing his sweat and tears from his eyes. She got herself up and slowly helped him to his feet. Finn pawed at Jerome's good leg. Jerome looked down and noticed the feline's wide, open eyes. It was a look of concern and curiosity.

Bending down carefully, he picked Finn up and cradled him in his arms. Finn nuzzled his cheek and was then placed in his vest pocket.

The two gathered their belongings and made their way to the glow of the lit flame. They expected another sign to appear. But none appeared. Jerome looked around for anything; Rebecca did the same. There was just the sound of the low crackling fire.

"Should we keep going?" she asked.

Jerome nodded. There was no other way around it. They had to keep moving.

FORTY-ONE

Together, hand in hand, they ferried their way through the impaled corpses. They were wet with rotted skin and exposed muscle. Oily to the touch. Both of them had made it through to the other side when they heard it. The terrifying screech that was death itself. It was like a thousand thunderstorms. Rebecca and Jerome covered their ears, trying their best to mute the horrifying siren of sound. There was something else. A gelatinous hand had attached itself to Rebecca's wrist.

"What the—" Rebecca said, looking at what had attached itself to her. A tug. Then another. The hand wouldn't let go. It had a firm grasp on her. Jerome saw this too. He burst into action. He grabbed the torch and jabbed it into the thing's arm. It convulsed and sputtered about, feeling the burning sensation, but it still held tight.

Continuing to tug at the disgusting, blood-soaked hand, she began to bash it with her fist. There was a moan. But it wasn't coming from the one holding onto her. It came from afar. There was another, and another.

Jerome raised the low-lit torch and saw what was happening. The Bastards were rising up from their impalement. The full-figured ones, anyway.

Rebecca continued hitting the Bastard's arm over and over again. She could feel her wrist losing circulation; the damned thing's grip tightened. Her bones were starting to crack. She howled in pain.

Seeing what was happening, Finn elongated his jaw. His vines burst forth, wrapping around the Bastard's mutilated forearm. With a sharp, precise jerk, the thing's forearm snapped in two. It moaned in pain as bone protruded through the dead flesh, while blood exploded immediately from the break. The vines retracted, but shot through the Bastard's milky-white eyes, exploding out the back of its skull. Its body limp, it slid down its impalement even more. Finn retracted the vines and his jaw became normal.

Rebecca grabbed Jerome and said, "Run! As fast as you can!"

The Bastards continued to rise from the entrapment, hoisting themselves up to attack and feast on the ample flesh of Rebecca and Jerome. It was a twisted and disfigured domino type of effect. Each one sputtered and flailed to life upon hearing the shriek from the shadowed distance. *No! Not again!*

The scream echoed throughout the cavern, shaking the walls. Lifting themselves faster, the Bastards foamed at the mouth, their teeth gnashing and gnarling for flesh. Some were even pulling themselves *through* the pikes, their abdomen and chest breaking apart like one would crumple a piece of paper. They turned their attention to the trio and began their advancement. It was an ocean of bodies, and the trio was being surrounded.

Shit! Shit! Fuck! Fuck! Jerome ran as fast as he was able to, taking Rebecca's hand, and headed into the unknown. Finn clutched to his vest, holding onto dear life.

Their only recourse was to head straight. Jerome thought about tossing the torch, but they needed whatever light possible. He decided to keep it and charge faster.

The Bastards kept coming, some falling over themselves, while others were dismembering their own, all in order to advance toward the team. Moans. It was like a swell of baritones sounding off all at once.

One Bastard took the pike it was impaled upon, and gutted another standing next to it. The one holding the weapon then opened its blackened maw and took one big bite off the gutted one's neck. Blood and ooze came pouring out as it fell to the ground, moaning in pain. Bones broke. Skulls split open, and organs were exposed and were devoured. This was only a small portion of the onslaught.

Jerome and Rebecca ran. He took a glance back and saw the Bastards gaining speed. Their eyes glowed as they moved quicker, picking up speed like one humongous locomotive barreling down the tracks. These were a different type. Faster. More ravenous.

Jerome turned his attention back to Rebecca and the task at hand. She looked at him, and out of the corner of her eye she saw them. Her eyes widened in fear. "Must go faster! Must go faster!"

They were almost about to be taken over. Their legs ached and burned. Jerome nearly tripped. Rebecca felt her legs starting to wear down as well. She needed to rest longer. Her muscles burned. Her brain kept persuading her to push through it all. With determination and a rush of adrenaline, she ran faster, helping Jerome.

Jerome. He was lucky to have her. In a last-ditch effort, he threw the torch into the gigantic horde. Rebecca looked at him and was dumbfounded. "Didn't we try that already?"

The torch hit a Bastard hard in what remained of its chest. It was set ablaze but did not create the effect Jerome had been hoping for. The throng kept moving.

"Hurry! Keep moving!" she ordered, as she could hear the moans becoming increasingly louder. They were closing in. It was just a mere hundred yards or so. Both of them suddenly reached a dead end, and turned around, seeing the coming wave.

FORTY-TWO

"Oh, you've gotta be kidding me," she said. "Are you serious right now!"

This was the end. They weren't going to escape; there was no way out. The wall itself was a smooth surface. They had entered into a narrowed-out canyon and were now stuck.

Rebecca felt around the smooth rock for any type of cracks or protruding formations she could get a foothold on. None were coming up. Jerome, too, was trying. And panicking. He tried to find any way to hoist himself up, but there was none.

The ground began to shake, then the cavern walls around them. Chips and small rock debris peppered onto their heads.

Them?

No, it wasn't the oncoming horde. It wouldn't make sense for the walls to be quivering. But something *was* happening. It was an earth-shake.

"Earth-shake! It's a goddamn earth-shake!" she yelled, looking upward, trying to see where the falling pieces of rock were going to fall. It was stupid, but they didn't have any cover.

The great horde kept coming. Nothing was going to stop their advancement and seditious hunger. Not even an earth-shake.

The rumbling grew louder. Rebecca and Jerome held each other close and looked into each other's eyes. They nodded. If they were going to die, they would go down fighting!

Finn hissed at the Bastards. His masters ran toward the oncoming wave, determined to take as many of them out as possible, come hell or high water.

The entire cavern quaked and shook ever more violently. What they couldn't see of the precipice, they heard. It was as if thunder had struck from on high.

A large, towering rock formation came crashing down, on top of the Bastards themselves.

Huh, Jerome thought.

Behind them, the wall started to crack and break. Jerome turned and grabbed ahold of a new opening that appeared. Rebecca followed his lead, and with his help, lifted herself up to an opening across the way. More debris fell as the earth-shake became more intense. This was the worst they had ever felt it. They held on with all of their strength, eyes closed, breathing rapidly.

Please, nothing in the wall! Please, nothing in the wall! That's all they needed, Bastards breaking through the rock and killing them on sight. Rebecca noticed something through all of the chaos. There was another sound emanating from the wall. It was a low rumble at first, but it was becoming more powerful as it got closer. Jerome could hear it too. He looked at her, a puzzled expression on his face. Out of the corner of his eye, he saw the army of Bastards climbing over the large formation that had fallen mere moments ago. He pointed, and Rebecca saw it too.

They were climbing over one another, fighting for their chance to taste the duo. Like a wave crashing against the shore, they finally overpowered the obstacle blocking the passageway. They had reached the wall and began to claw their way to the team.

Jerome kicked a Bastard off who was grabbing at his boot. The thing returned, even more eager to sink its claws into him. He shook off the decrepit-looking hand and slammed his boot on the wrist, breaking it, along with the other bones of the hand itself. Rebecca was doing something similar—using all of her reserved strength, she plowed her boot into the skull of one of the oncoming SOBs. It toppled back, losing balance, and fell on its brethren. It tried to get back up, to continue the chase, but the cohorts had other plans. There in the black, they ripped and tore into the fallen Bastard. Rebecca and Jerome watched in disgust as the thing was being eaten whole. Black goo mixed with blood exploded out of the thing's chest cavity as it was being devoured. Its skull was being torn open, like one would peel an orange skin. Piece by piece.

The two almost lost their lunch seeing the carnage below. They had to continue on though. More of the Bastards continued to arrive, ignoring the feast that was taking place. They were after sweeter meats.

Jerome found an opening where he could put his hands and feet. It wasn't much of a difference in height, but it was better than staying in the predicament they were in. Rebecca grabbed ahold of an indenture in the rock, lifting herself up.

The earth-shake continued. It hadn't stopped at all. But the inherent humming and rumbling coming from inside the wall itself had them worried. *What the hell is it*?

In an instant, they heard it. The noise was familiar. The high-pitched scream echoed through the cavern walls, and without warning, above where they stood, the wall exploded outward! A mountain of debris came showering down on them as they fell backward, on top of the Bastards. They couldn't see it, but they heard it. And it was like nothing they had ever heard before. A shape. One couldn't accurately describe it. But they knew it was a darker color than their surroundings. The high-pitched scream came again. However, this time, the scream did something to the Bastards. Their heads exploded. It was a red sprinkler of blood and gore.

Jerome and Rebecca both covered their ears and looked on as the mass overtook the giant ensemble of dead and began devouring them. Rebecca took ahold of Jerome's hand and led him to the newly formed opening. "C'mon! Hurry!"

They dove into the new entryway and hid. Holding each other tightly, they heard the loud screech coming from the other side. They had to get away. Everything was coming undone and crumbling around them. They blindly began to run. They didn't know where, but they knew it was away from the sheer disgust of what was happening in the narrow space they were trapped in beforehand.

Rebecca checked her vest pocket, and so did Jerome. Finn was curled in a ball, shaking and breathing fast. He was frightened. Jerome covered him, protecting his head and body as he and Rebecca ran into the dark.

FORTY-THREE

The earth-shaking had stopped. Nothing was following them as they made their trek along what they could only guess was a dirt path.

"We're never going to get to the surface, are we?" asked a tired and downtrodden Rebecca. Jerome closed his eyes, saddened that she was probably right. They didn't know where they were or if anything or anyone was following them. And to make matters worse, they were in complete darkness. There were shadows that crept along their path. But no signs of light.

Finn poked his head out and sniffed the air. He raised his body upward and hopped out of his hiding place. He was no longer shaking, but he was very curious about something.

"Mrow!"

Both of them followed the faint echo of the call as he raced down the path.

They had caught up to him, and he was pawing at an old contraption. It was barren and tilted slightly. They squinted hard and looked at it in amazement. *A lift!* It was beaten, and old. But it was still harnessed to the mechanical cable wires.

"Only one way to find out, right?"

They gathered Finn and turned the lift right side up. Jerome flipped a few switches on a nearby panel that was covered in dust, but nothing happened. It was decided they would have to climb. The lift itself looked stable and lite enough. Rebecca tugged the cable wire. It was taught. Jerome returned, and together they began the ascension.

FORTY-FOUR

The ride up was arduous, each arm burning like fire as they made their way upward. They were now seventy meters up, pulling and tugging at the wire. They didn't know if they were going to reach the outside or even hit the surface. Many questions formed in their minds, none of which yielded any complete answers. The two just knew they had to escape and this lift might be their way out.

Rebecca looked at Jerome, and he at her, as they both tugged at the lines. "At least we're not down there," she said. Jerome chuckled, but stopped immediately. It hurt to do that, but Rebecca enjoyed hearing any form of his voice. It was reassuring.

They continued their climb, in silence, looking at each other, pushing their muscles in their arms past the envelope. Finn popped out his head every now and then to make sure everything was okay. His ears perked up, and he jumped out of Jerome's pocket vest, circling around the rusted, metallic surface. He heard something and put his head over the edge, his eyes getting a closer look. Jerome looked at him puzzled. So did Rebecca. She signaled to Jerome if he could keep pulling. He nodded an affirmation.

She knelt down beside the cat, who was looking, and tried to see what he was looking at. "I don't see anything, little guy." Finn looked at her, and then back down. He gave a low whimper as he was picked up. He climbed up walked on her shoulders, wrapping his tail lightly around her neck, and then just lay, purring.

Some hours had passed. Each was now taking turns pulling the cable rope. Then they heard a faint humming noise. It was like a hummingbird beating its wings. They looked to see where it was coming from but couldn't pinpoint the exact location. It didn't matter though. Above them, an explosion of sound erupted. Large, heavy blast doors creaked open, and along with them came a rush of fresh air and *light.* Their eyes burned and teared as they ascended faster to the opening. Adrenaline kicked into overdrive, pushing them to reach the top!

Almost there! C'mon! Jerome thought, tugging faster at the rope. He didn't know who or what caused the newly discovered doors to part. He was just happy to see light.

"Hurry! We're almost there!" she said, tugging the cable again. The lift became stuck. They were only about six to seven meters from the surface. "Try the control panel again!"

He flipped a switch and pushed a few buttons. He didn't know what any of them did; the writing was faded away with rust and old age. He desperately tried again, in a different pattern. The lift suddenly dropped three feet and immediately halted. They held onto the bars.

"Not that combination! Like ever!"

He nodded in agreement. Trying again, he punched in another combination. They heard a chuk. The gears had unlocked.

"Shit!" she yelled. "Hurry!"

They wrapped their arms and legs around the cable and watched as the lift dropped to the darkened depths below, faintly echoing the sound of crashing metal.

With both hands and feet pinching the cable, they climbed up. The rays of light touched their skin as they finally reached the surface. There was a white haze over their eyes. Their nostrils burned as they inhaled the dry yet familiar sun-soaked air. They lay on their backs, taking the sun's vibrant rays. It was hot, but they didn't care. All they wanted to do was rest. But the two of them knew they had to continue onward. With a grunt, Jerome was the first to get up. He held out his hand; Rebecca didn't move.

"Do we really have to?" she said, finally looking up at him. She could see his eyes. They were full of hope and wanting to get a move on. "Fine."

She took his hand and got up, walking to the station that held the once old rickety lift. It was rusting, and while there were aged buttons, Rebecca noticed a large cracked button at the bottom. She pushed it. The blast doors groaned closed. As the doors completely shut, a faint high-pitched scream could be heard.

The two put on their goggles from their packs and headed due west. It was the most logical direction they could think of. It was where Eden lay.

They did not talk about what had happened. It was all so surreal. It took a few days to reach the entrance to the Garden. When they saw their familiar blast door, they ran toward it. The sun was high in the sky, and the sand blew lightly across the far-scape.

They flipped their respective panels and put their thumbprints on the sand-laden pad. The mechanism churned and whirred. On the screen next to their panels, a message read:

ACCESS DENIED

A second command prompted:

COLONEL HENDRICKSON SCAN NEEDED

Rebecca shifted a panel to her left. It was a metallic keyboard. She input:

DECEASED.
OVERRIDE command:
MASTERS/BETA117

A few whirs and beeps later, a screen prompted:

ACCESS GRANTED

The door slid open, sand falling from the ceiling as they walked through. They were home. In front of them was the familiar pool and sleeping arrangements. Jerome looked to his left and saw Caleb's things. Rebecca pushed the button next to her, closing the door. They looked back at the vast desert wasteland, the blast door almost completely closed. "Lights."

TWO WEEKS LATER

squak

bzzzz

"*Hello? Anyone? Can anyone he**bzzzz* *me*?"

squaaaaak

Rebecca stirred in her sleep and opened her eyes.

bzzzzz

"*It's*-bzzzzz-squaaaak-bzzz!"

She immediately got up and raced to the sound. It was coming from a spare walkie-talkie in the corner. She picked it up and pressed the com switch. "Cal? Cal! Respond!"

Jerome entered from the other side of the cavern, wondering what was happening.

Squak! Bzzzz! "*Who? Who's Cal? This is Fr*-bzzz-*Comstock! Do you copy? Frederick Comstock! Can I come in?*"

"Live with a man for forty years. Share his house. His meals. Speak on every subject. Then tie him up, and hold him over the volcano's edge, and on that day, you will finally meet the man."
- Shan-Yu